THE TAPESTRY

BY
AUDREY N LEWIS

Dedicated to the human beings who lost their lives too soon because of hate. May they all hold a place in our hearts and never be forgotten.

TABLE OF CONTENTS

PROLOGUE

U rban legends have always intrigued me, I love how many layers they have, how many times the stories change. How often they have been embellished. I love how with each generation, with each individual, a little something gets added or taken away like peeling off layer after layer of old wallpaper. I love discovering each layer, always hoping I might find the original and hear its tale.

I had thought that the story I am about to tell was just another urban legend, but then I became a part of the story.

For years I would hear stories of a colorless person who wandered the countryside. A person with wild white hair and glaring red eyes. A person who was full of deceit and magic, playing the part of both male and female. A person who was without sight, but could indeed see. A human chameleon, whose many roles included living forever among those who walked before it, beside it, in front of it and behind it. A person whose challenge it was to live life forever. But then, I have to ask, "What is forever?"

And so it was on a day when thousands came together that I bore witness to an event that would change everything. It was not just the power and speed of the wind as it arrived. It was the roar that accompanied it. A force so incredible, picking up and grabbing hold of the thousands of colored fabrics. Stories that had been laid out and sending them into the Universe.

It was in that roar I could hear the call to those we do not know and cannot see. Yet as I stood there, it was not fear that I felt. Surrounded by the power of the wind, I could feel the Universe allowing this person to be set free.

Her name was Justice, with a capital J.

It could have just as easily been Faith or Hope, but she chose Justice. After all, it was Justice that defined the act of being. It was how, without thought, without choice, she reached out, and lived life. It was the ability to seek out and offer others the opportunity to truly live theirs.

Like an urban legend, this story, too, had so many layers, making it difficult to determine what was real and true and what had been fabricated or embellished. Each storyteller held on to their memory, believing they alone knew who Justice was. It was a memory that most were usually more than happy to share. The story of how it was that Justice had become a part of what defined them. For me, it was a privilege and honor, as I listened to each of them. A gift that allowed me to keep a little bit of each of the memories they recounted and store away.

In the end, I suppose that it doesn't matter much. Each story is theirs alone to hold on to. To tell and retell as each person so chooses. After all, no one has the right to take away a memory. It is with some commitment to their memories that I feel compelled to tell the story of Justice. I believe that the legend of Justice should be kept alive so that it may continue for generations. The story I am about to tell is my version. The story that lies beneath all of the layers to the place that it all began.

Parts of it, Justice herself recounted to me scattered in conversations I was invited to be a part of. Other pieces I gathered from scraps of paper I found among her and Maia's things. Scribbles of thoughts filled with emotion, parts of Maia's diary, journal entries that had been torn out and scrunched into boxes, and envelopes hidden here and there in drawers, in books, and gathering dust on shelves. I am sure each of us who had the privilege of being in her presence was forever changed.

PART I

MAIA and JUSTICE

Chapter 1

The simplest of joys the wonder of nature sometimes are interrupted by unexplained storms.

The wind rushed across the county road, the only road that led out of and into DeSoto, Mississippi. It had no mercy as it hit the thick woods that hugged the opposite side, causing it to bounce right back. It was the kind of wind that if it got angry, no one wanted to be in its path. Fourteen-year-old Maia could not be concerned with the power the wind held. She was too engrossed in the kaleidoscope of leaves, a magnificent artists 'palette that she couldn't resist. It was from this vast assortment of fall colors that an exceptionally bright red leaf cascaded downward. She focused on it alone as it descended, hoping that it might be the one that she could claim as her own.

Maia had a grand collection of fall leaves. It was her need to add to her collection that she had finished her school work and chores early. Not wanting to get stuck doing any additional chores, Maia had ignored her mama's warning of the strong winds and blustery air. She had even ignored feeling a bit more anxious than usual. She wondered if her stomach doing somersaults was its way of saying it too couldn't wait to find that perfect leaf. She could hear her mama's words. Each year the same "What are you going to do with those dirty leaves? Maia ignored the question realizing that like all previous years, she really didn't know. She started down the road.

Despite her dislike, mama would conjure up a potion just for me. A potion that would keep my leaf beautiful forever. We would place it between the pages of "Peter Pan in Kensington Garden," one of our favorite books. -M-

Now the perfect leaf literally landed at her feet. Its brilliant red coloring could not be outdone by the pink and green marbling of the veins that ran through it. It appeared a bit disappointed by its own demise. A prize specimen, as Maia bent down to collect it pain enveloped her. With both hands, she clutched her abdomen and doubled over, pain consuming her. She found it difficult to even take a breath and was relieved when she could feel a moment of calm as it wrapped its arms around her, and the pain subsided a bit.

I made sure no one was looking, don't know what mama would have done if anyone saw me. Bet she and Pappi would have thrown me over the border to Tennessee. All DeSoto folks threatened their young uns with that. No one knew what those Tennesseans would do with us, and I for sure didn't want to find out. -M-

Standing upright again, she looked around to make sure no one could see her. She pulled her jumper up to her waist and then sticking her thumbs into the tops of her bloomers tried to loosen them, hoping that would take some pressure off of her stomach. She didn't want to have to untie them. It was at that moment without warning that water poured out of her as if her bladder seemed to fully empty itself. Her bloomers were soaked not having had time to remove them first, which now made them difficult to untie. She needed to get them off so that they could dry before returning home. She couldn't wear them home wet, and she could not return home without wearing them. Once removed, she found a sapling to hang them on, hoping that the wind might dry them faster. She pulled her jumper back down, smoothing it out a bit, and then with nothing more she could do, she resumed her collecting. She was so grateful that the wind had not swept up the leaf that still lay at her feet and carried it away. Once again, as she bent over to retrieve it, she was consumed by pain, and she dropped to the ground screaming in agony. Before she knew it night was coming, and she wished she had listened to her mama and taken a sweater. She was getting cold. The night was coming, and yet no one had come looking for her.

I was sure if it were past suppertime, mama would have sent someone to get me. -M-

Maia screamed louder in pain and with fear. She lay there alone. Feeling as if something had crawled inside her and was now trying to claw its way out. It had to have been several hours that she was lying there, scared, screaming in torment each time the pain increased.

I had tried to rewind what I had done. What was it that was so terrible that the devil had been summoned to punish me? -M-

She wondered if it was wrong for her to pray that someone would hear her as she screamed louder than she had ever screamed.

When nightfall came, she lay still. She had never before felt so afraid. Beyond anxious, her stomach was no longer doing somersaults.

Instead, it felt as if something had been brewing inside of her, and now it was trying to push its way out. She was sure that her organs were being ripped loose from the walls of her stomach. Something was trying to expel them from her. She crossed her legs as tightly as she possibly could, trying with all her might not to allow her body to expel anything, even that which was rightful to do. She was afraid parts of her would just fall out. In an instant, the pain subsided, and she contemplated trying to go home to her mama.

Mama had a potion for everything and could always make one feel better no matter what was ailing. -M-

But there was no time to leave. There wasn't time to even broach the thought. As the pain once again increased, debilitating her. In between her bone-chilling screams, she tried to breathe. Her stomach twisted, and all she could do was go with it. She pushed as if that might accelerate the inevitable, emptying itself of the poison that must surely be growing inside of her. The pain did not ease up when she tried to hold back, so with all she had, Maia pushed not once worried about the bowel movement that she had expelled. Hoping that perhaps it might relieve her, but there was no relief. She could feel the pressure of something trying to escape her. She screamed even louder. She felt her vagina ripping, feeling herself opening up, and something that she could not imagine emerging.

Maia could see the shadow of what she was sure was a buzzard circling above her. From the corner of her eye, she could see a pack of coyotes. She imagined them hungry, waiting for her to die. She bit her lip, wondering if death would be better. Would they rip her apart, leaving nothing left of her to be found? She continued to scream when she heard the splat sound as if a sponge exploded and the heaviness of slush poured from her. There was some small comfort when the pain subsided. Maia was able to force herself into a partially sitting position, sweat dripping from every pore only to see that among the blood and mucus was the silhouette of what she knew was a baby.

In the darkness it lay there, I knew it was a baby but didn't want to believe it. -M-

The moon wasn't yet quite full, but that did not stop the celebratory howling that the pack of coyotes sang out in unison. The moonlight was just bright enough for Maia to see the translucent shadow of an infant, which she was more than sure had come from within her. It was a baby so luminous that it seemed to cast a glow even though the clouds had moved in, blocking any light that the moon might cast. Maia pushed her hands into the earth, her fingernails filling themselves with dirt. With what little strength she had, she forced herself to sit erect. Sitting as upright as she could tolerate, she reached down. Instinctively and protectively, using only gentleness she grasped the tiny body. Slowly dragging it up her outstretched legs. She pulled until she could rest it on what was sort of her lap so that she could hold it in her arms. She held it close, uncontrolled tears running down her cheeks. Having witnessed the birth of so many of her siblings, she knew that the color of its skin and the absence of a cry could mean only one thing; that it was dead. Yet she could feel the tiny body expanding with every breath. Maia's tears fell on its translucent skin. As if awakening it, it took a deeper breath and cried. Allowing herself a moment of relief, with difficulty, she lowered herself slowly back so that she might rest a bit on the ground. Never once allowing herself to loosen her grip on the baby. As Maia took a deep breath, she realized that she had been holding her breath, and as she allowed herself to breathe, she focused on each breath she took. In that way, she learned she was able to calm not just the baby but also herself.

Chapter 2

Darkness not only hides things it allows believing in what can not be seen.

M aia lay quite still there on the ground in the dark of night, the infant in her arms. She watched, observed, listened to all that was around her. It was not the coyotes who advanced that she feared; they appeared more curious than aggressive. What she feared was the single large bird whose shadow she could not only see but whose presence she could feel as it flew overhead. Swooping and circling, causing her to fear for the baby.

It was a bird so large that I could feel the air move as it flapped its wings above me. -M-

As she lay there watching, holding onto that baby, she had to question what she did not entirely understand. Maia's mama had spoken to her about the birds and bees. She had explained everything in great detail; so many details that Maia was more than confident that nothing had filled her with a child.

I know how babies are made. Mama told me all about that, those birds and bees. She would tell me, warning me each time she birthed another brother or sister. -M-

Where it had come from? How had it come to be? Was its existence even possible?

I look at this baby and do not know. I do not understand how it could have come to be. -M-

Yet there was no denying that this baby had come from her. As she held it, there could be no mistaking that she and this baby were breathing in unison, taking each breath as if they were one. She took a deep breath and inhaled as did the baby. It was so calming for both of them. How could she allow herself such calm? When holding this baby, she could only feel an obligation. There were no thoughts of sorrow or joy, rather worry and sincere concern. What was she going to do?

Chapter 3

Gender is what often complicates life's simplicity.
While natures wild is the glory of all that is unconditional love.

Holding this baby, Maia thought about her mama. She thought about how her mama would always take a moment as if doing inventory after birthing one of her siblings. Taking time to examine them closer. Maia took a moment and counted to make sure that it had all ten fingers and all ten toes. Staring at this baby, Maia sighed, relieved by its physical perfection. Yet she couldn't help but feel pained. She knew it shouldn't matter as she tried to fight back her curiosity to discover its gender. It seemed more important than understanding the essence of its being.

I should not have cared. Its gender should have been of no importance when it was so physically perfect. -M-

She felt weak, both physically and emotionally, which made it difficult for her to comprehend what she would soon discover. With slightly shaking arms, Maia had held it up over her chest, an arm's length away. She hoped that the moon might peek through the clouds long enough to illuminate more than just the light that appeared to come from the infant itself. She was ever so cautious. Afraid it may fall as she attempted to identify its gender. Undoubtedly, it was the translucency of its body which must have caused her to be confused. For as she looked, it was not just with feminine or masculine anatomy; instead, she was sure that it indeed had both.

She tried to recall her mama's babies, her siblings. Had they looked so colorless when they were born.? Had their genders been so easy to identify? Perhaps, they had been washed clean quicker than she was now remembering. Maybe they hadn't looked so soon. Her mind was muddled. She slowly lowered the baby back down, stopping only so that she might lay it across her hips, allowing it to rest for a while. She too laid back and closed her eyes so that she might sleep, and make it all just go away.

Letting herself sink into the soft ground to find comfort, the coyotes took that simple act as an opportunity to begin to inch closer. She was relieved as she watched them. It was not hunger that prompted them; it was their maternal instincts taking over. Instructing them to eat away at the cord, which was still attached and the afterbirth that lay on the ground, some of which was still not entirely expelled.

I am honored to have witnessed the coyotes using such caution as they fed themselves. It almost seemed like love. -M-

What a sight that must have been, wild coyotes so uncharacteristically using caution to feed themselves on the miracle of afterbirth.

When they were satisfied that their job was complete, there was no inquisitiveness, only knowledge, and compassion. Cautiously so as not to frighten, they continued moving even closer, until they were within a breath away of mother and baby. It was with only gentleness as Maia lay still in and out of sleep, that she watched with slight apprehension and awe that the coyotes licked the baby, still laying across her clean. Neither the baby nor Maia uttered a sound. Maia waited for them to finish hoping the gleam would diminish. But as they licked it clean, it appeared that it only made the newborn appear brighter.

Chapter 4

There is always, a leader making way for others to choose to follow.

(It is this part of the story that the layers do not change. The story remains consistent from storyteller to storyteller.) On the night of the infant's birth, one coyote stood out from the pack. This coyote, without fear or order, took charge. This single coyote was not afraid to bare her teeth as she showed the other coyotes she was alpha. As if it was her responsibility alone to protect this infant and Maia. It was this coyote who ever so gently lowered her head that night and carefully nudged the baby, pushing it closer up towards the mother's breast. It was this coyote who, with teeth clenched, using caution only it knew how pulled the shoulder strap of the jumper Maia wore as well as the cotton blouse underneath it. It pulled until they ripped. And then it tugged just a little bit harder until Maia's breasts were fully exposed. Satisfied that it had succeeded in what it set out to accomplish, it was able to push the newborn inch by inch to the mother's breast until it reached her nipple. It then stood back, waiting and watching ever so thoughtfully for it to feed.

As Maia fed the baby, the pack of coyotes took it as an invitation to join her. Accepting her welcomeness, together they lay down next to mother and infant, surrounding them with softness and keeping them warm. It was this warmth that mother and baby would need from the cold night air. The coyotes moved close, heating them so that they would surely make it through the night. As the clouds filled the sky, they lay in total darkness, except for the glow that the tranluscency of the newborn gave off.

The coyotes stayed close that night, forming a tight circle around mother and baby, making sure that they would keep them warm and that they might also keep them safe. It was the coyotes that understood what darkness might prowl the woods and what predators might be flying overhead. It was those above that they knew were the greatest of threats.

Before the first rays of sun lit up the horizon, the coyotes rose. Led by the one who had declared itself alpha, ceremoniously made one final circle around mother and baby, before together, a united pack silently ran off back into the woods.

All I wanted was for it to be a dream, a nightmare, but it was real. The scream in my throat lay still afraid to speak out. -M-

Chapter 5

From whence they come til whence they go devil or angel you'll never know.

I t may have been when the earliest of light grew from the horizon that Maia awakened. Perhaps it was the baby who had begun to feed on her now full breast, either way, she was startled out of sleep. She began to rise, tempted to push the infant away, and flee. A scream formed in her throat. When as if without choice, but with obligation, all she could do was stay.

As Maia allowed or perhaps forced herself to look down at the infant, she noticed tiny wisps of white hair covering its head. She placed her open palm on top of them as if she might pet her dog, gently wanting to see if they were soft, hoping that touching them would ignite some feeling. It was not what she had hoped, and while she liked the softness and the warmth that rose from its crown, she found it difficult to feel anything else. The void of emotion made it especially challenging for Maia. It was difficult to know how to respond to it. Despite acknowledging that they seemed to breathe as one, she couldn't identify feeling anything else. Maia closed her eyes. Had it been wishful thinking that it had been a dream? She had thought it might have been a nightmare, yet here they were.

In church, they spoke of Jesus's conception, it made me laugh, how could it be so. Even now, as I hold this infant that came from inside of me, I do not understand. -M-

Still not understanding how it had happened or how it was even possible, it was very real. In all truth, while Maia had never told anyone or spoken the words aloud, she had often found the story of Jesus's conception hard to believe difficult to understand and hen the univers commands it to happen again

Now, as she held this infant, she thought that it was neither a dream nor a nightmare, but perhaps it was both. As the baby fed, Maia scanned the area, only to find the emptiness of the road and the stillness of the woods. It was then that she knew she was all alone, even the coyotes who had been somewhat of a comfort and company were gone. Feeling scared with such a grown-up responsibility, she realized that she needed to develop a plan.

I wanted to go home. So much of me needed that. But I knew I couldn't. There would be too many questions, and I would have no answers. There would be no forgiveness. -M-

She could not go home. There would be so many questions to which there would be no answers. It was a difficult dilemma as Maia contemplated what it was that she was going to do. Did she have any real options? Where was she going to go? She felt that her choices were limited and knew that no alternative would be simple. She was beginning to understand. Whatever her final decision, it would most likely determine her future, and the fate of this infant forever. She realized that whatever choice she made was her responsibility alone. In choosing, she would have to base her decision on what it would mean to be alone. What efforts she would have to make. What tasks it would take if indeed they were to survive.

She glanced down again at the nursing newborn connected to her for its survival. She attempted to allow herself to feel something, anything. She tried to calm herself, taking slow deep breaths, realizing that she and this infant seemed to breathe as one. The longer Maia gazed at it, the more she noticed its brightness, but it wasn't exactly white, it was colorless. She contemplated if the choice she made not to return home had been the correct one?

Glancing down at the baby, Maia was confident that it was not her decision alone. That someone or something was making the decision for her, for both of them. Finding herself in a more-than-compromised position. A position that she did not fully understand, she knew that if someone asked questions about this infant and where it had come from, she would have no answers. She pondered her dilemma, attempting to make sense of it. Playing over and over again in her head what answers there could possibly be that she might give. But as far as she could tell, there were no answers, not even for her.

All along, I feel like it is not me; someone or something is pushing me, making the decisions for me. -M-

As the sun continued to rise, it was that early morning light that Maia welcomed. It was when one could see the sun's rays dancing as if the sun were waving and saying, "Hello! Here I am!"

Chapter 6

Are we being punished when in God we don't believe? Or are we experiencing miracles to make us believe?

In the sunlight, Maia hoped she could see better what she had noticed about the infant the night before. Even the small tufts of hair that covered its tiny head were white, and when it took a moment to stop feeding and looked up at her, she could not help but gasp. For as white and colorless as this baby was, its eyes were just as red. They were not frightening, like the devil, but slightly soft and pleasing.

I think Jesus is punishing me for not believing, or maybe he is teaching me to believe...red eyes? -M-

She had never heard of any person having red eyes. She had never even thought that humans could have red eyes. Maia smiled and let a tiny laugh out; truth be told, it was not anything she could have imagined. It was something she had never thought about or even considered possible. She laughed out loud, thinking, "why would she?" But now, she did. Its red eyes reminded her of some of the rabbits that she and her siblings had raised and loved. A memory that brought a tinge of sorrow, knowing it would not be home to which she would be returning.

Maia cradled her baby, trying not to disturb it too much as it once again began to feed.

It seems all this baby does is feed, I don't remember mama's babies ever feeding so much. It is difficult to do anything without fear of making it cry. It is a special baby, and I must be sure to protect it. -M-

She was afraid of what might happen if it should start to cry. More importantly, she was concerned about how it would make her feel if she had done something to cause it to cry. It was at that moment that Maia knew the baby she was holding must indeed be very special, and it was her responsibility to protect it. Just imagining that it was she who inflicted any sort of pain was more than she could bear. The idea alone brought her tremendous stress, as did the thought of ever witnessing it in pain. As she pondered the steps it would take to protect it, she laid her hands gently on the infant and let them move over its body protectively. She caressed it as she tried to memorize every bit of its tiny body.

I want to know each bit of this infant. Someday, this knowledge may be important. But it is hard to understand why it is so different, and I wonder what that might mean. -M-

Still wanting to understand the unknown, she explored, not missing a centimeter of its being, hoping she had merely imagined things the night before. Now fully awake, she believed it would be an opportunity to determine its gender. Once again, still hoping that what she had seen was not real. As she let her hands and fingers touch and feel the infant, she forced herself to look. She could not help herself, and as she did, from deep within her, a scream of sorts exploded. There was no mistaking; not only was this baby she held colorless with red eyes and wisps of white hair, but it had both the genitalia of a boy and a girl. It had not been the outcome she had hoped. Without meaning to and without thought, her body uncontrollably shivered. That slight unexpected movement was all it took to startle it and cause it to cry.

It is so important that I not hurt this baby that it never has to experience unnecessary pain. -M-

Disturbed by what she had done, the pain she may have caused, all Maia could do was to hold it closer. Then tugging on her already ripped blouse, she ripped it more, trying to make more space. Once satisfied that she had made enough room, she tucked the infant inside. Pulling the salvaged piece of cloth over the baby, covering it as best she could, protecting it and keeping it warm. For one split second, she imagined what her mama might say in respect to the destruction of her clothes. Without further concern, she shrugged the thought away. It was then that she was clear, there was no decision for her to make. It had already been decided for her, for both of them. Maia was beginning to understand perhaps too well that there were powers higher than her trying to tell her something, trying to guide her. She would try and listen, to pay closer attention, and to be more watchful.

I try to hear the words, to understand the guidance. I am thankful for the help I am given. Grateful that it is not me alone to make all of the choices that need to be made. -M-

Chapter 7

*Is it possible that we are not alone, that forces we do not know,
we do not understand guide us?*

Maia thought that she might understand a little but had a difficult time trying not to think about going home. It was equally hard, if not harder, to think about, to imagine what would most likely happen if she returned home. There would be too many questions. Even worse, she knew that if she took the infant home, there would also be so much fear. Maia had often seen that nothing was worse than fear.

As the sun continued to rise higher over the horizon, she knew she would need to act quickly. With daylight making its way around her, that also meant that people, farmers, and such would begin their travels. The road would soon be busy, Maia was sure that could not be good.

I could not go home. What would I say? How would I answer the questions that would be asked? How would I protect the baby from those that would want to hurt it? Those that would want to make it suffer? -M-

It was the potential questions that worried her the most. She knew with no uncertainty that she wasn't ready for anything that would be asked of her. She wasn't prepared for the shame that would undoubtedly be directed at her. Perhaps, even more, she wasn't ready to face the inquisitors, whom she feared might attempt to steal the infant away. She feared that they would use it to cast spells. They would try to protect themselves from the likes of the infant itself or some other self-indulged fancy. She held the infant a wee bit tighter as she ed at the thought of what unthinkable acts they might perform on it if they were able. Maia cringed, thinking about how many church services she had sat through where they spoke of witchcraft and devil worship, sacrifices, and potions. She wondered if such sermons had any purpose other than scaring the congregation. She reckoned that it really didn't matter. For now, all that mattered was protecting herself and this infant.

Chapter 8

Memories to be etched into our very essence to be drawn from and allow us to move forward.

Holding the infant tightly, tucked against her again, hiding it as best as she could insider her blouse, Maia began to run. She ran until they were at the edge of the woods that she still recognized but stopped herself. Then as if without control, Maia turned, running back to where it all first occurred. The reason she had ended up in the woods, to begin with. To the leaf, she had so wanted for her collection.

I had chosen today to find the perfect leaf to add to my collection. There must be a reason for my choice. I can not go further until I collect what is meant to be mine. -M-

It was a challenge to allow herself to turn back, but emotions and need defied explanation, she had to have that leaf. She had no choice. She needed that leaf. She needed to hang onto it and to keep it close. Someday she would give it to this infant. One day she would tell it the tale. Maia was surprised she found it with such ease as if it were just waiting for her to come back to claim. Having no satchel or pockets made finding a safe and secure place for such a treasure a bit tricky. In the end, Maia tucked it gently deep inside her blouse away from harm, beneath where the infant's body rested. When she felt confident that it would indeed be safe and secure, she turned back towards the woods and continued to run.

Maia ran with purpose, but not direction. As her path took them further and further into the woods, she found herself questioning. How would she manage alone? Realizing the woods around her were becoming unfamiliar, she had no idea where they were and where they would go. Maia wasn't even sure what she would do or find. All she knew, all she was sure of was that the further into the woods she could take this infant, the safer they'd be. She felt pretty confident of at least that, but as they got deeper into the woods and the trees became denser, fear began to follow her.

I believe I have been given a remarkable job. I think I have been chosen to protect this baby. -M-

Someone or something was watching them, stalking them. She was sure of that. It was with the slightest of hesitation that she did not stop. Caution becoming a more significant part of the journey than Maia expected. With fear beside her, she found it a challenge to keep running.

How could she run? She knew she must watch, pay close attention to every detail. In the wind, Maia could hear her mama's voice as it danced through the trees, telling her, "Your instincts must lead you." She wrapped her arms around her chest as she hung onto this baby and, following her instincts, proceeded to run again. It was with confidence that Maia discovered her feelings and instincts were correct. Stalking them in the shadows of the tree line, was a pack of coyotes. Her fears lessened, hopeful that perhaps it was the same pack who had bestowed their gifts on them the previous night.

Chapter 9

Trust in the path you are being led, often it is the kindest.

N ow from a short distance, remaining somewhat hidden, the coyotes slowly followed, watching. Maia could feel eyes upon them. She found herself holding the baby closer and closer, not necessarily tighter and tighter. Every step she took, so too did the coyotes. They were waiting for just the right time to make their move and show themselves. Thanks to the fullness of daylight, it wasn't long before Maia was able to see the entire pack of coyotes and knew that her hopes had been granted. It was indeed the pack from the previous night. However, she was not comfortable having them see her looking at them, unsure how they might respond. As nonchalantly as she was able, she continued moving along, no longer running but attempting a cautious fast-paced walk. She was making sure that she positioned herself in a way that, at all times, she could see the pack out of the corner of her eye. Walking quickly, she continued to watch. What she saw was curious, for indeed, they were not only moving, but they seemed to be moving in unison with her. Each step she took, they too took a step. If she stopped, they stopped. As they moved, it was as if they proceeded with purpose. It was a purpose that only they seemed to understand, a reason that she would soon learn included both her and this infant.

Maia continued to keep watch; continued to move this way and that so as not to lose sight of them when they changed direction. She wasn't expecting them to turn and start to move towards her. They were no longer parallel with her but coming head-on. Simultaneously, a large bird began circling Maia and the infant. Perhaps, it was the same bird from the previous night. It was swooping down and flying back up, continuously moving closer as if trying to get a better look or an opportunity to feed. As the bird succeeded in getting uncomfortably close, Maia stood still, frozen, ready to crouch down to the ground should she feel too threatened. It was then that the alpha coyote from the night before turned on the bird and bared its teeth. Then leading the pack in concert, they all began to howl until the bird quite irritated flew away. The coyote, now able to focus its attention on Maia and the baby, moved closer. Soon, it was so close that she could feel its breath. It lowered its head and nudged her, although it was more like a push than a nudge. She held the baby closer, protective.

I had been so afraid that I had hurt this infant. I could feel the dampness against my skin and worried about what I might have done. It was a little funny when I realized what it was.

-M-

Feeling moisture run down her chest, she panicked, afraid to look, afraid she had held the baby too tightly.

In that instant of preoccupation, the next nudge caused her to lose her footing. She began to stumble backward, twisting her ankle as she righted herself to stop from completely falling. Half amused, half disgusted; it was a relief to know that the baby had only relieved itself. That it was not blood nor injury that she had felt and that she had not caused it. It was with that knowledge that Maia found the courage she needed to stand her ground.

I need to remember my Pappi's words,
I need to act upon them. -M-

She thought of her Pappi and remembered how he had taught her that "when in a situation that brings fear, one must stand tall and come face to face with the source." She stood there for a few seconds, trying to slow her breathing. She focused on the baby's breath until once again, they breathed as one, allowing her to regain her composure. When she felt confident, slowly, she straightened her back, pulled back her shoulders, and stood tall, holding the infant with what might have appeared to be pride, she allowed herself to take a step forward. The coyotes responded to what they must have interpreted as aggression by moving into place, forming a straight line behind the alpha, the one Maia now believed to be in charge. Together as soldiers, they began marching towards her. Each step they took towards her, not backing off, she took one towards them.

It is crucial to make these coyotes see me as their equal. -M-

She was without fear and determined that they not only understood but acknowledged her role. While she wanted to make sure that they knew she did not fear them, they needed to know she stood as their equal, not as an aggressor. It was crucial that they did not consider her actions a threat. Maia did not feel threatened by them either. With each step she took, she began to feel as though she was being directed as if her actions were not her own. When they were almost nose to nose, she stopped. Keeping her eyes directed at the alpha, not so much surrendering or retreating, but lining up so that they would be followed. The coyotes changed their formation and then, like soldiers lined up in a single file. Ready to move out, marching in place, waiting just long enough for her to understand, she should follow.

Maia was a bit concerned about where they would lead her but feared what might happen if she didn't follow them. She feared what would happen if she were left alone? Alone in woods, she did not know. She had never been so deep into them and was quite sure she had no clue where she was. She had no idea which way to go. Following them was the only responsible thing that she felt she could do. It was as if following them was her duty. She didn't yet know that it was their duty to lead her. Temporarily putting all concerns aside, she followed them. Zigzagging through the trees deeper and deeper into the woods, trying not to allow herself to acknowledge that while not with fear, she no longer felt safe.

I was so confused. I tried to wish the fear away. It took all I could muster to trust in the coyotes and protect the baby. -M-

Even the growing fullness on the trees, still holding onto their brightly colored leaves, would typically bring Maia joy. But it did not help, and it wasn't long before she could no longer delude herself. Both the fear which began to surface and the confusion she felt won as they consumed her. It was not the coyotes that she feared. She was quite confident that they would not harm her or the baby. They had proven their kindness and compassion more than once. What she feared the most was fear itself and the ugliness she had learned it could produce. As she had heard in sermon after sermon, the venom of fear could strangle a person to death. She was uncertain how to keep the web from wrapping itself around her, wondering who then might save her.

Chapter 10

One must not allow themselves fear after they have accepted hope.

Maia felt helpless. She was losing her sense of direction. The fullness of the tree canopy blocked out the sun, making it impossible to know if she was headed north or south, east or west. She was afraid that she would be lost forever, that even if she wanted to, she would never be able to find her way back home. It was the weight of this fear that began to slow her down more, her legs and feet heavy with fear, making it difficult for her to even take just one more step.

As if frozen, standing in a pool of muck, like in the pigsty at home after a heavy rainfall, she could not move. She watched in horror as the coyotes continued moving forward until they were just specks lost in the trees. She remained motionless. Panic covered Maia like a blanket ready to cover the body of a newly dead soul. A fear that began slowly to fill even her lungs, making it hard for her to breathe. In her head, she was sure that the coyotes would not knowingly leave them behind, yet she was having a difficult time listening to her head. As she watched them disappear from sight, she wondered if they knew the situation that they were leaving her in. Maia tried to call out, but even her voice was frozen with fear.

I was so alone, my hope vanished. When the baby cried. It screamed, and for a moment, I let myself believe. -M-

She allowed herself to sink further into despair, and just as soon as she was sure she could see them no longer, the infant she held onto with every ounce of strength, cried out. It was a cry so loud and so piercing that it echoed through the trees. It brought Maia a moment of renewed energy and hope as she was sure that it was a cry so loud and so shrill that the coyotes would surely have had to hear it. A cry that was so mighty that it released her from the hold that fear had taken. And while it was with great struggle, it allowed her to lift her feet once again and take a step. She knew that she would need to run, run like the wind if they were to catch up to them. Determined to do just that she tried. Pushing herself to her fullest capacity, she stumbled, almost losing her grip on the baby. Her arms stiffened as she held on to keep it from slipping out of her blouse. She knew that it was her alone that must protect them both. Sinking back into the muck, she forced herself to stop and readjust. She was protective, with sincere concern that she might have indeed dropped it. Tears welled up, blurring her vision. She could not stop her emotions from devouring her. For the first time since it had all begun, she started to cry. She cried until tears took hold of her, and she allowed herself to be drained of all hope. She fell backwards, hopeless, hanging onto the infant as if that were all that was left.

Maia lay there, her arms wrapped around the baby while allowing herself to be caught up in the endless flow of her own tears. She lay there and cried. She cried for all that was lost. She cried for being lost, and she cried because that was all that she could do. She cried until there were no more tears. Empty and drained, she lay back still holding the baby, with only an ounce of hope, sinking deeper into the muck she waited. The coyotes had since stopped, having realized that their charge could not be seen anywhere. Concerned, they circled back. It was the shadows overhead that caught their attention. They could see several birds circling in the distance. They could feel the wind from their wings pick up, so strong that the fallen leaves beneath their feet began to dance swirling about in play. Still, they stayed in formation.

As they got closer, even the coyotes had to give thanks, for it was the birds that unintentionally led them to the spot where she lay. They had not expected to see her so exposed and appearing so defeated when they came upon her lying there. They stopped. A small group separated from the pack to once again fend off the bird, although now it was an entire flock. The remaining coyotes sat back on their haunches. They patiently waited, for it had to be her decision to accept the challenge and continue. She was the one who had to choose whether or not she wanted to finish the journey. The coyotes waited for quite a while without moving. One could barely hear the reverberation of their breath. Maia was herself, elated to have them return. Still, she found it to be difficult before she was able to acknowledge them and the birds that swooped down taunting her.

Using a small corner of what was now a dirty, ragged, and wet blouse, which hung off of her shoulder, keeping company with the strap of her jumper, she wiped her eyes. Finding another small corner of her blouse that was still clean enough, she carefully wiped her nose. She blew it ever so gently so as not to startle the infant. The baby's face turned up towards her, and she could see a small smile, almost comical as the corners of its mouth opened to yawn. It was that tiny yawn that held a smile, that was all Maia needed to inspire her. She held her head down, protectively attempting to avoid the birds who had not yet been frightened away.

I know I must gather my strength if I am able to protect this baby and myself. -M-

Using all of the energy she could conjure up, she pulled herself together. Trying to steady herself, she secured the baby. Then finding a spot out of the muck and pushing her left hand down, she pushed herself upright, ready to push on. She understood she would need all she had to keep up with the coyotes, whom she knew that she needed to follow once again.

Having warded off the birds, the coyotes prepared to move on again. An army of soldiers in formation circled Maia and the baby several times before continuing on what was undoubtedly a path they knew well. Taking their time, often checking to make sure that they didn't get too far ahead, making sure two coyotes followed behind to watch her back.

I am grateful that the pack came back for me. Thankful that they let me follow them again. Happy that they waited for me. But I am a bit worried, they seem anxious, and I wonder what they really want. -M-

Chapter 11

Can one be too cautious when accepting help?

Maia was grateful for their concern, their guidance, and their companionship. Still, a bit of her couldn't help but wonder if perhaps they seemed all too eager to lead the way. It was a feeling that made her just a bit uneasy, and she wasn't sure if that made her a bit more cautious or curious. Either way, she followed them, unsure what else she could do, and grateful that they had made concessions so that she would not again get left behind. As they walked, she continually watched over her shoulder and above her head, making it difficult for her not to stumble a bit. They walked for another hour or more, her feet aching and blistered, the baby heavy as it rested on the waistband of her jumper still tucked securely in her blouse. She was wet and smelly. She cringed at what she might find when she finally took the baby out and removed her blouse. Again, she was almost ready to give up, allowing herself to fall prisoner to her body. She worried she could not take another step, sure she would have to give in to her own exhaustion as fear had since escaped. As if they knew she could go no further, the coyotes came to a stop. It was with more than relief that Maia let her legs stop holding her up. Her body slowly sank down to meet the ground, her arms remained securely wrapped around the infant; she allowed her eyes to close. Having fallen asleep, when her eyes opened, she knew it wasn't just a dream. How had she not awakened? The coyotes had once again licked the baby clean, but now they had done the same for her. She would worry about finding a place to wash her cloths later. They did the best that they could even with that. For now, it felt a bit refreshing just to be semi-clean and not quite so smelly. She put the infant to her breast to feed, taking the opportunity to look around, hoping that something might look familiar. All that Maia could see were the endless rows of trees, each looking like the one right beside it. There were so many, and they were so close together that their branches had begun to interlock. A full canopy had been woven, blocking any light that the sun might share. Inevitably making it almost impossible for even a bird to get through, a comforting thought. As the coyotes formed a line to once again move on, she wondered how much longer she could continue, although she had been afforded sleep, she was still so tired. Thankfully, it wasn't long at all before they stopped again. Relief filled her as she found a tree stump to sit on and rest. She welcomed the motionlessness only to be dazed by a glow that the woods seemed to be dressed in, a whitish glow that seemed to light up all of the space around them, holding them in its center. Maia wasn't quite sure she trusted how it felt. It was warm and welcoming, and it seemed to fill her, which under the circumstances made her not fully trust it.

The glow seemed alive as if it were breathing, its brightness fluctuating. Maia was fascinated as she watched it dance around. She tried to follow it to see what it may expose. She certainly wasn't prepared for what she saw.

Was there any possibility that it was a dream, a hallucination, that in my sleep I walked? Was it possible that heaven had opened its doors and was inviting me in? -M-

Chapter 12

No matter what one believes Miracle and Magic are the same.

B linking several times, she rubbed her eyes; sure, she was just too tired. She was definitely too hungry. Perhaps she was hallucinating or daydreaming. Maybe she was sleepwalking. For a split second, she wondered if she had arrived in heaven. The baby began to squirm, its small hand pulling at her hair, which had long since fallen out of the clips that held it in place. Now it lay loosely over her shoulders; that slight pull of it awoke her senses. What she saw before her took her breath away; a cottage just like the one that she remembered seeing in one of the fairy tale books her mama used to read to her. She remembered it well as it was a colorful page, unlike all the others that were black and white. Now, just in front of her, she could see it. It was something she couldn't possibly have expected, too beautiful to find words to describe it.

She stood up slowly, worried perhaps it might vanish if she moved too quickly like a mirage. But it did not disappear. She stood there, holding the infant, frozen in disbelief, not sure if she should try to move closer to get a better look. She could not fathom where she might be. She did wonder how far they could have traveled, feeling a twinge of pain, thinking that she would never find her way back home if that was what she chose. She wondered how anyone would ever find her, that was if she ever wanted to be found.

Maia stood there quite still for several minutes while the coyotes busily formed a perfect semi-circle behind her. It seemed to be a standoff as they awaited her next move, and she awaited theirs. She tightened her grip on the baby because it was all that she had to hold onto, and turning around to face the coyotes head-on, she asked them, "What have you done? Where are we?" She waited in silence as if she expected one of them to answer. Their silence left her to ask herself, "What have I done? Where have I allowed them to take me?"

Chapter 13

It is natures way with life comes death. Both must be nurtured.

I have never seen anything like this. Everything is dark, but not cold. There is a glow that welcomes. I feel like I have stepped into the enchanted forest. -M-

Here they were, deep in the woods, definitely deeper than she had ever been. A place without sunshine. Without the sky. Under a canopy of branches and leaves, someone or somebodies had built a small and beautiful cottage. It stood before her looking enchanted. The white glow seeming to shine directly over it made it more inviting, and it appeared to be even more magical.

An aura existed, encapsulating her so that she might feel just a bit of the magic intended only for her. But as she looked down at the infant, who was so peaceful, she couldn't help but wonder if it was this baby for whom all of it was meant. Taking a step closer, the glow did not just expand its perimeter. The light intensified, allowing the entire cottage in all its glory to be exposed.

Everywhere I look the magic grows. -M-

Maia tried to remember if she had ever seen anything so magnificent. Every stone that made up the bottom half of the cottage looked as if it had been hand-picked. Each stone was remarkably uniform. Stacked, the staggered joints perfectly lined up, the crevices filled with mortar to keep them secure. She could see that each log making up the upper half of the cottage had been cut into perfect lengths, a challenging job in itself. Each log fit perfectly into its neighbors, and they were perfectly stacked and intertwined. It flowed carefully and artistically into the stone base on which it rested. Meticulous chinking had been done, full and even, smoothed to perfection. Awestruck, she remembered watching Pappi build his own log cabin. It had been difficult for him and those that had stepped in to help.

Who could have built something so magnificent? Without access or resources, which I do not see. How could it come to be? How am I even here? -M-

She took a moment so that she could have another look around. So she could check out the surroundings. Mesmerized, she had to ask," how could it be?" There was no sign of a quarry. It was not only tricky but incomprehensible to imagine that each stone would have been carried. It was easy to stand there, still in the silence, and admire the craftsmanship, but harder to understand its existence.

Inspired and elated, she held onto the baby with new enlightenment. She was no longer feeling the pain in her feet as she stepped closer. The glow expanded its diameter with every step she took, following her and lighting the way. It was a new experience for Maia as she not only saw but could feel the energy that the glow seemed to emit. A power that she appeared to be in the midst of. Taking small, slow steps, she continued until she was within ten feet of the cottage where she stopped again in amazement. All she could do was stare at it, attempting to breathe in the beauty.

There is so much detail. The flowers are so real, I am sure that I can smell them. I want to touch them, to trace my fingers over them and feel them. -M-

She held the baby and feeling the need she tried to find words that might describe what it was she was seeing, but she had no words. The detail that surrounded each window, as well as the door, left her speechless. Symbols and designs that she had never seen graced the cottage. The variety and intricacy of the flowers so detailed, each petal and stem meticulously handcrafted. They looked so real that she was sure she could actually smell their scents.

She tried to envision the people or peoples who must have worked so hard to create this. It wasn't just the artistic ability she admired. She couldn't imagine the time it must have taken. It was hard for her to control herself; she wanted to reach out and touch each piece, feel the life she was sure it held.

She scoured the surroundings again, looking as far as she could see within the glow, while the coyotes continued to wait. Hoping that the coyotes might really see her, not just watch her, she allowed herself a bit of boldness. Bravely she took several more steps, this time moving closer towards the courtyard, which occupied an area directly next to the cottage. Glancing at it from a distance, she was sure she could see more elaborate carvings on the small wooden and stone fence. As she moved closer, it was evident that the fence had been built to lovingly protect what was a garden, so full of fruit trees and vegetables. As she took in the enormity of it, she had to wonder. How many people was it intended to provide for?

My heart is skipping. I can feel my stomach begging me to feed it. I can see so much waste and think I may cry. I know that I must control myself, it is not mine to touch. -M-

Still cautious, she pushed open the gate and walked through into the garden. She walked around, slowly taking stock of its yield as she moved about. She stopped moving, sure that she had heard something.. She stood still and listened. She could hear her Pappi and Mama's disapproving words, "Can you believe such waste? So much rotting on the ground. Surely not a passage to heaven." As she tried to maneuver through the almost non-existent rows and avoid stepping on all of the rotting fruits and vegetables, Maia thought she would have to agree with them. She had been taught that there was order and reason in planting. Now making her way through the chaos, she had to think that someone had evidently made a mistake. They must not have planned for growth or understood the need for space. Certainly, they could not have anticipated the challenge necessary to care for so many plants. The overcrowding and growth of so many plants could definitely be overwhelming.

She pulled the baby closer. Covering it as completely as possible with her blouse and somewhat with her arms. She worried about any insects that might make their way to it. While she attempted to take some sort of mental inventory of the garden's contents. She didn't have the patience for it. The plants seemed to be interwoven, making it difficult to tell where one started and another began. Each pushed the other out of the way as they struggled for room to grow.

I believe this may be the very first time I would like the chore of weeding. Of gathering that which is ripe and ready. -M-

Throughout the jungle of stems and leaves, she could see that there were bunches of vegetables that looked ready to harvest, maybe more than were rotting. It would be a challenge, for sure, to collect everything that appeared ripe. Even the few things that weren't ready looked as if they might be a challenge. For now, she knew she had to practice restraint, no matter how often the sin of wastefulness had been beaten into her. It was not her place to interfere with the owners of the garden. It was not her place or privilege to harvest anything or assist healing among the plants. It was how she had been raised. "Never forget the gratitude for the Lord's bounty. Never to be wasteful." She tried not to concentrate on those words and thoughts, hoping it would help her to control herself. Hoping she might look at the garden in a different light. Attempting to push back those words that had been instilled in her and now caused her pain. She tried to imagine that the Lord might have had a hand in the garden. She had to believe he did, for there was no other way to explain so many vegetables. Vegetables that were still harvestable in the dead of fall. As her mouth began to salivate, she realized how hungry she was, and how suddenly everything looked so good. She stood there among "God's glory," and wanted to harvest some of what was ready, not steal it, but save it, or, in this instance, devour it. Awestruck with such possibilities, she could feel her stomach screaming to be fed. She wondered if she could muster the self-control needed for such a challenge. She must have stood there for a long time holding the baby. Contemplating, when the alpha coyote ventured into the garden.

I think I should be more watchful of the coyotes. They seem to be more than just coyotes. I think I will need to learn to listen. -M-

It invaded her space without a sound, nudging her from behind, moving her toward the gate. She was quite confident it was now more of a push than a nudge as she stubbornly dug her feet into the dirt in an attempt to hold her ground. The coyote, equally stubborn and tired of waiting for her, moved closer. So close that Maia could feel the heat of its breath. She wasn't sure if it was fear trying to wrap itself around her or if she was allowing this coyote to irritate her. Similar to her parents, this coyote was continually trying to direct her actions. Either way, she found she had no choice but to obey, no matter how irritated it made her. The coyote continued to push as she tried to pause with every few steps. They kept this up, pushing and pausing until they were back at the cottage, standing at the front door.

Chapter 14

They walk among us always, it is just that not everyone chooses to see or hear.
Not everyone chooses to believe.

"Never go somewhere you are not invited" she thought. How many times had she heard that rule? She tried to dig her feet into the ground, her arms protectively wrapped around the infant, her knuckles centimeters from touching the front door. Standing there, working with all her might to hold her ground. She was sure she could feel the symbols and designs that adorned the cottage, breathing as if they were alive. The coyote would have none of Maia's stubbornness. It turned to the pack who sitting back on their haunches, watching. They were awaiting the single, a reminder that they needed to be at attention. The alpha then continued to push until, with teeth partially showing, it used a low pitch growl as if to say that it meant business. Unsure if it was her fear of the coyote or the fear of parental disobedience. Standing in front of the simple, beautiful wooden door, she paused. The door had been left open just a crack, inviting. Then, unable to restrain herself or the pushing of the coyote. Maia let hunger and exhaustion guide her. She used her foot to carefully push the door open a little wider. With the coyote directly behind her more than just encouraging her to go in, she pushed a little harder, opening it a bit further.

With the door open, my whole being has been filled. -M-

Maia had felt that the glow emitted energy when she first saw it. But now it elicited a feeling she had not previously experienced. It was a feeling that she did not think she could explain to herself or to anyone else. Just stepping over the threshold more than filled her with warmth. It was as if love had just wrapped a blanket around her and was holding her close. A feeling that she welcomed, filling every center of her being. Her body tingled. The infant reached its tiny hand up as if it too were receiving or asking to receive something. More significant than the warmth that filled her. That filled the space around her. Maia was quite sure that the energy had become a part of her. Not moving away from the threshold where she stood as if frozen just inside the doorway, she perused her surroundings. With the same awe that she had experienced when she first saw the cottage, what she saw took her breath away. Had it not been for the coyote who had followed her in and pushed her into a waiting chair, she would most definitely have fallen. She was quite sure that the fall alone would have caused her to drop the baby, and she wondered, "What then? "

Safe, gratitude consumed her. It was more than once that she gave thanks for this coyote. This coyote who she knew was responsible for saving them both, not just once but several times. It was embracing that gratitude that she let herself give in to its direction. She sank back into the overstuffed chair, surprised that the simple task of sitting did not bring her discomfort. "Laziness had no room at the inn," words her parents pounded into her and her siblings. Words that were always followed by some punishment or another, if they appeared too lazy.

I believe someone wants me to be queen.
I think I really like this. -M-

But here and now, in this cottage as if it were the only place she belonged, sitting in the overstuffed chair felt right. Never before had she sat in something so comfortable. She felt as if she were floating and sinking all at once. She imagined how it might feel if she were a queen.

Delighting in the comfort, unconsciously, she held the infant to her breast. Without thought doing what should be natural, she let it feed. Temporarily at peace, she sat there, closing her eyes, allowing everything to find its place, to sink in. Upon opening them, she wasn't sure what to look at first. Just from where she sat, there was so much to take in. She began to study everything that she could see from where she sat. She found it hard not to imagine that someone must have been waiting there just for her. So many of the things she could see seemed to have been put there just for her. And as if that weren't enough, she thought that she could hear someone calling her name.

Maia glanced down at the infant who was still feeding, hoping it would soon be full. She did not want to disturb it and thought that it would be so much easier to walk around if it was content. She felt like she needed to have a closer look at everything the cottage offered, perhaps then it would make it simpler to understand, all she thought she saw.

There is too much to see. I am sure that everything has been designed and gathered with me in mind. With this baby. The scent of food is making me lightheaded. Maybe this is all just a dream. -M-

As she walked around observing, even the smallest of details seemed to be personalized for her. She took her time. Examining every corner of the room, slowly and stealthily, so as not to give warning or not to disturb, should perhaps someone be hiding somewhere among the things.

What she found most intriguing were the smells. The scents were intoxicating, permeating every crevice of the cottage. As she stood there searching, she could feel small droplets of saliva begin to flow from the corners of her mouth. She could not stop herself from salivating. She let her eyes wander until they came to rest on the table she had tried so hard to avoid. Sitting on top of a beautiful embroidered tablecloth was a spread of food like she had never seen before.

Surprisingly, hungry as she was, it was the tablecloth that captured her focus. It looked just like one her Granny had made, and she began to wonder if perhaps it was. In disbelief, she started to walk away. Thinking maybe hunger had made her a bit crazy and that the food laid out was just her imagination in full bloom, maybe working overtime. But even after blinking several times and rubbing her eyes, there was no mistaking: it was real. She had never seen so much food in one place. Not even the exceptions of holiday fare, Christmas, Easter, a special occasion, none had ever come close in comparison. Yet, here it was. Everything appearing to be freshly made, she could see steam still rising from some of the dishes, as if someone had just finished cooking, in time for her arrival.

She looked around again. Stretching her neck, trying to see over her shoulder and in front of herself at the same time. Unable to comprehend how everything could be so fresh, look so perfect. Not able to wait any longer, she carefully stuck a finger in a bowl of mashed potatoes. It was still so hot. Skeptical and wearily, she continued to look around, sure that someone must be hiding. Surely they would have to be somewhere close by for everything to be so fresh. Perhaps it had just been removed from the small wood stove that sat in the corner of the room. Surely that would make sense, she thought. But she couldn't explain, even to herself, how they would have been able to lay everything out so exquisitely while keeping it hot. It would have taken some time and several people for such an accomplishment. A scenario that she was quite familiar with. It reminded her of home. Of all the times, her mama and sisters helped the church women set up for a feast, and how long it took when they were asked to decorate too.

I cannot help but wonder. Like all of the materials that make up this cottage, where could they have come from? Now so many fresh flowers, some I have never seen. All abloom and no sign of flowers in the garden. And how could that even be this time of year? -M-

Each detail elated her. On the table were baskets of freshly cut flowers. Each basket full of her favorite colors, predominantly orange and red. In fact, there were fresh cut flowers placed on every table in the entire cottage. She couldn't fathom their origin. Where would one locate such beautiful flowers that would grow this time of year? Someone had, indeed, given a lot of thought to the planning and setting out of everything.

Beautiful, full lavender plants had been purposely placed on both sides of the bed. Already the scent was working its magic, having a calming effect on her. Then there were the books. Books seemed to be everywhere. She had never seen that many books in one place. Maybe the library, but she wasn't even sure there were that many books there. There was a writing table with writing tools, an inkwell, and a sharpening device carefully positioned on top. Who would have known how much she loved to read? How when she wrote she felt important? There was a small, but apparently, very efficient stone fireplace, whose slow-burning fire produced just enough heat to make the cottage a comfortable temperature. There was enough dry wood to keep it going for hours, maybe even days. She remembered what Pappi had taught her and would have to make sure to arrange them correctly.

There is so much beauty. -M-

Over in the corner was a beautiful wooden cradle. Each spindle intricately carved with designs she recognized from those on the door frames and the exterior of the cottage. It wasn't just curiosity, she felt compelled to concentrate on each character. The longer she looked at them, examining them, the more she was sure that they might actually be words- ones she could not yet make out or understand-but words just the same. These words appeared to form sentences or sayings. She would try to remember to look through the books and see if she could find something that might explain their meaning. Inside the cradle were perfectly sewn and designed cloth baby dolls, colorful rattles, coverlets, and a fluffy white sheepskin.

Not to be forgotten, there were baby clothes, lots of them: little blue and pink outfits as if someone knew the baby was both.

Did someone anticipate her arrival? Did they know that this little baby was different, unique? Had everything been prearranged? Was she a player in someone else's game? Perhaps, whoever it was understood more than her. Maybe they understood how this baby had come from her.

On a small, but extra long table next to the cradle was another beautiful lavender plant, the smell producing the same calm to the baby that it did to her. Carefully, Maia held the infant. She removed everything from the cradle and placed it neatly in a pile on a beautifully carved rocking chair that sat at the cradle's foot. Maia laid the baby gently in the cradle. A cradle that seemed to have undoubtedly been crafted just for this newborn. She gave it a slight push to start it rocking. Comfortably it rested there, finding its hand, it began to suckle, and its eyes closed. Maia took a deep breath, and for the first time since the baby arrived, she felt more than relief, she felt calm.

Wandering through the cottage, she took in every detail. A beautiful simple spinning wheel with a skein of yarn already started stood next to the cradle. A basket full of wool lay waiting close by. Nothing had been forgotten. She cautiously looked around to make sure no one was watching. Then, she reached out to touch it just to make sure it was real.

She was growing ravenous, she glanced back at the table full of food. Trying not to be too anxious, she still worried that someone might be watching. She was afraid that they might stop her, that they might tell her to leave. With that thought in mind, she made her way over to the table, continually scouring the surroundings, wanting to make sure that there could be no one hiding and watching. But as she got to the table, all the scents and variety of foods did not matter.

I think today I understand that hunger
can have no rules and no manners. -M-

Forgetting all of the manners that she had been taught. Forgetting to behave correctly, she did not bother with a spoon or fork; instead, she began grabbing at the food that lay before her with her hands. Fingers furiously grabbing here and there. She stuffed her mouth with chicken and jerky, potatoes, cheeses, candied fruits. Eating them as quickly as she could get them into her mouth. Eating as fast as she could, just in case someone should try and stop her or she was to awaken and find it all a dream. She couldn't swallow fast enough, and the juices ran down her chin. When she was thoroughly full and content, she took handfuls of food and fed them to the waiting coyotes.

She did all of this successfully while the baby lay quiet. It was as if the baby knew she needed the time to eat time to savor the food. Just after she had filled her stomach and was feeling quite content, the baby began to stir. Its movement caused the cradle to rock. The rocking motion unsettled the infant, and it started to cry.

With my stomach full I can feel a little something
when I hear this baby cry. -M-

With her stomach full, Maia found it was much easier to respond. Walking back to the cradle, Maia wanted the infant to know she had not forgotten it. She had only needed to refill herself, her body. Maia peered into the rocking cradle and put her knee up against the side to make it stop. Using the blanket she had covered it with, Maia reached in and wrapped it around the baby before picking it up.

Holding it close to her, Maia breathed in its scent, realizing how much holding it, at that moment, brought her joy and gave her a sense of peace. It filled her heart as much as the food had filled her stomach. It was as if they were one and at that moment she loved it with all her heart. Maia held it to her breast and let it feed again. When it too was full, she kissed its white wisps and held it closer. Rocking it in her arms as she walked around the cottage, holding it lovingly.

It was a cottage whose interior seemed anything but small.

Chapter 15

Beauty of the unknown is often a gift.
A new beginning of which memories are made.

I will tell it each thing, and then maybe
it will begin to learn. -M-

Maia walked around the cottage yet again, even slower than she had before. She stopped in front of each piece of furniture, each piece of wood, food, flower, everything that the cottage held. In a quiet and calm tone, whispering, she began introducing the infant to each thing as if she knew that the cottage and its contents were a lesson to give. Maia concluded the experience by walking back to the rocking chair, where she sat and rocked. She rocked as if she were full with new pride. She rocked with joy until she could feel her eyes grow tired, and her lids feel heavy. Maia became fearful that if she rocked too long, she might fall asleep. She forced herself to get back up and holding onto the baby; she began to pace. She paced, letting her mind replay all that she had observed. Remembering everything she had already learned, what every corner of the cottage had to offer, every gift, every luxury. She let her eyes move to the wall of shelves lined with books. A particular book's bright green spine stood out. Calling to her to touch it.

I do not understand. How do they know?
The book is our book, mama and mine. Something is telling me
it is time to preserve the leaf. -M-

Without thought, Maia reached deep inside her blouse. She reached under the baby, where she found the leaf she had been protecting. The one that she had picked up and carried with her from the beginning. Holding onto it, she could feel a connection to her home and not only her family but her collection of leaves that she had left behind. Cautiously she pulled the book from its place on the shelf. Reading its title took her breath away. It was a story her mama had often read to her and her siblings." Peter Pan in Kensington Gardens", one of her favorites, and the very book that housed her collection at home. However, unlike the book her mama read, this copy was new and full of color. She found a place in the center and laid the leaf on the page, knowing when she closed the book, the leaf would be pressed and preserved. The beginning of a new collection and a record of what had been. Of how it started.

Now even with this joy, I feel only sleep. I must not sleep.
What should happen if they return and without question take
back what is theirs? I will need a plan. -M-

As happy as Maia was to have found such a perfect place to begin anew, it was not enough to awaken her. She held onto the infant, hoping that its breath might keep her awake. As sleepy as she was, she was afraid to stop, afraid if she let herself stop moving, she might fall asleep. She was afraid of sleep. She was fearful that if she fell asleep, she would have to wake up. Nervous if upon waking, she was to find out that it was only a dream? She had no clue where she was, and she did not have any idea to whom this cottage belonged. What she was most fearful of was that whoever it was that the cottage belonged to would return. She feared that she would be asleep, and they would return and find her. What would happen if they arrived and found her without allowing her any time to give an explanation? And what would her answer even be? She looked around for an exit plan, just in case she was fortunate enough to have time to flee. The worry was at least keeping her awake.

She asked herself. "What if there was no way out?" "What would happen if she had to face her worst fear?" "What if they would want something from her that she would not or could not give?" It was because of all of these questions that instead of sleep, she continued to pace, whispering sweet nothings to the baby as they paced back and forth. Over and over again, she walked, afraid to stop, fearful sleep would win.

I don't know how I let myself fall asleep. I didn't hear a thing. I didn't feel a thing. If it is a mama I am, then I am terrible. What would I do if something happened to this baby I have been entrusted to care for? -M-

Never remembering how or when she fell asleep, sleep must have won because Maia awoke, unable to move. She was panicked, finding herself swaddled in a blanket under the coverlet. Maia did not understand how anyone could wrap a grown person so tightly, yet, she lay still, swaddled as if a mummy. Not only had she fallen asleep, but someone had cleaned her up, washed off the baby's excretions that had become caked onto her, and washed and replaced her clothes. Even replacing the underwear, she had left behind.

How did that not awaken her? They certainly would have had to carry her, for she was nowhere near the bed as she paced. They had taken such good care of her. Swaddling her to keep her safe and covering her with the beautifully quilted coverlet before leaving her to sleep.

The baby was not there with me. Nowhere in my bed. Beyond panic, beyond fear. All I feel is shame and the need to find it. To know that it is safe. Or is this all a nightmare and soon I shall wake up? -M-

When she was finally able to free herself, using her hands, she gently felt around for the baby. The baby was not there. Maia became overcome with panic, realizing she was alone. Had someone taken the baby, or was the reality what had become her greatest fear that it was all a dream, a nightmare?

There was no baby with her. Had someone taken the baby? Even with the adrenaline kicking in, an attempt to get up quickly did not work. They had tucked her in so well, that she found she couldn't get out. Struggling a little too much with the covers only caused her panic to escalate. She had to stop fighting and simply move with slow determination before she finally freed herself. Her heart was beating furiously, and she was having trouble catching her breath. Once free, Maia wasted no time as she attempted to get out of bed but found herself falling hard to the floor. She hit her knees hard, causing them to be banged up and bruised. This made it difficult for her to steady herself as quickly as she wanted, needed. A tear involuntarily ran down her cheek. She stumbled as she made her way to the cradle in search of the infant.

Chapter 16

There cannot always be an explanation.
Pure unconditional love has no rules.

I would hear mama tell us when we were at our worst behavior that she only felt love. Now seeing the infant safe in the cradle, maybe that is what I feel. -M-

Relieved, she discovered it lying there sleeping. Like her, someone had placed the infant in the cradle, where it lay swaddled, sleeping so peacefully. Maia admired it as it lay there. It, too, had been washed off and dressed before being perfectly wrapped and tucked in. It appeared to have been lovingly cared for and now lay cozily under a coverlet or its own. Someone had put a diaper on it and left extra diapers, which were carefully folded and ready to use on the table close by. They had also left a box which, when opened, revealed it had been filled with extra safety pins. There was a jar of salve which looked similar to what she remembered putting on her siblings when they developed a rash.

I would hear mama tell us when we were at our worst behavior that she only felt love. Now seeing the infant safe in the cradle, maybe that is what I feel. -M-

Maia unswaddled the infant and picked it up. She pulled the blanket out of the cradle and wrapped it around the baby as she held it close. It smelled so good. She walked over to the woodstove, where the firebox had been filled, and the stove had been started. The fireplace's embers still burned, making the cottage comfortably warm. Fresh food had been prepared and sat on the table, which had been cleared of the previous night's leftovers.

The best surprise was the large galvanized steel tub in the middle of the room filled to the top with water. Maia knelt down, resting the baby against her as she touched her elbow to the water to determine the temperature. She was just semi-surprised that it was not hot but warm to the touch. Apparently, someone had taken the time to use the stove or fireplace to warm the water before filling it. Maia knew it would not have been a quick process full as it was.

Someone or someones are doing a very good job of taking care of us. I wonder what it means. I wonder why. -M-

As excited as Maia was with these new gifts, it did not prevent her from being cautious and concerned. She was troubled that she had not heard a sound. There had been someone or several someones in the cottage with her. Obviously, they had worked very hard cleansing them both so thoroughly and to prepare so much food. Her inability to hear and be aware that they were not alone was what scared her most. What if it was the infant crying out in the night that she did not hear? She questioned herself. Should she allow that concern to be her priority, or should she let herself enjoy the moment? The moment she thought she deserved. She continued to look around. She wanted to make sure that she hadn't missed anything. The cottage was strangely still when she realized that the coyotes were missing. She looked around the cottage before looking outside, where she found that they had been put. They now stood watch, as sentinels surrounding the cottage. Remnants of food showing that they too had been cared for.

I am not accustomed to being so cared for. At home it is always my chores that award me care and kindness. Yet here I have done nothing. -M-

She found it a bit uncomfortable. She wasn't sure how she felt about being so taken care of. She was curious and confused, and part of her felt violated. She continued to come up with questions. Were the coyotes left to protect her and the baby? Or was it their job to guard them? She felt sure that she should feel somewhat afraid that would be a reasonable emotion. Yet for reasons she couldn't explain; instead, she felt comfortable and safe. Comfort and safety were feelings that distressed her a bit. She wasn't sure that she liked feeling that way. If she thought about it, it didn't make sense. She had never been away from home. Now here she was away from home. She was sure she was incredibly far away. Alone with a baby, and no mama to seek advice, no one to tell her everything would be okay.

She remembered thinking it was a difficult place to be. How was she supposed to understand so many conflicting feelings? Feelings that filled her with a mixture of emotions. There was a part of her that was empty and wanting. Another part that was thankful and full. She wasn't sure if her Mama or Pappi had ever made her feel so taken care of. It was hard to put it into words. She felt a weight was being lifted off of her. Could she rely on the unknown? Was it safe to believe? To think that there was someone or several someones there to watch over her and the infant?

I have to wonder could the story of Hansel and Gretel be real? Am I being prepared for something terrible? – M –

Could she be sure that it wasn't the story of Hansel and Gretel? A tale that her mama had read to her and warned her about. It was definitely a memorable story, one that now put the thought in her head, What if someone or someones were just preparing her for something terrible?

Torn, Maia looked at the baby, knowing that they had to survive. And so she let herself believe because that was all she had. Thinking that she wouldn't have to do it all alone gave her a chance to breathe. It made her understand that alone or not, they would make it. With a sigh of relief, the fear was gone, gratitude replacing it, giving her the confidence she needed to know that she would be able to provide for them both.

No matter what I am feeling. No matter how afraid I am, I do know that I am beyond grateful. I am beginning to believe there is a plan for me and for this baby. – M –

Chapter 17

*One must open not only their eyes but their hearts
to accept the gifts bestowed them.*

Maia knew how fortunate she was. She understood that she was within walls that protected her and hid her. A place that kept her safe from all of the questions people would have asked. It gave her not only a sense of peace, but strangely, she felt as though it gave her a sense of power. Still, there was so much she did not know, and there was no way she could answer the questions that she did not understand.

As those first hours, that first night turned into days, she became aware of a hole that she could not fill. A longing for what had been so familiar, and now felt lost. It made a small part of her hold on to hopefulness. As if she were almost sure that her parents and others would come looking for her. Maia felt divided. While she did not want to worry her parents any more than she was sure she already had, there was a part of her who knew that it was the only choice she had. If what she really wanted was to be found, it would not only be an effort, but it would be a struggle and take real-time and work on her part. As she stepped outside the cottage and looked around, it was the reality that made her ask, "How would they find her? How would anyone ever find her?"

The woods that surrounded the cottage were always dark despite the time of day. Yet the glow remained visible. The glow seemed to feed her, and she could feel it within her reach. Maia imagined that if she followed it, sometimes she could see something in its trail. She thought that maybe it was something familiar. If she decided that she would choose to go back, she would have to find a way to reach out to whatever it might be. She had no idea where she was and no idea how to get home. She would stand there looking around, understanding that it made sense to accept that if she didn't know where she was, they too would most likely have no way of finding her either. Perhaps, she didn't really want to be found. That thought frightened her every time that it came into her head. It was a fear so intense that she knew she must always try to push it out. To keep it at a distance, that would be safer. Remembering that fear was never good.

Some days she acknowledged that the reality was, in all probability, she would never be found. On those days, she imagined that her desire not to be found made up for her fear of never going home. Either way, she understood that it was she, alone, that would need to prepare both emotionally and physically for such an outcome, such loneliness.

Today like so many others I am alone. I seek out something I might recognize, but still do not think I want to be found. I am beginning to feel as if this is where I belong. -M-

There were days, too, when she would ask herself, "How could she just give up?"

In the early days, she spent her time scouring the cottage and its surroundings, hoping each new day would offer her some familiarity. But the familiarity seemed to have gone. Just an occasional feeling that she was where she belonged. Then, just as quickly, second thoughts would overcome her, and she considered how she might leave. It did not take long for her to understand that any attempt to leave would only make things worse.

Nothing ever changed. She had no idea where she was, so even in a moment when she thought she might want to leave, to go home, she had no idea which way she would even go. Instead, she looked for places where she could find the faith she would need to allow her to believe in something. It was the success of finding that place that she held onto.

Other times, Maia would spend hours hoping beyond hope that her family would find her. That someone would be looking for her. In the early days, every day, she would go outside, she would listen. She would listen to the silence that lay beyond; she would listen and hope, in case they called her name. She would sit in the silence, hoping to hear something, sitting quietly and still, waiting for hours. Waiting to hear something so that she could answer back. On those rare occasions that she thought she heard something. Someone calling her name, the coyotes would begin to howl: one and then the next, loud piercing howls that didn't allow her to hear anything else.

I thought I heard someone calling for me today. But the coyotes howled so loudly I do not really know. –M–

When she took the infant and left the cottage, to tend the gardens and prepare them for the winter or just to explore the woods, it was always with a coyote or two trailing close behind. It was as if they were not only protecting, but watching over them. Guarding them, preventing them from wandering off too far and getting lost or maybe-preventing her from trying to leave.

Every day was like the previous- the leftover food each night would be taken away and replaced with another full day of meals. The wood stove and fireplace would be filled and almost always lit. More often than not, she would try to stay awake while pretending to be asleep. She was not just compelled to do this, but she needed to. She needed to catch a glimpse of those she now referred to as her "fairies". Thirsting to see and know those that were so good to them. But each time she would fail, sleep calling to her, and unable to fight it, she would have to surrender-each morning awakening to what seemed even greater joy.

I can tell much time has passed. I am having a hard time keeping track of time and days. -M-

As time went on, days and weeks passed. She felt the need to keep track of the days. How long she was there, perhaps just as much as the time she had been gone. She attempted to be consistent. To make marks on a sheet of writing paper with every new day. It was getting colder, and the days were getting shorter. There was a light dusting of snow on the ground, and her baby was growing. In no time, it would roll around on the floor as fast as words could roll out of her mouth.

It is growing so quickly and doing things so early. It is already starting to crawl, yet winter has not yet arrived. -M-

She watched it and wondered how soon before it might begin to crawl. Maia didn't have to wait long, for as different as it was to look at, it was physically way ahead of schedule. She tried to remember if any of her siblings or charges had crawled at such an early age. So very young, so very small, this one was beginning to crawl.

Chapter 18

Those gifts that seem the most practical, are the gifts that secretly contain the most love.

As she watched it wriggle across the floor, she worried that it might get hurt. She feared that its bare colorless legs on the cold floors might lead to sickness. Trying to use what she had available, she attempted to make leggings out of the diapers. She attached them to one another with safety pins. She would roll a diaper into a cylinder as best she could and using several pins, attempt to secure it together. It gave her a sense of accomplishment. It made her feel good when she had created something. Even if temporary, even if they looked ridiculous, it was something that might bring comfort and safety to the baby.

She hoped she could figure out a more practical solution, a way to sew with the materials that were lying around in the cottage.

She hadn't quite learned the knitting skill, although she had spun more than her share of yarn from the wool that had been left. But she found the yarn too thick to use to push through the material. Then like magic as if they could hear the words in her head, the very next morning, a new wardrobe had been left for it. Sewing needles and thread lay neatly on the table for her. The blue coveralls that had been left were so soft, and extra padding had been sewn into the knees. Nothing had been overlooked.

She wondered if they had seen her design and had a laugh. Then she thought not. They were too kind. When she pulled the coverlet up to make her bed, she was more than delighted to find that she also had been left with gifts.

I am not sure of the reason, but the gifts keep coming. Everything I need and think of somehow seems to appear. -M-

Maia's heart was warmed by these gifts, thinking that maybe it was their way of accepting her and letting her know that she, too, was genuinely welcome. New clothes for her that had never been worn. Clothes that allowed her to wear something other than what she had arrived in. Other than what they had so kindly dressed her in on the night of her arrival. It was exciting for Maia to be given items that were for her alone.

She had a hard time keeping the clothes she had clean since they were the only things she had to wear, and the one she had arrived in was quite tattered. Now folded in neat piles were several blouses, a couple of jumpers and a few pairs of leggings. Maia held them up to her face to feel how soft they were. She had never had a pair of leggings before, not ones that hadn't been worn and handed down several owners. In truth, Maia had never had anything that hadn't previously been worn. Among the gifts that they had left was a beautiful knitted sweater, she was sure that they had used the wool she had spun, as she looked and noticed it was missing. It made her feel useful that, perhaps, she had in some small way contributed. There were matching mittens and a big fluffy fur hat. The sweater and mittens were perfect, they fit her as if they had been made for her alone, and she thought perhaps they had.

I am concerned maybe they don't fully understand. I would never hurt an animal or person I considered my friend. -M-

The fur hat made her a bit weary, almost queasy. She tried it on anyway, it was soft and felt so warm, she could only imagine what the animal who had owned such beautiful fur must have felt like covered in it. With that image in her mind and pain in her heart, she quickly removed it. She was thinking that, perhaps, the coyotes would be upset if they saw her wearing it as she felt they rightfully should. She spent quite some time looking around for a place that she could hide it, knowing in the back of her mind that someday she might need it.

Chapter 19

What's in a name?

Time is moving quickly. Days and nights over and over again. It is a good sweet baby, but it is very odd. It is growing so quickly, I don't think that's normal. But so sweet. I believe it is time to name it. To christen it a boy or a girl. With Faith and Hope and Justice. Yes it deserves a name. It deserves to be strong and it deserves the opportunities it will earn, the only role can be to raise it male. -M-

So it was that the days grew into night and with night always came sleep. With morning it was all new once again. The infant rarely cried but filled the cabin with laughter and song. When it began to pull itself up and start to walk at such an early age, she realized she could no longer refer to it in such generic terms as baby or infant.

It was such a sweet and perfect baby, and it deserved a name. Maia knew it was not right for her to call it baby or infant or it forever. She had given it some thought, and there were several names which she had anguished over. She'd thought Faith. It had more than taught her to believe in something and not give up. Hope was a possibility. So many times, she felt there was nothing left when it had given her reason to believe in the power of hope. But those were more feminine names, and she didn't want a name that was too gender-specific. She didn't want to add any more turmoil for this baby. She was sure that its future already promised to be quite confusing.

She knew that this baby was extraordinary, and was sure that it would grow up to be righteous and fair. As sure as she was that she was not guilty, she had never known that she was with child; therefore, she had not sinned. The baby needed a strong name, a name that would bring pride, a name that would fit a boy or a girl. And so she decided to name it Justice. As she contemplated her decision, she couldn't help but wonder what it all might mean-being born with the genitalia of both girl and boy. It was luminescent and had red eyes. Eyes, which she was to learn, could not see. Yet, when gazing into them, they were more soulful and reflected more truth than one might wish. As she breathed in the fullness of her decision, it felt good, for all of this was true justice. Justice, for this infant, whose heart was full whose soul appeared so pure. She believed that even with all the unanswered questions, perhaps there really would be justice for them both. Justice was a strong and righteous name, and she was good with that. She was comfortable with her choice. As she looked around at her surroundings and what they had, she spoke aloud and reminded herself of the glory and truth that was Justice.

Chapter 20

It is possible that in the darkness it is the brightest of light.

I think about the canopy often.
Was it planted just to keep the birds away and the sun out to
protect Justice and keep him safe? -M-

When Maia thought about her arrival at the cottage, the reality was that fear held her tightest. Forlorn and cold, without cause or answers, it was to the cottage that she was led. A beautiful cottage located in a remote area of the woods. An area so deep in the woods that she did not know that it even existed. She had never traveled so far.

She looked around, not sure if it was really magical but allowing herself moments to believe. It was definitely a place that appeared to be made safe just for Justice. She wondered how it was possible: that a canopy of trees surrounded the cottage and the area around it. A canopy that hid them from the sun seemed as if it was not only planted but installed just for them.

Sometimes I miss the birds' songs.
I think that Justice would like the music they make. -M-

The canopy provided protection, a hiding place to protect them, to keep away the birds, to keep away anything that could fly. For it was birds that could fly, that she understood presented the most significant threat. Given the opportunity, especially when Justice was small, it was the birds that had been awarded the ability to carry Justice away. It was the birds that could steal Justice not only from Maia but from those that protected and cared for Justice; it was the birds that could steal Justice from the Universe itself. There was little that could protect Justice from the birds other than the safety of the canopy alone. It was a place that allowed darkness to protect Justice with its lack of sunlight but filled Maia's world with a constant glow of light. It was here that they had been cared for and felt loved. They had been allowed to love back in any way they could or chose. Although it was difficult not ever knowing who it was that they were giving their love to.

Chapter 21

*The Universe wraps its arms around us so that
we may know that we are protected*

In the early days, Maia had decided that having a penis and being male was a better choice than having a vagina and being female. She hoped that in doing so, it would offer Justice greater opportunities and less pain, should they ever decide to leave the cottage. She had always been taught, in her house, in the classroom, and in the church that it had been boys who were stronger. Boys who were given more opportunities had greater privileges, and all too often were the ones who made the decisions. These were all things that she would want for Justice, wishing only the best for this baby, and before she knew any better, Maia had chosen to raise him as a boy.

Justice proliferated; she had never seen a child grow so fast. It wasn't long before Justice went from crawling to walking to running. With the coyotes always around to watch over him, the trees to hide him and the darkness to shade him, Maia found comfort, still believing he would be safe.

I wish I had recorded the first day I let Justice run free alone. He was so very small really just so very young. He would run with his entourage of coyotes. He would always come back with a treasure or two. I could never understand how he could find such treasure. -M-

It was hard to remember how little he was when she first let him run through the woods with only the coyotes and how he had returned home in no time flat. She tried to remember how such a small child could make such a quick journey, and never come back empty-handed. Justice would always return, bringing back treasures he had found along the way.

In the beginning, she would ask him where he had found such treasures, but he would just laugh and putting a finger to his lips, whisper "shh" as the coyotes drew in close to him. It was in those early days that she not only knew but learned never to question. Still, she always wondered how it was that he could find such things, a gold button, a silver coin, a pair of eyeglasses knowing surely he had no sight. In the beginning, his hands were so tiny.

I am thankful that they have gifted me such a fine chair. So beautifully carved from a tree stump. I love how comfortable it is so that I can wait for Justice as he runs and explores -M-

Usually, every day, sometimes more than once a day, Justice would choose to run, and when he did, Maia would sit outside of the cottage and wait. She would sit on a chair carved from a tree stump that they had left for her one morning. It was beautiful with the same intricate designs that had been carved on the doorframe, the cradle, the fence posts all over the cottage. It was a chair designed to make her feel invited to do just what she did, sit and wait for his return. It never seemed to matter if he was away for five minutes or five hours she would sit there. She would sit watching out over the yard until he returned. It was in this time that she would come to learn and understand that by bringing her here, to this cottage, it allowed Justice true freedom. A place that protected him and made him safe. A place where the gifts and the quiet stillness of Mother Earth made his senses keen. She understood the absence of birds, but she missed listening to their voices and wished that it was a sound Justice could hear. She knew he would love it.

Chapter 22

Allow letters to turn into words. Put words together to form a sentence. Form sentences together to tell a story and absorb them as if a sponge.

When Justice wasn't out exploring, he would sit by Maia and wait for her to pick out a book so that she could read aloud to him. He loved it when she read to him, but as he grew up, she found she couldn't ever read fast enough. Justice seemed to absorb each word as if it were his own. As he grew a little older, he would often stop her mid-sentence to ask a question. When he was very young, he would wait until she was finished before asking any questions. They were almost always questions that she could not answer. The inability to answer his questions made her question her abilities to raise him. There were times that, if she weren't reading fast enough, Justice would finish the story word for word before she even had a chance to read them. It was his thirst for more that often left her feeling inadequate and lost. After all, it had been her knowledge she had felt was what it was that she had to give him. It was on those days when he asked too many questions that she felt the most troubled. It was on those days that her self-esteem was at zero.

I am having a hard time answering Justice's questions. If only the "fairies" that look after us would respond to my request and leave me a message, a note. -M-

 She would sit down at the table and write a letter to their "fairies". She would take her time. Using only her very best handwriting, making sure each word was chosen perfectly to convey her appreciation. Perhaps a new book might help her find the answer to a specific question or maybe a book on the same topic. When she completed the letter, she would read it and reread it several times before leaving it on the table where they always placed the food. Sometimes, she would feel brave enough to request that they leave a note in return with the answer.

It was just a single word that she hoped for, an acknowledgment, that they existed. A word written on a scrap of paper would be enough for her to know it wasn't all a dream. That she hadn't died, and there really was a heaven or hell. More often than not, when she asked, a brand new book would be waiting on the table in the morning. Sometimes it would be wrapped up like a Christmas present, but there was never a personal note or written word in response to her request. Sometimes her letter would still be there, appearing unopened, making her wonder if she was caught in limbo, and that none of it was real. But then she would pick up the book or package and wait to open it. She wanted to share the excitement of whatever laid inside with Justice. It was on those occasions that reality would whisper in her heart.

Maia cherished each book she read to Justice, almost as much as he loved hearing them read. Each story would find its place in her heart to store as memory and make her smile, as she hoped it would for Justice. Sometimes if the words were too complicated or maybe she was too tired, she would attempt to make something up, improvise. She would tell the story with a twist all her own. But it always failed: Justice would always catch her. Even when he was very young, he would know, even if he had never heard the story before. But he would never say anything. In the beginning, he would lean back against her while sitting on her lap. He'd lift his head as if he were looking at her and smile, a silly little smile that said, "Really?" As he got older, he would sit next to her and lean up against her. He would become very still and gently place his hand on hers or in her lap as if letting her know her efforts were appreciated.

Sometimes I find it difficult that Justice is so smart and I can't give him more. Sometimes I find myself wishing that he had never come to be. That I didn't love him so much. –M–

The older Justice got, the smarter he became. Although she couldn't quite remember how early, he seemed to surpass her in his schooling. She tried not to allow it to bother her so much, but the truth was, it did. It bothered her that she couldn't give him better knowledge than he could give himself. It was at those moments more than anything she wished that he could see, and sometimes, although she tried to suppress it, she wished that he had never come to be.

Like Maia, Justice shared his love for a good book almost more than just a good story. Like a sponge, he would soak up the contents of each book she read to him. Books had begun to take up so much space in their borrowed little cottage, that Maia tried to think of ways she might consolidate. And Justice began to worry that with so many books soon, he would have a difficult time finding his way around.

But the knowledge the books offered was what Maia knew that Justice needed. It was more than she could offer. Justice never said it with words, but she was sure he knew it too. As often as she would sit and read to him, she was convinced that the feel and smell of the books alone were just not enough for him.

My reading of words somehow does not seem enough. But that time we spend "reading time" is the greatest of our time together. It is our time to share. -M-

Still, it was the times that Maia read to him, what they called "reading time" that she felt was always their greatest time together. If pressed, she was confident that Justice would have agreed. Whether it was that they had just shared a book, read a new story, learned a new definition, or a new lesson. It was "reading time" that they afforded one another with the most fabulous conversations. It was time that they communicated.

Their conversation always opened doors when they discussed issues that they might otherwise never talk about. It was the best time for Justice to ask questions and gave Maia time to seek the correct way to answer. It made her think, and she liked that. In the years that followed, there were many times that either Justice or Maia would pull out a book just so that they might converse. When Justice was awarded the ability to learn to read using his fingers, it was celebrated with an assortment of unique books that were left just for him. This new knowledge allowed the doors of communication to open even wider.

Over the years, Maia's desire to identify the "fairies" who cared for them did not diminish. Instead, her desire to see who it was that took such good care of them increased almost becoming an obsession. She would do everything she could think of to force herself to stay awake.

So many nights, I try to stay awake. I so want to see who our "fairies" are. Last night I succeeded, but this morning there were only leftovers. I will need to remember how to create meals of our own. -M-

On the nights that she succeeded, there were no visitors. In the morning, it was she who had to prepare something for them to eat. She would use the leftovers from the previous night. Leftovers that hadn't been cleared away and that they hadn't yet fed to the coyotes. It was on those mornings that Maia took the greatest of pride. It was an opportunity for her to show off her creativity while providing something for both herself and Justice to eat. It was those times that she was able to let go of feeling inadequate in the intellectual department. Most every day, she felt like she was failing him in his education.

The joy as I listen to Justice's laughter and see the enjoyment that covers his face as he savors the food I have created for us. He tells me how delicious it is and gives thanks. That warms my heart. -M-

It was those days that she surprised even herself when able to demonstrate her creativity. With the absence of the "fairies", it was Maia who had to cook. It was then when she most enjoyed the delightful sound of Justice as it filled her with warmth. Justice would giggle at the deliciousness of her creativity. He would let the flavor linger as long as he could, dribbles of saliva dripping out of the sides of his thin mouth and down his small perfect chin. He would always show his delight by giggling. On those mornings, when he delighted in her cooking, he would giggle until he burst into full-out contagious laughter. Laughter that turned into snorts and had them both just short of rolling on the floor. It was these experiences cooking, preparing meals for her, and Justice that reached inside and pulled at her emotions. It was one of the only times after having lived so long at the cottage that she was emotionally torn. Did she want them to come back? Or was this experience, this edible passage enough to let them go? Or to let go of them? Ultimately, she did not have to worry, for as quickly as they stopped, they would return the very next day.

Chapter 23

*Is it possible that no ones life is truly their own,
simply borrowed for the time they walk among others.*

*Sometimes I think that Justice is not mine alone. That there are others with
a higher power, who think they can do better for him than me. Sometimes
I think maybe they can.*

Returning as if they were there to remind Maia that Justice was not really hers alone. It would be them that made sure that Justice would never need or want, that he was watched over and taken care of whether she could or couldn't. Maia saw this in everything that they did and was troubled by the fact that it might be true.

They added to his wardrobe every time that Justice grew another inch. Somehow, they knew, and his old clothes would be replaced with new ones, often leaving a few items behind for Maia so that she might use them for sewing projects of her own.

*I am learning to accept that it is not me that actually
summons the "fairies". That it is Justice for whom they watch*

over and provide. I am lucky that often times, they can make me feel important. I am thankful to them for their gifts. -M-

Maia never had to worry when she didn't wash Justice's clothes because he would always have something new to wear. In fact, he had what seemed like an unlimited amount of new clothes. It was a difficult concept for Maia to grasp. Growing up, she had always felt she was lucky if she had a single new outfit. She was so accustomed to being grateful for decent hand-me-downs. She couldn't remember ever having more than three different outfits in her wardrobe at a time, never would they be new. When the occasion arose that they would bring a new piece of clothing for her, she would hold it up in front of herself, sizing it. She would look at Justice, and she would wonder how they always knew the exact size of clothes to leave. How did they always seem to know what she needed, or what would suit her best? Maia enjoyed all the attention and attentiveness to her needs. She loved it when she had someone to take care of her and not just Justice. There was little she ever had to do, except to see to it that Justice was happy and entertained, and most importantly, she believed, well-read. It was a comfort that she was beginning to take for granted. Sometimes allowing herself to forget her role in their survival.

She was sincerely without worry, comfortable, and secure that they would always be there, and then things changed.

Chapter 24

Even angels must be tested

I have never been so cold. It is unimaginable, our breath freezes before it leaves our mouths. Our bedsheets and cloths are frozen and now we are all alone. They have left us here without any warning or words. I am frightened for us both. -M-

It was one of the coldest winter months that Maia could remember, undoubtedly the coldest since they had arrived so many years ago. It was in that month that it was so frigid that their breath froze before it even left their mouths. It was in that month that they found themselves unprepared for what lay ahead and in the greatest despair. The cold didn't just blow, but it ripped through the cottage. Icicles formed on the stove before they could even heat up the water. The coyotes came into the cottage where they gathered together. They took turns warming one another as well as Maia and Justice. The bedsheets and some of the thinner clothing they layered, (shirts upon shirts and pants upon pants) cracked at the touch.

There is no relief even the food must first be thawed before we can eat. And the glow seems to be vanishing. I think I can understand Justice's darkness. -M-

What food there was had to be thawed before they could even touch it, let alone eat it. The glow seemed to disappear as if it, too, had frozen. As the tiny bit of light would disappear, Maia thought she might understand what Justice must feel in all the blackness.

Maia was most fearful during that arctic month when everything seemed to be frozen still. She was afraid when for days, they were all alone. When they did not come, that maybe they never would. The cottage feeling more like cold storage than a place of safety and protection. It was during that bitter cold time that the Universe chose for Justice to grow. To sprout up like some mega weed. Justice was growing out of his clothes. His sleeves and pant legs were too short, making it hard to move, especially as the cold had forced them to wear so many layers, which in itself was challenging.

I hate them, I hate this place. Why me? What do I have to do. I think I wish Justice never was. -M-

It was during this period of freezing weather when feeling abandoned, Maia allowed herself to be angry, really angry. She stomped about the cottage, full of self-pity and resentment, looking at Justice and wondering why. But then, all too often it was something Justice did or said to bring her back to the realization of how fortunate she was. Justice would find a book they had not read. His cold hands fumbling with the pages, and as if he could see, he began, "A gift wrapped up for no one to find, holding the secret of all mankind. Little was it known that hundreds of people had already unwrapped it only to discover the true meaning of this gift."

I am wrong to feel so much hate?
Justice is such a gift. He is my gift. -M-

Maia stood back and watched him, and just that would remind her that she needed to let go of her resentment. She looked around the cottage and realized that although they had not come, somehow they were there.

Today I am so thankful. They do not visit but
they have not forgotten us. -M-

They did not bring much-needed clothes and food, but they had not been entirely absent, and most certainly, they had not forgotten. As she went from stomping to pacing, she found there was no room for anger, for it was gratitude she should have, and she allowed herself not only to look but to see. It was then with new eyes that she noticed. They were not there in the physical sense; still, they had most definitely thought of everything that they could. They needed to assure Maia that they would not leave her unprepared should anything come in their way. As Maia refocused both her eyes and her mindset, she could see how obvious it was, they had indeed planned well.

She could see that they had prepared for times when they would be unable to come. They had left provisions to ensure that neither Maia nor Justice would ever truly be in need. As Maia could see, they had thought it all out. She looked at Justice, appreciating his words, and she wondered how she could have missed it. They had filled a shelf in one of the newly installed cabinets. They stocked it full of black, white, and blue thread, providing various sized needles and pins, even an assortment of buttons. Bottles of dried spices had been intermingled where they would fit. They tucked away in the back almost hidden several small bags of dried fruits and vegetables. While they did not come to her aid, they had made sure that she knew they were there and that they cared. It was impossible not to laugh out loud with joy. Feeling her happiness made it easy for Justice to join her in her excitement and sense of relief. Together they laughed and danced, bringing warmth briefly to the cottage.

I believe that this is my opportunity to prove to Justice I can take care of him and of me. -M-

These newly discovered gifts allowed Maia to prove to herself and to Justice that she indeed had the ability and drive to survive. More than just survive, they would flourish.

Chapter 25

Frozen hearts still feel

.

The cold does not allow anything to be simple and I must learn to sew with my fingers frozen. -M-

Maia gathered the clothes that Justice had outgrown, making sure that she left him enough to keep him as warm as possible. Needing to remove the threads from the seams, she couldn't decide what was harder. Her hands were so cold. Trying to work barehanded, it wasn't long before she could no longer feel them. Wearing her mittens, kept her hands just warm enough but didn't help her fingers very much. It was difficult to manipulate them and do the work she had to do. She opted for the mittens and had to work more quickly than usual while she diligently removed thread after thread holding the seams. She made an effort to keep the threads as long as possible as she removed them, knowing she would need them to sew with later. Next, she began cutting the used fabric into large pieces so that she might begin creating new garments. Designing each piece so that it would come together to create new clothes for Justice, and if material permitted, would save some for herself. She was extra careful sewing the pieces together. It was a difficult task not only wearing mittens, but they barely kept her fingers warm enough to sew. Perhaps it was the cold that caused her to think about before, something she hadn't done for some time. Maybe it was because it was taking so long for each stitch that her mind began playing tricks. Pausing too often as she stitched the cloth together, she would remember, thinking of her own mama.

Mama taught me so much. I wonder if she thought I listened. I wonder if I ever thanked her. Mama I miss you. -M-

Maia remembered how she had sat by her mamas side, watching her as she sewed clothes for her and her siblings. She remembered how her mama had so patiently taught her to sew. Showing her tricks she used to make it easier, like doubling the thread so that she could just pull it once through the eye of the needle. She had taught her to keep the stitches consistent and the seams even. It was in those minutes of her remembering that she was sure she could feel the warmth of her mama, grateful for the time they had spent alone. She was also sad as she recognized how much she had taken for granted. Recognizing how at the time those moments they were just that ,moments. But now she realized that they were lessons remembered, lessons that gave her knowledge, knowledge that gave her an advantage.

I cannot help but wonder if Justice and I will ever have that. Will he think of me with joy or sorrow? -M-

She looked at Justice and wondered perhaps worried a bit if someday the same would be true of them. Would he remember or understand what their time together really meant? She would remember her mama, and through held back tears, she would understand the magnitude of missing her. She would look at Justice in his silence, in his darkness, and in silence, she would continue to sew. Making her ask herself, "What was it that made her so shallow and self-absorbed?" It was as if her world and space alone were all that mattered? Maia would sew for hours and days, alternating sewing and cooking meals to get them by, to pass the time. To keep them warm. To make sure that they would survive.

I have no time to read or talk. There is much to do. I need my time and my space to remember. -M-

Maia did not take the time to read to Justice, nor did they speak. Her memories did not allow her to. Besides the sound of her needles pulling threads through the cloth as she happily created, or the sound of the spoon mixing what was in the bowls, there was silence. Meals always contained water as the base of whatever Maia made. Water was abundant as buckets were left to collect the melted snow. It was incredible how she was able to add a concoction of spices, dried fruits, and vegetables to the pot of collected water. Its aroma not only filled the cottage with a tantalizing smell but tasted almost as good as it smelled.

Justice makes it fun to design and sew for him, and cook for him. He makes me laugh. Together we laugh and dance and sing, in that moment I can forget about the cold. -M-

It wasn't just her ability to design and complete various clothing to make an outfit that made her proud of herself. Instead, it was how Justice responded when she finished, which made her the happiest and gave her the greatest satisfaction. After each meal or when giving Justice a newly completed piece of clothing, Justice would smile that contagious smile and belt out a song of thanks. He would try on his newly designed clothes disregarding the cold of the cottage and strut around to model them for her. It was in this way that he knew he could make her happiest as she admired him displaying her handiwork. It gave her joy and gratitude that she could withstand the conditions and prove to herself how capable she could be. Proud that she had overcome the discomfort the cold caused. Grateful that she could find a way to disregard the pain that the cold caused her hands and fingers and allow her to complete the delicate work that was necessary to sew. As she watched him strut about the cottage in his new clothes, she couldn't help but notice how pretty he was becoming, how tall. It was difficult for her to grasp how long they had actually been there, how long she had been away.

So many years we have been away.
We have been in this cottage. It is sometimes hard for me to understand that he is from me. -M-

Chapter 26

We need to learn to communicate to use words and actions that express us

Maia looked at Justice with a mixture of pride and anxiety. There were times that he made her feel like they were connected, yet more often, she felt distant. She paced, wondering where the time had gone wishing that she could see herself. She thought about what the years might have done to her and how she had changed. Would she even recognize herself? Would anyone remember her? She wandered over to the desk and looked at the pages and pages of checkmarks she had made. It was a painful reality to see how many years had passed, a fact that she found hard to believe. She watched Justice, thinking about how much he had grown, inhaling his very essence, she was thankful that at least they had each other. At least she wasn't all alone.

It has been too long since we have eaten anything of substance. I am beginning to feel weak and I watch Justice and know he too is being affected by the lack of meat. -M-

It was during these times when realizations and feelings made her the most fearful and caused her the most worry. It was a time that she allowed herself to be vulnerable. Now, they had been alone for so many days, without visits or any real help. She knew that both she and Justice needed more nourishment than what the concoctions she had been preparing could provide. Although they had been left with items that were indeed helpful in preparing rations, she couldn't help but be concerned. What if they never came back? She still had no idea where they were, or how to get home, how to get out. She worried if they had to, with what they had, how long could they hold out?

Maia spent hours studying their surroundings, always looking for something she might have missed over the years. Something that might give her a clue as to where they were so she would know how to get home should they ever have to leave. During these cold days and trying times when she felt deserted, she knew the importance of looking around and taking it all in.

I must remember all that there is around us perhaps I'll find a way out. I am so afraid that they will never come back. I am afraid that their gifts will cease and we will be alone with nothing. -M-

To remember all they had, all they had been given. It was why fear enveloped her as she not only worried, but sincerely thought about the day when they would stop coming altogether. Hoping beyond hope that that day had not already passed. If it had, she was not prepared. What would happen when all of their care and gifts stopped? She worried about what she would do, what they would do. She had read to Justice, played with him, studied and explored with him, but she had never really talked to him. She had never really discussed with him about her life before, about what there was somewhere else. They had never talked about what lay beyond their cottage or the woods. She had never thought that there was a reason, and Justice would have had no idea to ask.

I think about out there. Away from here, I wonder what it would feel like. What it would be like. I wonder if I would remember how to speak and react with others. Justice and I are here together. Mostly silent I wonder what are we to one another? -M-

Maia was sure that they were both quite content with where they were. Content maybe even happy with how it was. It was all Justice knew. It had been so long since she'd had any human contact that she wasn't sure how it would feel. No human contact except, of course, Justice. There were too many times that Maia would look at him and wonder if he was really family or just a stranger passing the time with her. It was those times when she questioned their relationship, how they came to this place? How he came to be? It was those times when she would question, and without words, Justice would walk away.

I do not know how to make my thoughts go away. I know they make Justice very sad. -M-

It was as if he could read her thoughts. He wouldn't say anything, he would just turn away, his back to her and walk out the door. Some days, she would watch him leave and let him go. Other times she would go after him, following him out the door to walk with him and speak in silence because she didn't know or have the words.

On the days she let him go, in solitude, she would sit or stand and shudder. She would think about before, about her family, about life before and without Justice. She would sit in that solitude that grew dark, and she would wonder if her family still looked for her, ever? Had they given up all hope and moved on? Did they think she was dead? She would sit in the darkness and remember her little sister, the one she barely knew. She wondered what she was like. Was her mama okay? Her mama had also been with child, that day that she went to collect her leaves. On that day, her mama's health had been wavering, she hadn't been well since the previous birth of her sister. Maia found it hard to imagine that if she had gone home instead of running away, she and her mama would have raised their children together. Maia let her mind wander as she imagined that. They would be such good friends, she was sure of that. She and her mama would share their secrets and cook and sew and talk. That was what she needed to believe. It was a dream she needed to keep.

Maia tried not to question what her mama would have really done. She didn't want to think of how she would have reacted to an infant-like Justice. But as time went on, it was not her questions or wondering that triumphed. It was in those moments, those thoughts, in times of solitude that she realized that mostly she was terrified.

The year before the big freeze, the garden had begun to wither up. They had used it to supplement what had been gifted them. Maia knew it no longer produced nearly enough to sustain them should or when they ever needed it to. She worried, knowing that they could not rely on it alone. At one point, she had started gathering what she could when she realized she hadn't started soon enough.

I am grateful that I thought to store some food from the garden but it is Justice whose gathering has been the most helpful. –M–

There had been many times; a day here, a day there, that they used the garden as a supplement. It had certainly come in handy. She knew the harshness of the winds and frozen air of winter could take its toll and wondered, no feared, nothing would be left. What she didn't know was: while she was fretting about, Justice had been gathering, too. He had collected and stored several bushels in a cold, dry area that kept it fresh.

Now without their return, she wished she had not been so fast to act and so anxious to use what she had gathered. She should have thought to preserve some. As she sat at the table, she worried about the next meal, allowing herself some self-pity. It was often an easy thing to do when Justice had wandered off. The stillness was more of an enemy than a friend. When Justice returned, it was not with his usual quietness. She looked up only to be totally surprised as he unloaded onto the table what he had been hoarding. It was those unexpected surprises and treats that they gave one another that ultimately was what kept them going.

They have left us a pile of books, books whose purpose is to teach survival. Are they telling me they will not be coming back? -M-

Chapter 27

Sometimes we are forced to be alone and we must ask ourselves who we are

It was a painful reality that even with all of the potatoes and other roots, beets, carrots, onions, their bodies needed more. They were both beginning to show what the lack of protein was doing to their bodies, and Maia worried.

She worried and wondered as one of the coyotes put its face in her lap. As she sat stroking him, she knew she was ill-equipped to hunt, and she didn't have the heart. As she rubbed the coyotes head and looked around, she noticed a pile of books she hadn't remembered seeing. For the first time, it was with fear and caution that she reached for them, and it left her even more fearful when she saw their titles. Able to sense her discomfort, the coyote placed a paw on her lap, attempting to calm her. Justice joined them and stood by Maia's side. Words still did not exist, only feelings.

She should have been happy and content to know she was so loved. But all she could think about was what would happen to her? To the coyotes? To Justice? They had been absent for so many days, leaving them alone. All she could think about was without their help, she would be alone. It would be her soul responsibility to protect him and keep him safe.

Her hands faltered as she picked up the book on top, "Guide to Survival" and as she began to examine it, she wasn't quite sure if it was excitement or anxiety she felt. For the first time, there was proof that someone or someones was there. With anticipation, she started to flip through the pages. Pages that actually had handwritten notes and diagrams stuck between them. It was the very first time that she had seen another person's handwriting in as long as she could think back to their beginning, in the cottage. She had to look at it carefully several times before she could read them to Justice.

It is a beautiful thing to see that they are real. That they have words like ours and communicate with love. I worry that I will be unable to trap as they have described, but know that really I have no choice. -M-

They were full of encouragement and included quite detailed information on how to trap, how to gut, skin, and prepare. The thought of doing any of that turned her stomach and pulled at her heart. It was one thing to prepare it and cook it, but an entirely different one to have the job of catching it and killing it. She looked at the coyotes that had stayed so true over the years and wondered how she could ever cut into a living thing, not to mention trap and kill it. How would she explain performing that act to Justice? But with each new day that they did not arrive, with each new day that they were not there to help, they did not forget. Each day, there came a new handwritten note, and Maia knew that soon they would be on their own. She knew that it was only a matter of time. They were getting close, leaving personal messages, words of encouragement, lessons to be learned and practiced. It was difficult not to be a bit angry and a lot afraid. They had been so well taken care of, so provided for. At the same time, they had been so isolated, lost, left without answers. She was having a difficult time, not letting anger take hold of her, getting so angry at them. She became angry. She was mad at herself for allowing such an unflattering and ungrateful emotion to surface. So much had been given, but also so much had been taken away. And, now, she understood that she would need to prepare for when there would be nothing. She found it increasingly difficult to hide her fear and anxiety. She knew Justice would know something was wrong, he always did. Reading emotions was one of Justice's many gifts. This is what added to her anxiety. She knew that Justice would most definitely begin to question. She was quite confident that there would be questions she could not answer. Just the thought of what he would ask added to her stress. How could she even begin to explain something she, herself, didn't understand? She had no answers.

Chapter 28

As if one could take flight we are reminded what is meant by freedom

I have not spoken to Justice about leaving. I have not told him we will need to trap, as we to prepare for moving on. -M-

Being alone without the extraordinary help that had been bestowed on them was one of the many things that they never talked about. One day as she worked to prepare for their independence, Justice's greatest gift showed itself.

From early on, Justice had expressed an immediate interest in whatever it was that Maia was creating. He was especially intrigued each time she would gather her threads and whatever cloth that she found available. Justice would put his hands on top of her handiwork and let them flow over the fabric. His fingers exploring the threads and each of the stitches. As if he were reading a story that she had created.

Always excited for something new, he wanted to learn. Each time Maia would begin to work on a piece Justice would stand or sit beside her. When he was very young and had just started to crawl, he would crawl up on her lap and place his hand over hers, their fingers moving as if they were one, just like their breath. The needle would move in and out, the thread following along. It wasn't long before a very small Justice felt comfortable enough to use his voice to ask for a needle and threads of his own. When he felt it could be his work, with confidence, he was ready. However, it did not go well when at first, Maia told him no. It was her sincere concern for him that made her worry, afraid that he might hurt himself. But Justice was just as determined as she was concerned, and it did not take long to plead his case and win. And so it was, Maia allowed Justice to have a needle and thread of his own. Like anything Maia taught Justice or that he learned on his own, it was no time before he mastered it, bypassing her in skill, perfection, and design. This was no different, and he quickly began using the needle as if it were an extension of himself. Often she would find him with needle and thread-making intricate designs on the scraps of cloth she had left for him, each more beautiful than the one before, each with more detail. Maia would wonder how he could create something so accurate and real if he could not see. She wondered if perhaps he had help, she would have to watch more closely while he created.

On this particular day, Justice had been playing in the front yard, spinning in circles, arms outstretched as if he were inviting the Universe to join him. When from out of nowhere, it seemed as if he had. An eagle landed in the tree just above him. Maia saw it fly through the canopy of trees and tried not to panic. She couldn't remember ever seeing a bird, let alone an eagle enter the space that was now their home. As always, the coyotes were in the yard with Justice, they rose quickly and began to pace, cautious as if they were waiting for a signal. Regal, the eagle, perched itself on what was surely its branch directly over Justice as if it had landed there specifically to watch him. To wait for him, or perhaps in an attempt to take him. After several minutes of being perched there observing, it began to call. Justice heard it, he stopped spinning. And then as if he were being controlled, he lowered himself slowly down until he was sitting cross-legged on the ground. He sat very still and quiet, his hands resting palm-side-up on his knees, his head bowed down as if in prayer, and in that way, he did not move but simply waited. In no time, the eagle took flight and flew down, perching itself in front of him. Justice raised his head as if he could see. For a bit, they were face to face. Neither moving, until the eagle inched forward, slowly almost too cautious. And then did the unexpected, it lowered its head and gently laid it in the palm of Justice's hand. Justice had the most peaceful expression. The eagle waited patiently for him to turn his palm over. Giving Justice permission to reach out and touch him. He stayed perfectly still and allowed Justice to not only feel but explore its body, its feathers, its beak. Justice was so gentle, so awed. With Justice's fingers still touching it, the eagle turned its head slowly, allowing Justice to feel the mechanics as he did so. It put its talons in Justice's hand, letting his fingers explore its claws showing him ever so gently how sharp they were as if a warning. Justice lowered his head until his nose was in the eagle's feathers, he inhaled so that he might breathe in a bit of his majesty and then gently he kissed the back of its neck as he gave thanks. The eagle flapped its enormous wings, yet Justice did not flinch. Then it flew away, once again calling to Justice as it disappeared back out of the canopy.

Justice remained still for quite some time as if he were allowing the moment to etch itself in his being. The coyotes too were still, an air of confusion seemed to hold them, all but one. One single coyote lay separated from the rest, watching and perhaps understanding that a message had been delivered for Justice alone, a warning. A voice that fooled, seeking Justice's trust so that when it returned, there would be no battle. The coyote knew that in the magnificence of the interaction she had just witnessed, there was deceit. Maia, too, had been watching. She had stood at the window bearing witness to the awesomeness of such an encounter. Yet knowing inherently that it could bring no good as it was the birds that the canopy was there to protect Justice from. Yet she could not move, no matter how hard she tried, she could not protect him.

Maia stood still watching and waiting, not praying, but wishing with all her might that he would come inside, that he would know to join her in the security of the cottage. She stood and watched and waited. He was full of cautious joy and excitement like she had never seen him before when he finally stood and came running in. He did not stop but ran right past her, and she watched as he gathered his fabric and the box of black threads she had given him. But as he began to sew, the black threads changed to yellow and red and white, gray and blue and green. The thread actually changed color before her eyes as Justice gave life to his most recent experience. He did not stop until he was finished creating what had touched his soul so that Maia too might see. He simply wanted to share so that perhaps she too might know. Maia stood awestruck, she did not say anything at first. She couldn't. She was speechless, unable to verbalize. She watched and admired his talent, the detail. All the while, she was trying to understand what the message might be and what was really being said. She wondered if Justice even knew. As it was completed and Justice laid it down for her to see, all she could do was to tell him what a beautiful picture he had created. She did not know what else to say. She was afraid to ask him for an interpretation, fearful of what he might tell her, afraid of its true meaning. She was scared to ask him, did he even understand what had happened?

These gifts that Justice has I must keep hidden.
There is no place outside for people to see. -M-

Most of all, it was the unknown and the possibilities of what-ifs that scared her. She was afraid that if anyone else ever saw what she had just witnessed, they would think Justice a witch. She remembered the stories from the Bible that she had been told in church. It took considerable effort for Maia not to forbid him altogether from creating. For her to take away all of the fabric and threads that he had been so happy to receive. But she reminded herself that no one would ever see. Who would ever know? In this place, they had called home. It was only them, the coyotes, and the ""fairies"" who had cared for them. Maia was quite sure that such a talent, such a gift, should be admired, and so with admiration and awe, she made sure to keep it close as if it were a book in a language she could not read. Hoping that as she examined it time and time again, she might understand its full message.

Each time Justice continued to create, it was always more intricate and detailed than the time before. She would watch, and each time her amazement grew, and still, she was without explanation. That was how it began.

Chapter 29

Perhaps it is not ours to question what we believe

*I worry how long will they be absent this time.
The ground is beginning to thaw and it's time to work on the
garden. It will be so much work this year.
The garden is beginning to fail us. -M-*

The ground was thawing, and too quickly, things were making their way above ground. Maia knew not to question how nature was somehow altered in this place they knew as home. She also knew she could not question when once again, they had been left alone. Their "fairies" had once again been absent for more than a week. This left Maia finding herself working tirelessly in an attempt to prepare the garden. The importance of making it more productive was crucial. However, it wasn't long before she realized that no matter how hard she worked, the garden was no longer capable of producing enough for the two of them.

I have read and reread the books on survival that they left.
I know that assuring our survival is my duty but
I don't think I can follow the instructions.
Killing does not feel like an option. -M-

With trepidation, she asked Justice to help her as she began to gather twigs. She was careful not to tell him that the purpose was so that she might build and set some traps. She was hopeful that doing so would provide them with a much-needed source of food and protein. But even without telling him anything, she was quite confident that he understood. She was greatly concerned that their time at the cottage was running out. It was essential to her that she figure out a more humane way to trap, one that she and Justice would be able to live with. She had read and reread the book on survival. The instructions, along with the notes that had been handwritten in the margins of the book, described a trapping technique that would just not work for them. Maia wondered how they could even think it would be a viable possibility for them since it seemed that they would know them better. While Justice understood the need, he had a difficult time in assisting with any part of trapping. He was happy and satisfied with the little that the garden would produce.

Justice is happy to feed from the garden,
he is not concerned as I am. -M-

While they both enjoyed the meats that an animal provided, it was a difficult concept for either of them when it came time for trapping and killing it themselves. In the end, they found they need not make such a decision. The decision was made for them, reminding them again how grateful they were for the gift Justice had received years earlier.

One of the coyotes who had been with Maia and Justice since the beginning, a coyote who had helped with Justice's arrival, was pregnant. It was her first litter, and towards the end, she had been hanging close to Justice as she prepared to deliver. It was his gentleness that was most comforting to her. It was the peacefulness of his lap that she so often chose to lay down her head and wait only seconds before Justice would place his hands on her and stroke her.

The day she delivered was no different, his small hands served as warmth to the pups waiting for her to take them and lick them clean. One pup, in particular, stood out, a bit smaller than the rest and a bit off, the bitch would most likely have let her die as the litter was so big and she was so weak, but instead she left her in Justice's hands. Nudging her each time, she tried to get away. Like her siblings, the pup was looking for a place to feed. But it would be Justice who would need to nurse it. Justice who would learn to love it and feed it and call it his own. It was Justice who named her Dakota.

Maia had watched Justice feed Dakota not only milk but confidence and love. It was in no time at all that Dakota was strong enough to keep up. From the very beginning, they became inseparable. There wasn't anything one did without the other. As it turned out, Justice was Dakota's ears and Dakota, Justice's eyes. It was this combination that allowed them the comfort of knowing that there was nowhere they couldn't go together. It gave Maia the comfort she needed knowing that wherever they went together, they would indeed be safe. The truth was there was nowhere that they didn't go together.

There is no better gift than that of friendship. For the gift of sound and sight has connected them. Joining them so that in one another they give all of themselves. –M–

On rare occasions, when Dakota wandered away, Justice would wait patiently. He would try not to pace while singing softly and tapping loudly, sending vibrations out to Dakota to bring her home. If Justice wandered, Dakota would pace back and forth in front of the cottage howling without pause so that Justice would hear her voice and bring him home. Maia was grateful to the coyote for giving Justice such a gift, and to herself for sharing the burden. The companionship was what Justice so needed and helped her, too, especially during trying times. She wondered how they had managed together alone for so long without Dakota, especially Justice.

Now in a time of need, Maia was confident she couldn't manage anymore. The garden scarce and the anxiety of trapping weighing heavily on her being, it was Dakota who left Justice's side choosing to go out with the pack, a true blessing.

It is the first time Dakota has left Justice and joined the pack. They have been gone for hours and Justice seems so lost, there is nothing I can do to ease the emptiness. –M–

On Dakota's return, it was at Justice's feet that she lay both a rabbit and squirrel, proud of her catch. Maia carefully skinned and dressed them. She prepared them in ways that were sure to surprise the grandest of chefs, always making sure that Dakota got fed first and that there were still enough scraps to go around for the rest of the pack. She felt indebted, for it was Dakota who always made sure that it would never be their blood on the food she prepared.

It is difficult to write. It is difficult to do anything.
I would be happy to lay down and just sleep. -M-

After being alone for so many days, weeks, without a visit. Without a note, without anything, Maia was beginning to wonder how long they would be able to sustain themselves. Even with Dakota's gifts and Justice's stash. The frigid temperatures had taken their toll; her spirit was on the verge of breaking. She felt hopeless and lost.

There were times she was so cold, so deeply worried that she could not even get out of bed. Justice and Dakota would join her as they tried to keep one another warm and keep her from falling too deeply into a depression. Even with hints that the weather was starting to change, it was difficult for Maia to imagine what life would be like. She did not expect them to ever return. It was an endless string of worry as she feared not just for herself, but for Justice and Dakota and the rest of the coyotes and worried about what might become of them all. Lives lived and then forgotten as if they never were. Would that be their story?

For a minute I let my heart dance. But now it is broken. -M-

Chapter 30

It can be a difficult task to discern between fear of the unknown or fear itself and the meaning of love. Both can fill you with the need to run

For an instant, Maia celebrated how wrong she had been when finally they did return. Instead, she realized her fears would not be calmed. Their return was not what she thought it would be. It was not what she had hoped for. So rather than celebrating their return, Maia's greatest fear had come to be when she learned that they would only be returning one final time.

She knew she had to be grateful. It could have been in the midst of those frozen days. Then it might have been the end of them. All of them.

Spring is coming. I love to watch the plants begin to sprout. Everything new and alive. I wonder when it was Spring that became my favorite. Now there is nothing to celebrate with Spring. It will no longer be filled with joy and new beginnings. Today they came with gifts that I would need to survive. Gifts that I alone would need to use. While the aromas from the

feast that has been prepared are intoxicating. I fear they may
be poison. Perhaps it is my wish. I choose not to suffer. -M-

Gratitude was her only choice as she looked out the window at the small green stems poking their heads through the earth readying themselves for spring.

The same day she awoke to a feast bigger than the one which had greeted her on the day she and Justice had arrived. In addition to a table full of every food she could imagine, there were neatly piled stacks of new books and a satchel full of writing utensils and paper. There were big bottles of seasonings and salves.

There was so much to see and take in that Maia did not know where to start. Just like any other time that they received a special gift, she wanted to take inventory but not until she shared the bounty with Justice and Dakota. She found it unusual that they were not there and figured that they must have left very early for a morning run. Maia anxiously waited for them to return, she wanted to know if they had heard anything. Had Justice smelled the glorious smells that accompanied the food? Was it possible that she alone had once again slept through it all?

Maia grew impatient as she waited for Justice and Dakota to return. Pacing only made her more anxious. It had been such a long time since their "fairies" had come by that she couldn't contain herself. She began examining an unusual amount of new clothes which they had left in two neatly folded piles. They had also left several additional rolls of new fabric. Maia was sure Justice would love how they felt as much as she loved how they looked.

There are so many gifts this time. -M-

Enthusiastically, Maia began unfolding each piece of clothing. As if she should be guilty should Justice catch her, she was extra careful. She made sure that she would be able to fold them quickly and put them back in their place. She was enjoying the softness and smell of each item as she held it up to her face, rubbing her nose in the fabric.

However, as she unfolded the last piece in the second pile, she found herself quite confused. Actually concerned. She was sad, and feeling hurt when she realized that neither collection included anything for Justice. She was confused, both piles were most certainly for her. What she didn't understand was that the clothes in the bigger pile included sizes that certainly would not fit her.

Shedding the guilt, Maia hoped that Justice would not sense her disappointment when he returned from his run with Dakota. While she could not hide her confusion, she hoped that he would not be upset with her. She hoped that he would forgive her for not waiting for him before examining everything. Maia acknowledged that she was definitely more worried and stressed by these unusual gifts. It was the stress that made her pace. As she paced, she caught it out of the corner of her eye. Lying on the table next to her bed so easy to see.

How is it that they know my name? So beautiful.
They have written each letter as if it were special and perfect.
I will take my time to see what is inside.
What it is that is for me alone. -M-

As if it had been there forever, an envelope. An envelope that had her name inscribed in beautiful cursive letters. How did they know her name?

It was the first time that they had left something so personal. Maia knew it must be important. Her hands shook as they reached out to pick it up. The envelope thick felt uncomfortably heavy. She turned it over several times, letting her fingertips enjoy its texture. Using a finger, she traced over the letters that spelled her name. And then carefully broke the seal on the envelope and pulled out a neatly folded piece of paper, wrapped around a large stack of documents.

She trembled as she carefully unfolded the letter, making sure not to allow anything to fall out. She could not believe that someone had actually written to her. It wasn't just a message here or there, a side note in the margin of a book, instructions meant to be followed, a lesson to be learned.

No, it was a personal letter, addressed to her. She found it difficult to control her hands, which continued to shake as she read it out loud. She wanted, needed to hear the words that someone had taken the time to write to her. She tried to imagine the voice to whom the words belonged.

To you dear Maia, we give thanks.

For sharing your beautiful child with us, we are grateful.

For allowing her to grow, and create and share is a tribute to your sacrifice, your caring, and your kindness. She will be a great teacher and loved by all, you must never be afraid to let her go.

Our blessings are with you, and we are honored and humbled to have served you both. Now it is time to move on. Close the door and don't look back. The world awaits her.

For the many years that you have shared her with us, we offer you a token. May it be the beginning of what awaits.

We leave it up to you to see to it that it is with wisdom that you spend this gift and that it is you who must make sure that it last long enough.

Be careful, and remember she is exceptional. Others will try to take her. We can no longer protect her under the canopy.

Understand that you need to move on.

P.S. We are not "fairies", Maia, and this is real, but if you would like to still believe, that is just fine with us.

Included with the note was $5,200.00. It was more money than she had ever seen in her life. More, she was quite sure, than even her parents had ever seen.

I do not understand. They write about "her". Have they forgotten all this time? They watched Justice grow and participated in that growth. And so much money I do not understand. But I believe I need to hide it. -M-

A bit shaken and anxious, Maia heard laughter. She looked out the window, Justice, and Dakota had come back and were playing in the yard. Not too far from the garden entrance, she could see that they had left another gift: a brand new four-wheeled cart. At that moment, she gave thanks for Justice's lack of sight. She was grateful that Justice could not see it. Standing at the window looking out, she realized that she was still holding the money, leaving it tightly wrapped up in the letter in her hand. She pulled the money out and using her thumb and forefinger fanned it just to feel if it was real.

The reality was, it wasn't just money. It was a message, they were sending a message that she understood. They were not only asking, but they were telling them to leave.

Holding onto the stack of money, she wondered. What they had meant when they said: "long enough." And who would try to take her? Who were they talking about when they spoke of her? Were they calling Justice her? After all these years of providing him with all he needed, why now? What had she missed?

Maia continued to watch Justice and Dakota playing in the yard and wondered what was meant to happen next? All these years of raising Justice as a boy. They must have agreed that it was true for they had always left Justice boys clothes, making sure he was well taken care of as if they knew him. So why now did they call him, her? And who were these folks who would give them so much money, so many gifts while at the same time tell them that they had to leave? She could not believe anymore that they were "fairies". "fairies" would never do such a thing.

With all my might I watch Dakota and Justice dance. Their joy making magic. But I do not see what it is that they speak about. Must I continue to look? -M-

Maia continued watching as Justice, and Dakota danced about and soon found herself lost in the moment. She was pulled into the magic of his laughter and Dakota's howling. She welcomed how it warmed her heart and, for a minute or two, made her forget. She tried to look closer at Justice, maybe a bit differently. She squinted her eyes, thinking that it might help. She was very unsure of herself. Afraid of the possibility that after all this time, maybe she had missed something. But no matter how she looked, she couldn't imagine what that might have been.

Chapter 31

Changes may not always be welcome nor may they be wanted

As I pack it is difficult to imagine no more of this. This place we have called home. It is difficult to think what might be. Where we will go. I have never spoken to Justice about before. Never mentioned what might lie beyond the woods. -M-

The following days were like a cyclone, even the coyotes were restless. Justice was quiet as Maia gathered things to pack up and load into the cart. She had been cryptic about what they would do and had not yet told him that she might have made a colossal mistake. So, mostly to avoid conversation, she let him be. She watched him, sure it was painful for him yet unable to make conversation that might excite him. She hurt too, and more than that, she was afraid. She needed to think of herself.

Justice seems to need to remember as if he is making the reality last forever. All I can do is stay out of his way. -M-

For Justice, it was as if he not only wanted but needed to etch every inch of the cottage into his soul. He slowly walked about the cottage, trying to stay out of Maia's way while touching everything, inch by inch. He touched and smelled and listened. Maia watched him feeling some relief that she had already hidden the money away. She had sewn a pocket on the inside of her favorite of gifts. A lavender patterned dress that was so soft and so comfortable, as if it belonged on her body alone. Securing the pocket with several small buttons, she knew it would be safe.

I am grateful that Justice has found peace and time to sew.
It is in this skill that talent has appeared.
But now I fear something may be off. -M-

Maia was grateful that for once, Justice wasn't insisting on helping. Instead, he sat quietly and sewed. Inviting the fabric to sing out in a mixture of colors and emotions. Sorrow and anxiousness had never been so beautiful, Maia was sure of that. When the packing was almost complete, she took the time to clean the cottage. She cleaned until it appeared to look as good as she had remembered it when they first arrived.

Dakota began to howl as she paced. Justice had taken a seat at the table, sat there as if frozen, a tear falling down his cheek. He did not move, not even to put his hand on Dakota, whose head lie in his lap. Even his sewing had stopped, and the unfinished work had fallen to the floor.

When Maia bent down to pick it up, she saw it. Red blood had seeped through Justice's pants. Maia thought she was able to understand, yet wondered what it might really mean. It was a much harder transition for

Maia than it was for Justice, who, after the initial ordeal and stress of the experience, expressed that she suddenly felt whole.

As I bent down to pick up the fabric Justice had been sewing, I saw his womanhood emerge. Now I understand why they spoke of her. -M-

Justice was excited when Maia gave her the pile of new clothes that had been left for her. It was lovely to have a new wardrobe to help her celebrate what she would later describe as actually feeling reborn. She tried on each blouse, skirt, dress, slip sweater, modeling them for Maia as much as for herself. While she could not see them, she could feel them. She could feel how well they fit and how comfortable they were. As if each piece had been made only for her, and indeed she knew they had. Justice modeled every item of clothing. Each piece of apparel felt so perfect and was so comfortable. It was as if she had been practicing and preparing all along.

I wonder if Justice will ever forgive me. I watch her celebrate her new identity, sad that she had to wait so long. -M-

Chapter 32

We may not always see ourselves as others see us, nor may we be who they see

Justice was excited with this new identity, and it gave her enjoyment as she prepared to share intimacies with Maia that she wasn't comfortable with before. While Maia was not as comfortable sharing, she was happy for Justice, and together they rejoiced as they celebrated life.

Maia looked at Justice and was pleased with herself. She was happy that she hadn't felt like doing much extra over the last several months. A reason she used for not cutting Justice's hair, now it was so long. Maia noticed how beautiful and white it was. Carefully she reached out and ran her fingers through it, combing it to the side, Justice lifted her chin and faced her as if she was not only looking right at her but as if she could see her.

Maia's heart sang. For the first time, she allowed herself to see Justice as a girl. With all honesty, she could see what a beautiful young woman Justice was. She wondered how all those years she had made such a mistake. It was Justice who reached out to make it right. Justice held Maia's hand, telling her, "You did not make a mistake. You gave me a lesson in strength. I can not thank you enough for that."

I do not know why Justice is so kind, with such patience and understanding. Does she know that I would have been fine with her gone. Fine had he never been. -M-

Maia encouraged Justice to help her as they completed the last of the packing. Together, they decided that they would stay a couple of extra days, although Maia knew that they were pushing their welcome. She could see shadows lurking in the trees, and the coyotes displayed confusion, unsure as to where their loyalties lie. In the end, it was a bittersweet goodbye when they piled up the cart with all that would fit.

I will lock up the fabric squares. The stories that Justice created and were told over and over again. I will lock them up so that they will remain safe until he may visit them once again. -M-

Overflowing with years of memories, food, jugs of water from their hosts, and all of Justice's fabric squares, which seemed to breathe with life. Maia had packed them safely, putting them in the locked box that had been saved for that purpose alone. Everything had its place and purpose, and so it wasn't surprising how well it all fit together like a puzzle under tarps that covered the load. Maia looked back one more time before she and Justice each took a handle and, in unison, moved out, Dakota never leaving Justice's side. The remainder of the coyote pack paced until they too were ready to leave. Then as if they had been given orders, they left the cottage and prepared to lead Maia and Justice out of the woods.

Once again we shall allow the coyotes to lead us. - M -

Having no clue where they were or how to get out safely, both Maia and Justice decided that they would let the coyotes lead them wherever they chose. Maia didn't think she could ever go back home, despite the ache in her heart. The truth was, after so long, she had no idea where home might be. So, putting their faith once more in their guides, who had brought them to this place, they were quite sure that they could trust them to lead them out and lead them well.

These were difficult times, and there were difficult times. When they departed the cottage, it was not just that they were leaving a home or place they had cared for that had cared for them. They were leaving the protection that it provided, the protection of the thick trees that shielded Justice from the sun, and the canopy that kept out everything and anything that had wings, minus the incident with the eagle. They were leaving the care, love, and gifts. They were leaving their life.

There is no protection from the elements and I must watch Justice suffer. There is so little I can do to ease the pain. - M -

Now, as they walked, the sun shone over them. Without the canopy the trees provided, even the slightest sun was too much for Justice. Along the open roads and fields, there was no shelter. There was no protection. Maia would stop every few feet. She would kneel down and gather a bit of dry dirt because that is all there was. Carefully she would add a bit of water from one of the jugs making a mud paste, which she used to rub on the parts of

Justice that were most exposed. Maia was finding it challenging to keep up as blisters quickly formed on Justice's lips, nose, and ears. Justice never once complained, but surely the blisters and her burning skin were painful. Maia attempted to pat them if that might help, and she stopped often to use the salve. It was soothing, Justice told her, but Maia could tell it did not really help. Neither of them spoke very much. They both knew that this new journey and chapter in their lives was sure to be a challenge. For Justice, the most frustrating part of the journey was the inability to access or have access to her sewing materials. It was sewing and creating and telling a tale that Justice most wanted and felt the need to do each night. But when they stopped to rest, it was rest they must. Despite that, Justice nearly begged for these things. Maia had a difficult time telling her no. But Maia knew that time was everything and that to unpack for just the night, really only those few hours, all the begging would not change that it would have to wait.

Maia took the time to explain that there was just too much that would have to be unpacked to accommodate her wish. With so much pain, it was difficult for Justice to sleep, let alone rest, making the travels and their bonding just that much more strained.

We should be working together instead
we are driving one another apart. -M-

Now with the sun visible. No longer hidden from the protection of the canopy, it was so much easier for Maia. For the first time in so many years, she was able to tell direction, and she knew that they were traveling west.

I want to scream with joy! I want to dance. I do neither. Today I celebrate in silence as without the canopy I can actually tell in which direction I go. -M-

She felt in her pocket and pulled out the small books that they had left for her before sending them away. She remembered how good she had always been at identifying flowers and plants back home. It had been one of her many chores. For as long as she could remember, it had been her job to gather plants for her mama's cooking. For ingredients for making medicinal potions. But now, as they traveled, this new environment had so many plants and flowers that she did not recognize. She scoured the illustrations in the books but was not confident that the details were sufficient for her to feel comfortable using them. She worried that if she made a mistake and used them, her worst fear would be a reality. She feared what might happen if she or Justice or any of the coyotes were to ingest something she prepared using a wrong plant. So, when they stopped, and Maia was preparing food, it was a difficult chore to make anything with variety. Maia instead settled on a limited diet, which was to use the dried fruits and vegetables which had been packed up and brought with them.

Additionally, she worried about rationing. It was challenging to ration when she had no idea how far they were headed or how long it would take. She was afraid of what would happen if they ran out.

Chapter 33

It is essential that we understand it is not food and
water alone necessary to survive

It was the jerky that she had made from the squirrels Dakota had gifted to them that was the most delicious treat of all. The squirrel jerky was the one food that, no matter how hard she tried to discipline herself, was the hardest food to make last. Maia had gotten very good at physically stretching the jerky to make it paper thin and longer than it was in its original dried state. It was the one thing that she was sure everyone wished was more plentiful. Each of them, including Justice, devoured every morsel that they were given. Wanting the jerky to last, Maia was more cautious with how much of it they could eat, more careful than she was with fruits and vegetables. It was also the one food that she felt was a true gift that she could give back to Dakota. She would make sure that Dakota always got just a bit more than she or Justice and always got the first and last piece at a serving.

Each of them, Justice, Maia, and even Dakota, were happy when at dusk, the pack of coyotes would wander off for an hour or two, leaving Maia, Dakota, and Justice alone. It allowed Maia to feel less guilty when she chose not to share with the other coyotes. However, there were several nights when Maia had selfishly wished that Dakota would join them, hoping she would bring something back, but in the unfamiliar surroundings, Dakota would have nothing to do with leaving Justice.

So, it was more than a pleasant surprise when one night out of the blue, the coyotes returned from their outing, each bearing a gift of their own. Maia was elated to see the abundance of squirrel and rabbit when one by one, they each laid their gift at her feet. She was more than thankful. Their contributions allowed her to make a hearty meal full of substance. It also gave her the ability to restock their supply of jerky as she prepared several squirrels and rabbits for drying. This was also an excellent opportunity for them to make camp for a few extra days. Both she and Justice were exhausted, and she was sure that Dakota could use the rest as well. She looked around, feeling confident that it was a good place that they had stopped, a spot shadowed by towering trees and nicely sheltered with a small drinking hole close by.

Maia used several of the fresh rabbits and squirrels to prepare a feast of thanks for the coyotes.

*I believe we are family. The coyotes have blessed us
with gifts that I can use to replenish the jerky.
It is a very good day. -M-*

She knew that they would be grateful to have their stomachs full of such delicacies as they were used to at the cottage. She was thankful to them for staying close, always watching above to make sure that nothing would escape them as they dutifully protected Justice. Perhaps it was selfish on Maia's part when instead of moving on after all the meat had been packed up. The jerky was dry after they had repacked the cart and were prepared to move out, she had insisted on just one more day.

She just wanted another day of rest but insisted on telling herself and any who would listen that the jerky would do well with just one more day of drying. It was on that extra day that things changed.

Chapter 34

It is possible that when you love so much protection is all you can give even if it means sacrifice

The birds arrived, not only one or two, but what seemed like hundreds, making it difficult for the coyotes to protect Justice without some sacrifice. One of the older males met his end as he lept in front of Maia to shield Justice from a swarm of them. Maia and the coyote locked eyes as he was lifted upward. They continued until he was out of view.

I can not help but feel guilty for being selfish. I just am so tired and so needed that extra day. I believe I have caused great loss. As the birds lifted the coyote out of reach our eyes locked. Such beautiful piercing eyes. Such soulful eyes. Eyes like I have never seen but shall always remember.
I give thanks that Justice is safe. -M-

Silent and in mourning, the entire pack of coyotes was watchful as they continued to lead Maia and Justice on the journey. Each of them visibly a bit more anxious, worried about who or what might be next. They were not alone in this state. Dakota was jumpy, and her self-esteem at zero, she could not believe that she was not the one who had succeeded in keeping Justice safe.

Maia worried that it was she alone that they blamed and found it difficult to relax. Justice was sad as she knew she was the reason they all continued on with such heavy hearts. It was during this portion of their travels that Maia found it especially challenging. There was so much to remember, to watch, to organize. There was so much to learn; that alone was becoming a difficult task.

She had stopped making checkmarks at the end of each day. This made it difficult to keep track of the time. She was quite sure that they had traveled together for several months before they finally parted ways. It was a sad goodbye

My heart is heavy. So many good-byes
as our coyote friends leave us. -M-

Even the coyotes seemed to have sorrow in their howls as they turned and left. But not, Dakota. Dakota did not howl, and Dakota did not leave. Dakota stayed by Justice's side, not sure what emotion to express. She, too, knew life would inevitably change. Like Justice and perhaps Maia, she wasn't sure if she was really ready for life to be so different.

As the three of them continued on, they were alone, heading into an unknown environment. It was an environment even Maia did not feel comfortable in. It had been so long that she had been away, so much of what she knew or remembered had changed.

It had been a long time since they had left the safety of the woods. The further they traveled, the more civilized it was becoming. There was so much that Maia didn't recognize. It would be a life that they would indeed all have to get used to. Maia worried for both Justice and Dakota.

Maia spoke about the miles and miles of railroad tracks they followed, knowing that they would ultimately lead somewhere. When a train would travel quickly past, it was not without the accompaniment of the engineers' whistle. The train cars swayed back and forth as the wheels moved along the track clanging. At first, the new noises were like explosions, not just to the virgin ears of Justice, but to Maia as well. It had been so long that the quiet of the cottage had made her unprepared for what she had so obviously forgotten.

As they walked, she thought about all the gifts the cottage had presented to them. She was grateful for the books, for the time that they afforded her. The time that allowed her to read aloud to Justice whenever she wanted and inspired the conversations she and Justice experienced. She was thankful for the safety and protection that afforded them the time to have alone to experience Justice as a male and a female. She was grateful for Justice's wisdom, but she was uncertain as to why she had been entrusted with her being.

I find it a challenge to remember before. Before the cottage and all of its gifts. It is Justice I try to think of and as we walk it is difficult not to question once again why the Universe entrusted me with her. -M-

As they approached the city limits, Maia realized that there was so much they hadn't talked about. There was so much she had forgotten, and so much she had chosen not to share. She had never really had a conversation with Justice about cities or people, about communities or religion, or even about relationships. They had never really spoken of anything outside of their own little world, besides what may have come up in a book at some point, and Justice would have questioned. She tried to remember if she had ever really spoken much about her family. The family that she wasn't sure if she had left behind or if they had just decided to lose her. She wasn't really sure if Justice knew they were family.

As they approached, Maia realized even if she had talked to Justice about such things, she definitely would not have described them in the manner that they saw. The noises and congestion, the hustle, and bustle. It would not have been a description like the one they were about to approach.

Even Maia was not prepared or versed in the ways of such a city, the truth was Maia had never really seen a big city. After so many years in the cottage, she was not expecting to be led to a place so full. Full of sound and people and machines and smells. For Maia, it was full of excitement, awakening her, and she wasn't sure how she should address or contain that feeling.

She had forgotten and felt no need to tell Justice about the moving boxes. In the woods and the secure arms of the cottage, they had been safe from such things. Justice, who was usually so uninhibited and curious, reached for her hand and squeezed. Maia paused, inhaling the beauty of the commotion.

No matter how many books I have read to Justice. No matter if I had told her about before. About what laid outside the

cottage. I would not have described it as it was now.
I am not prepared. -M-

All of the things she had surely missed while in the cottage. Justice's hand, so frail and afraid, squeezing her hand brought her back to reality, and she moved forward with slow watchful steps as she squeezed back.

Holding onto Justice's hand, she used her free hand to pick up the handle of the cart and placed Justice's other hand on the opposite handle.

I am not sure what Justice wants or needs from me. She reaches out for me and I take her hand. But it is freedom I seek. There is a bit of excitement in what lie before us. -M-

She examined Justice's face looking for some sort of sign that she could let go before pulling her hand away from Justice. Justice was not comfortable without the security Maia's hand gave her. She liked the way it felt the support was comforting, but like so many times before she understood what was expected. She moved her head towards Maia, and obediently nodded. Without hesitation, Maia let go, and together they continued forwards. Dakota placed herself as close as she could, touching the side of Justice's leg. Not wanting to miss a step and letting her know that she would always be there. Justice smiled as it was Dakota's unconditional love that warmed her heart.

As they walked, Maia kept an eye on Justice watching as Justice continuously kept turning her head. Left to right, right to left, up and down and back again. Clearly, she was listening to the sounds, trying to make sense of them. As Maia watched, all that she could see was the pain and fear on Justice's face. As if it were happening all over again, Maia couldn't help but ask herself, What have I done? How had she allowed the not-"fairies" to force them to leave? And as if questions would right what she really felt, not tear her away from her own wants and needs so she could focus on Justice. She continued to ask herself questions she could not answer. *What made her decide it was okay for them to allow the coyotes to lead them away? What had made the coyotes lead them to such a place? Had they been instructed to lead them to such a destination? What happened to compassion and protectiveness? What was the plan?*

In the end, it was Justice's pain that tore at her heart, and in as much as she was awed by the city, it was no match for her sorrow.. And there was Dakota, who she knew would have to pass for a dog, and of course, the question of the money and what she would do with it.

Maia had read all of the books that they had given her. She tried to remember all that they had tried to explain. She played it like a moving picture being projected in front of her and could almost see the handwritten notes that they had left. She understood that it would, indeed, be an arduous journey. She was nervous that their instructions had suggested that they would need to listen and follow their own instincts, that of hers and Justice. They'd implied that it would be the outcome of their instincts alone that they must use to find their way. Standing back away from the street, it was evident that they were unprepared.

Chapter 35

It is a monumental task, this thing called love

They were just a stone's throw from the city itself, separated only by a narrow street, finding protection in the shadows. Even hiding, she could feel people staring. She was sure that the three of them must look a sight. She couldn't go forward, not yet. So, together, she and Justice turned the cart around. They knew that they would need to make a new plan. With Dakota's assistance, they found their way to a small wood not too far from the city. They worked their way through the trees so that they might go deeper and deeper into her heart. It was here among the trees and their protection that both Maia and Justice were happiest. This seemed to make Dakota happy as well. Most importantly, Maia was delighted that they could stop so that she might take the time to dig deep into the cart. Hoping she might allow Justice the opportunity if she wished to sew their fate.

Exhausted, and both full of so many emotions, they did not speak. Dakota laid her head in Justice's lap, attempting to fill her with the warmth and love that was missing from the city they had just seen. It was a place that appeared not only to lack both love and kindness but seemed to drain them of all hope.

As we settle for the night, back in the warmth of the trees I give Justice her thread and fabric so that she may sew our fate. As I get ready for sleep the one thing I have come to trust is Justice will know. -M-

Maia put the fabric and thread into Justice's hands, Justice was more than elated—throwing her arms around an unprepared Maia in an awkward hug of sorts. It was sewing that gave Justice peace, and it was that peace that they all so needed.

Over the years, Maia had allowed herself to let go and never to question. When she felt the need to do so, it was best to just walk away or turn around. It took a while before she understood, accepted, and learned that Justice's sewing creations were a gift, not a curse. In time, it allowed Maia the ability to completely overcome her fears. It was this gift that she could see not only brought joy with the bright colors but insight with what each piece revealed upon its completion. Often the finished piece would end up as what Maia believed was a prediction, or perhaps a premonition. There was no doubt each finished piece always came true or revealed the truth.

After spending the night amongst the trees, it was not a surprise when in the morning, Maia awoke only to discover that Justice had been busy. Maia examined the beautiful and vibrant colors of Justice's newest creation with both confusion and amusement. It was this latest creation that made her full of wonder.

I am not prepared for the picture that Justice has created. It is a wonderful idea I think and I know that it must be, but I worry what will be left for me? What will be left of me? -M-

On the fabric was a young girl who appeared to be Justice, a covering on her head hiding her face, her hands hidden with a beautiful pair of gloves. A clean and well-groomed Dakota sat close by and with them a tall, nicely dressed man. Maia looked at Justice and Dakota, and at that moment, she understood. She knew that what Justice had created was exactly what she must become, a bit of her wondered why she hadn't visited that idea.

She knew it would take additional planning. It would undoubtedly take extra time, and surprisingly or maybe not so surprisingly, Justice understood and agreed. After remaining several nights in the woods, it was beginning to look like they had a viable plan. They were ready to start moving forward with implementation. It was in the woods that they found comfort. They were grateful that the weather and privacy had allowed them to stay put for several more weeks as they continued to prepare.

Chapter 36

Sometimes choices aren't choices at all

Maia spent hours tossing and turning. She knew it would soon be her last night, and possibly the last time she might actually be identified as herself. In the morning, she awoke to find Justice busy sewing. (where the fabric came from, she was unsure. She dared not ask. It was best not to ever question, so like always, she would never know. She had to be content with that) Her hands busy with each stitch. Each stitch more perfect than the stitch before. A polished machine, Justice would hold the needle just so moving it in and out over the seams making perfect even stitches. The end result a beautiful suit, which was almost complete. Maia stared at it admiringly but frightened.

Maia knew as Justice completed the last stitch, her fate was sealed. Straining, she took a deep breath feeling as though it might actually be her last. With the suit complete, it was up to Maia. She knew she alone had to make sure she could succeed with what would surely be a real masquerade.

Maia found that cutting her hair was the hardest; she couldn't remember when it had last been cut. Now, as she looked at Justice's hair, which was already growing quite long, she thought about the twists and turns life had given her. She remembered how very blessed she should feel as she gathered up the clumps of salvaged hair which she chose to save.

I can not part with my hair. It has grown for so long, a part of me. As I hold it in my hands I have only one choice and that is to save it. -M-

She wrapped it up, carefully tucking it in on the bottom of the cart, thinking, part out loud, and partly to herself. One might never know when an extra set of hair might come in handy. Justice heard her and giggled. For a minute, Maia gave in, and she, too, found herself laughing at how ironic all of it was.

Maia searched her memory for her Pappi and his mannerisms. She thought about the other men she had known, but it had been so long ago. She wasn't sure if having watched Justice grow up as a boy counted. She practiced having conversations with Justice, talking to him in her man's voice. Still, it was difficult to be serious as each time she tried, it brought them both to the ground in laughter. For years to come, it was especially those moments that Maia would often talk about, she needed to hold onto that laughter alone.

She talked to Justice and, in the end, decided she would take day trips to the city to observe from afar. Observing for a few days would be a good idea. It was what Maia wanted, what she needed: day trips, extra time. It was a painful thought to transition in such a way, and she felt she deserved to give herself the added comfort she deemed necessary. Never once did she think about Justice's transition and the lack of choice she'd had. For Maia, it didn't much matter. It was her comfort that was important, that was necessary. Going on those day trips, she felt safe. She knew she would always return to the safety and comfort of the woods. Back to Justice and Dakota. After several day trips, there was no question when the time actually came.

We have been preparing for weeks.
I know that the time has come. Tonight I will say goodbye to
my Maia. No longer will I be a she. -M-

Chapter 37

The day that they walked out of the woods for the final time was the day Maia said goodbye to her female self forever. With her chest tightly wrapped and wearing the newly sewn suit, she forced herself to stand erect and show pride. As she took those final first steps, she knew she would never be able to turn back.

*With Justice's help we have chosen my new he name.
I shall now be known as Joseph. It is a good name and
I will wear it proud. -M-*

As it was, life as a man was more comfortable to acclimate to than Maia had anticipated. Her man self (who would be known as Joseph) was welcome in the community. He had no knowledge, no connections, and no understanding but still was more welcome than if he had been his she-self.

With each new introduction, each new interaction, Joseph found that he had made a natural choice because there seemed to be no other. As a man, it made the most mundane of tasks effortless. There were more choices than he could have anticipated. Just the task of finding a room to rent for himself and his daughter was so much more comfortable than he knew it would have been had he tried as a single woman alone with her daughter. It allowed all of them to stay close and as inconspicuous as they possibly could, which wasn't so easy with Justice and Dakota. Sharing a bathroom with other boarders, at first, did not present a problem since it had been years since he had even had running water. But Justice, who had never experienced running water, a bathtub, or even a real toilet, was having difficulty acclimating to the use of such things. She found it difficult when she had to wait her turn for their use. Joseph enjoyed the luxuries they offered but found that waiting for his turn and sharing the facilities was not easy. Some things seemed too hard to hide.

I am amused at how easy this masquerade is. I am grateful for the smoothness and ease I am accepted. -M-

As they settled into a routine and grew comfortable in their environment, deciding on how to live and support themselves seemed effortless.

Choosing a profession was not only quite a simple choice but seemingly the only choice. Both Justice and he had excellent sewing skills. It was these skills that were used to design and sew all of his suits. It didn't take long for the compliments to pour in on the suits he wore. People wanted to know where he got them and were amazed when he gave them the answer. He and his daughter would indeed be interested, he would tell them when they inquired how they too might have such a suit. It wasn't long before they got their first paying customer, who was soon followed by more than they could handle. Before long, they found themselves so popular that they were forced to put people's names on a waiting list.

They worked so hard as their business grew. Their fingers became blistered and bloody from so much sewing, yet they both continued without complaint. It was the tiredness that consumed them as the orders continued pouring in. They found that sewing each piece by hand became increasingly difficult to keep up.

The small room had become overcrowded with fabrics and patterns, threads, and needles. Joseph knew that they could not continue at the pace they currently were going, not without help, yet he knew they could not afford to bring in another seamstress. It was not the money so much as who they were and how much of themselves was invested. It would be too difficult to have someone work so closely. While they tried to keep the masquerade a secret. He had even mentioned it to Justice, who agreed there was a lack of options.

Justice never complained, but Joseph watched her. Justice looked so tired, yet it was Justice who was the one always ready to help, always with a smile, a word of encouragement, always giving her last of something to Dakota or someone or something else. Justice had so much to offer, and there was so much Joseph knew he could still learn from her.

Joseph had seen the machines that sewed. He had fantasized about what they might do, but he had never used one. He had never actually seen one in person. Their existence had been talked about before. He remembered his mama spoke about how incredible a machine that sewed would be.

"Can you imagine such a machine?" Maia's mama would ask.

I can hear mama talking to me. I can feel her hands I must allow my she self a chance to remember. - M -

But even in their dreams, they could never afford such a luxury. For a moment, Joseph allowed Maia to come out and gave her permission to go back. Maia closed her eyes, remembering how patient her own mama had been when it came to sewing. She remembered how many times she had sat down and shared her skills with her. Savoring, how wonderful it had felt the moment that she had learned. She had made her mama so proud. Maia ached to hear her mama's words once more. She wanted to hear that sweet but scratchy voice. The voice that could be feared by someone who didn't know her. She wanted to hear her tell her how smart she was, how quickly she learned. She wanted to hear her mama tease her that she was going to be a better seamstress than she was, and soon it would be her who was doing all the mending and sewing.

"Everyone will be asking for Miss Maia," she had said, "and you'll be taking care of your mama." That had given her such pride. Since her mama was known around the area for her fantastic sewing talents. Maia could almost feel her calloused hand on hers, guiding her as she took each stitch. She could practically hear her voice, rough but kind, loving in the only way she knew how. Maia took a minute to not just look but to try and see Justice, and she wondered if Justice would ever have such good memories. She imagined she could understand just how her mama must have felt. There was a part of her somewhere, a bit of something maternal that she was sure felt the same way now with Justice.

Once again, the female Maia was locked away, Joseph shared a bit of those early days with Justice. He left out the part about how proud his mama had been. He decided it was best to wait on that for another time when he might feel he could tell her how proud he was. He stayed silent for a bit, remembering how good it had felt, how similar perhaps they were. And, he let the memories etch themselves into a place he could visit at his leisure. He couldn't help but wonder what his mama would do if a machine were given to her. Now that he had so much success and so much money, he could easily buy two sewing machines: one for himself and one for Justice and even a third one just for mama. It was a good feeling, a proud feeling to know that spending that much money wouldn't feel like a burden in his pocket.

Joseph watched Justice sitting on the floor, fabric laid across her lap as she sewed. Her blistered fingers working their way across the seams, he looked down at his blistered fingers and could feel her pain. At that moment, putting all concerns aside, Joseph knew what it was he had to do. He had been a bit apprehensive about Justice using a sewing machine, worried about her sewing through a finger or worse. He knew in his heart that the worry was all it was, a worry.

He thought about how many orders they had to fill and even more were coming in. Overwhelming numbers, despite the long wait for the finished garment, and a waiting list on top of that business continued to grow. He had no choice but to procure a sewing machine for Justice too. Just the thought of what Justice's hands looked like was all he needed to decide that Justice would indeed need a machine of her own.

He felt good when comfortable, and without hesitation, he ordered two. Joseph was careful not to let Justice know they were coming, and for the first time, he had a hard time holding back. It was difficult not sharing, but that was different than what he was doing now, keeping a secret. He couldn't remember a time he had indeed kept anything from her, besides the money, yet now he felt it best if he would wait to tell her. It would be several weeks before the machines arrived and he had to wait too. He did not think it fair that they both suffer from such anxiousness and excitement.

Justice had never heard of a sewing machine, and he knew that it would be a difficult thing for her to imagine. Since he had never seen one either, only a picture, he did not think he could describe it adequately. Joseph did not expect that she would even begin to understand, let alone imagine the possibilities such a machine would offer. He wasn't sure if he was more excited to surprise her or to see it and use it himself. Either way, he knew she would be proud that it was something that they alone had earned and paid for.

The sewing machines have arrived. I think it will be a wondrous thing to use them. -M-

Both he and Justice were amazed at the ease and speed their new machines offered. It didn't take any time at all for either of them to master its use. The speed of the machines allowed them to work so much faster. It made it possible to welcome new clients, bringing them many new jobs. It was the speed of sewing on the machines that gave Justice extra time to work on her own projects. After a day of work and having completed a suit or two, she would begin. She would work alone in the dark, in silence. It was not just the darkness of her blindness, but it was in total blackness, it was then that she was sure he would not see, he would not hear.

It was here that, with unknown and unsolicited help, she began to weave on a loom that would appear without expectation. A loom that produced absurd amounts of fabric. The fabric was so beautiful that everybody wanted something made from it. It brought even more customers to their door, some who would come from cities far away. They would begin lining up early in the day, waiting to be fitted for a suit made from the newest fabric.

It is not mine to question. I give thanks for the fabric that Justice can produce. I will not ask. -M-

Then, at Justice's suggestion, they decided to offer additional days just for women, it was a frenzy. The women would push and shove one another in line, so that they would secure a place which would get them a fitting, assuring them a dream dress made from the newest fabric.

Justice has suggested offering days just for women. I cannot turn her down. She has earned this voice. -M-

Maia was genuinely beginning to let go of her old self. Forgetting her altogether and happy to allow Joseph to stand on his own, without interference, making him pleased. Joseph enjoyed how it felt. How his masculine charade had enabled him to support both himself and Justice. He liked how it had allowed him to buy sewing machines. He was amazed at the ease and speed that the new machines allowed them to complete and deliver finished garments.

Chapter 38

It is not always the dreams of others which we should understand

Their fingers healed, and their pockets were full. Reminiscent of what had been, of life at the cottage, once again, they were without want or need. Dakota, too, had the best cuts of meat to fill her, as she continued to stay by Justice's side, companion, protector, and eyes. She would watch closely as Justice too remained loyal as a companion, and cars.

They had found their place among the city dwellers, and the community welcomed them as one of their own. It was this acceptance and respect as a successful businessman that Joseph finally decided it was time to move out of the boarding house and look for a place of their own. It was in the house they moved into that Justice's gifts indeed grew.

It wasn't long after settling into their new house that Justice and Dakota felt safe enough to venture out alone. On some days, they would leave until dark, and Joseph would vacillate between being sick with worry and anger as he waited for them to return.

It feels so wonderful to be in our own house, but there are consequences that I did not anticipate. Justice and Dakota have decided they feel safe enough to go off alone. It isn't like the cottage where I knew they would come back. Their sense of freedom makes me angry. I worry too. But perhaps I worry because my own emotions are threatened. -M-

Unlike the cottage they once called home with the protection of the woods and its canopy, there was no safety in the city. There was no one to protect them, and so as far as he was concerned, there should be nowhere for them to go. Often he could be found pacing back and forth until they would walk through the door. The pacing never seemed to help. He had learned early on that others looked after Justice, but too often, that didn't help either. He did not know them; he could not see them, and therefore, there or not, in his eyes, they did not exist. So whether worried or angry, Joseph knew he had no control, sometimes he wondered if Justice had any control either.

Those first few times, when Justice and Dakota would come home wet and dirty, he was not happy. But then, Justice would explain to him how they had searched such a long time. How they needed to find just the right one, referring to a large tree limb that they had dragged home. Joseph didn't ask. He didn't want to know how the limb came to be wrapped with cords of raw sinew. Listening to her excitement and anxiousness, he couldn't stop them, nor did he want to. For days, they would go out, sometimes coming home empty-handed and with heavy hearts. It was weeks before they had four limbs that they were sure would work. He stood by and watched them working together. Justice and Dakota stripped the limbs clean. Dakota loosened the bark with her teeth. Then Justice used her fingernails to scrape away the balance before Dakota took it back to gnaw at the leftover until it was smooth and clean. Joseph watched as they worked together. They tied, cut, and secured what was soon to be a brand new loom. A loom that would be hers alone, a place for her to speak in colorful exuberance, a place where Justice would sit for hours if Joseph would allow her.

Justice would spend hours weaving black threads, creating pictures that would come to life. Colorful, animated, screaming with realism and emotion pictures. She would spend hours without stopping. Sometimes without eating until they were complete. He was always in awe as the only threads that he ever gave Justice were black ones, and yet the finished piece, each tapestry, sung out with color. Vibrant color alive. As if it had stepped out of the fabric and into the world from which Justice had woven it. Joseph never got used to or bored with her finished work. Each piece a new story, more intricate than the one before. But he was never entirely comfortable with them either. He would take them from her and lock them in the box that was for the tapestries alone.

Justice and Dakota have achieved completion. They have succeeded in the creation of a new loom. One that Justice is proud to call her own. I wait for the stories to be told so that I can take them from her, and lock them up. -M-

(It wasn't until years after he was gone and Maia too when Justice was on her own that it was discovered that when put together piece by piece it was more than a story. It was their life. It was every milestone, every event, every celebration.)

Chapter 39

When it is the pain of others we feel, it has a name

Once again I must sit with Justice in her loneliness and sorrow. Dakota has gone off and left her and the emptiness I must witness is painful. I can not help fill that hole I do not want to. I can do nothing but try to comfort and hope she believes my kindness is sincere. -M-

So many days had passed, the house was unusually empty and dark. Joseph tried to comfort, but without Dakota, there was no comfort. Justice could not wrap her arms around the quiet. This had been the second time that there had been such a void. The second time that Dakota had taken off without warning. Justice could not leave. She did not know in which direction she should send vibrations. Dakota was not lost, it had been her choice when she left. Justice could not move, all she could do was question. So for days, all Joseph did was listen. Justice replayed the hours, minute by minute, attempting to find answers. But even together, they could find nothing.

They seldom talked. It had been a long time since they had found the proper words. Still, he tried to comfort. He reminded Justice that it hadn't been so long ago that Dakota had left—how she had come back even more ready to guide, to teach, to share. Justice understood, but she did not want to allow herself to acknowledge her understanding. It was not so much the loss as it was the emptiness. How was she to express such an emptiness? Such a void? How was she to go forward with such a hole? How could Joseph possibly comfort, even he knew he could not fill that hole? Even with all Joseph had done, all he had given, all he had given up, and all he had sacrificed, there was no way for him to be what she needed. It was difficult for him to accept that. Although, if he was honest and sincere, he didn't want to be that either. Joseph would look at Justice and feel so inadequate while somehow feeling that perhaps he had willed it. Perhaps, it was he who did not honestly want to be the one she needed, that was too much responsibility and too much commitment. So on day four, when in the distance they were sure that they could hear the distant howling, Joseph looked out the window and watched. He was relieved when he heard Justice finally allow herself to breathe. She breathed deeply, and then she allowed him to help. She took a bite from the sandwich that had been sitting on the same plate for four days. The same sandwich that he had brought to her each day as they waited together. That he tried to encourage her to eat, reminding her that she needed to remain strong. As Justice let herself breathe, she listened, she allowed herself the possibility of hope once again. It was more than Justice could imagine when Dakota came back, full of love and bearing gifts. Following closely behind her were four coyote pups. It was the smallest that Dakota carefully carried in her mouth pleased with herself, gently laying it in Justice's lap. A tiny thing that was so full of love. Finding Justice's finger, it began to suck, spurring memories of that first day. The day Dakotas' mother had placed her in Justice's lap. Trusting in her care. However, this time it was different. Justice had a difficult time responding to this new pup when all she wanted to do was to shower

Dakota with love. She couldn't give or get enough. It was hard to fill herself with all that she had been missing over the last four days.

That sweet pup now in Justice's lap. So many memories of when Dakota herself was that little pup.
Justice saved her. Over the years they shared so much.
Not just love but sight and sound. I was an outsider who got to watch. Now here is another gift for Justice. A gift that will ensure she is never alone. -M-

Joseph stood back, watching, remembering. So many years ago. Yet here it was playing all over again as if it were yesterday.

Dakota's mother had opted to give her to Justice rather than let her die. She was such a small pup, and the bitch must have known there was something wrong. She also must have known, of that he was sure, that Justice would hold it dear and love it and care for it and share in the glory of its being. It had been Justice's simplest of gifts that undoubtedly saved that pup. Through the years, Dakota would stand by and give back love, compassion, and appreciation for all that they offered one another.

Joseph reached out and lightly touched Justice's shoulder. Remembering years earlier the first few minutes after they had met Dakota. Now it was happening again. He picked up the tiny pup from Justice's lap and welcomed her before putting her back, encouraging Justice to love her. Justice knew but did not want to admit that she understood, because she could never imagine life without her soul.

Justice decided the only thing she could do was to name this new pup, Dakota too. And so it was, with each new pup, each new introduction to grow her soul, they also were named Dakota. Unlike the first Dakota, they all had their hearing and their sight. But just like their namesake, they never disappointed, never deserted, and always shared with understanding and love. It was in this way that Justice allowed herself to believe.

Chapter 40

Without choice there are times one must glimpse into the darkness

Justice sat with Dakota in the dark, not just the dark of day that Justice knew, but darkness that she could feel as the room grew cold. It had already been two days, and still, Joseph had not returned. Justice was beginning to worry.

She tried to replay the voices, thinking perhaps she might remember something she had missed. Maybe, she thought, there was something that she might have recognized, but there was nothing. They had been voices that were not with the kindness Justice had grown to understand, but rather ones that made both her and Dakota uneasy. As the voices grew louder and angrier. As a deep growl began to surface, it was Justice who attempted to calm Dakota.

But then they left, and they took him with them. It was his quick departure and the distress in his voice that was so concerning. Dakota began to pace, and Justice took to the loom, working the spool of thread back and forth, back and forth as if it was she telling the story.

There could have been no way for me to know. There were no warnings. When they took me I was silent. I did not offer a goodbye. Justice must have been so scared. They were so loud and surely she did not understand. I had never spoken to her of such things. -M-

She took time out to feed herself and Dakota. She cleaned and bathed, all of the tasks that she knew were required to get through the days. But still, the cold came, and the darkness seemed to turn to black. It was on the fourth day that there was no longer the silence. She could hear his footsteps slowly and sounding defeated coming home. Dakota, too could sense his return and was quick to follow Justice as together they waited at the door. But it was not the joy that Justice expected, nor that he had hoped to give.

His clothes were disheveled, his head bent in shame, and for the first time, it was he who fell crying into Justice's arms. Pouring out what seemed like all that was left from all of the years. Joseph sobbed, remembering all of the joys. He cried, remembering all the heartaches, and felt his heart heavy, remembering all of the sorrow.

Not certain of which identity to hold dear, he thought of them both. He hoped that Justice never felt that her parent had faltered in making her feel cared for, protected, loved, not just by those in the cottage that cared for them, but by him/her personally. There had been few words, for there did not often seem that there was a need for words. Yet now the pain was so great, that not only could it be heard in the gut-wrenching sobs he made, but in the torment that seemed to suffocate his body, convulsions acting as a buffer. Without thought, with condition-free love, acting with a maternal need to comfort Justice wrapped him in her arms, holding him close, afraid for both of them to ever let go.

They had come full of anger and accusation, those had been the voices she had heard. They had been full of vengeance. There had been a woman. Joseph began to pour out words. A Miss Wanda Ty a customer whom neither Justice nor Dakota ever liked. It had been her voice, high squeaky grating, the way she spoke to him. It was the only time Justice could remember Joseph being rude. He always tried to look exceptionally busy when she arrived, often hoping Justice might assist her. But she wouldn't have it and would insist that it was Joseph alone who must do her fittings. Miss Wanda Ty was not easily put off. She was even less kind if she felt someone was not reciprocal in her feelings, let alone if she thought that she had somehow been rejected. Miss Ty was used to getting what she wanted, and she wanted Joseph.

It was not easy for him to be rude or standoffish. He did not think himself capable, yet with Miss Wanda Ty, there was no choice.

It was this rejection for which Miss Wanda Ty decided she would make sure that he would suffer. She accused him of rape. When they took him away, their only intentions were to lock him up, making an example of him, thereby having Miss Wanda Ty's revenge. For days they held him, they questioned him, they roughed him up. For days, all he would do was to plead his innocence and deny the accusation. It was only after he realized how long it had been and that it seemed hopeless to make them listen, for, without a doubt, they did not hear his words.

He thought about how they had taken him, leaving Justice all alone. There had been no warning or explanation. He knew what it was that he had to do. So when once again they stood him in the middle of the room, questioning him and pushing him. Pushing and challenging, he acted boldly. As he stood in front of them, he began removing his clothes—all of them. And then when there was nothing left, he removed the wrapping around his chest. The wrapping that held tight all that he had left of who he had been before revealing a full set of bosoms. With head bent, not so much in shame but in fear as well, he dropped his pants just long enough to expose himself and his apparent lack of a penis.

The policemen were unfamiliar with such a scene. They became angered by her deceit, their own manhood exposed for question. So without words, one by one, they took her as if she was their property to do as they wished without consequence, without repentance, without guilt.

It was difficult for him to find a place to make himself presentable after they threw him out while they laughed at the irony.

They took what they wanted with no recourse. They left me more empty than I could have ever imagined. I stripped myself bare and they took me, laughing without care. How can I explain such an act to Justice? Although I feel somehow I must. I have never spoken to her of such violence, I have never spoken to her of relationships. Has my entire life been a series of lessons to punish me? Yet it was for Justice that I exposed my entire being. That surely must have been an act of love. -M-

He was sore, bruised beyond the physical, and yet love bound him to stand tall. He wrapped his chest even tighter than before. He smoothed out his suit to the best of his ability and drew in a breath. It was a long way home, and yet when he arrived, it was not as tall as he had hoped. Perhaps it was love itself that was actually what allowed him to let go.

For several days he stayed in, hiding in the solitude of his room. He would not only allow Justice to speak to the customers but encouraged and urged her to do so. Without lies or excuses, business went on.

Weeks went by before he felt strong enough to return to what he felt were his responsibilities. It was upon his return that Justice allowed herself to feel his pain and understand that a bit of him had died before his returning home and that as hard as he tried, he could not hide it. As Justice adjusted to his return, life went back to the way things were. Justice found she was once again taking a back seat to the comings and goings and the day-to-day business aspect of what was. Joseph had built an even higher wall of solitude in those days, and he had placed Justice on the other side. There was no reason to break through; it would never have been allowed. So Justice and Dakota spent more time seeking out and reaching out to those whose stories needed to be told, those whose storytelling would set them free.

Every day they were together, Justice would sit with him in the silence, the silence that they had allowed to take up so much of their time together. The silence that had filled so much of their space. They each went through the motions that made their day full, but without acknowledgment of feeling, it was merely empty space filled only by the silence that screamed at them both. It was during these moments when he waited in pain for Justice to reach out. Joseph waited for her to offer him the gift which she had given so many others. He waited for the opportunity to tell his story and set him free. It was the gift that he did not receive that brought him the greatest anxiety. Would he even be able to accept such a gift, or would he reject it out of fear of what his story might tell? Still, he wanted her to offer him the opportunity so that he, alone, could choose. He felt that was the least she could do. She owed him, she owed him at least that. So, in the heaviest of silence and less than patient, he waited.

I watch as Justice invites those to tell their story.
I watch but have jealousy in my veins, some anger in my
heart. All these years, so much sacrifice and she has not yet
invited me to tell my story. -M-

What he learned after all those years of observing from the outside was that there could be no request. After all the years, that much he understood. She did not offer for perhaps she too was afraid of what his story would be and what it would mean to set him free.

It was the silence that brought Justice the most fear, for, in the silence, there was time for her to question. What would become of him? What would become of them? What would become of her? What would it be like if everything changed? Over and over, these questions played in her head. The clients continued to come, but the work became a burden, the money almost a curse. Dakota would sit by her side, knowingly. Often she would nudge her, but now, all too often, Justice would ignore it until she knew she could wait no more. Then, gently she would rub behind Dakotas ears or scratch under her chin.

It was an exceptionally cold day. There was snow on the ground—a freezing chill in the air, reminiscent of the cottage years ago. The wind blew fiercely. Joseph stood at the window, feeling shaken. He felt like the little man stuck dead center in the middle of a just-shaken snow globe. Trapped inside with no way out, unless fate would have it that somehow it might break. Remembering, it felt like those months in the cottage when they had been left alone. Now, he stood in their house looking out the window feeling cold and alone. Justice could hear him slurp purposefully loud from the cup of tea he was drinking. It was one of the first times, Justice allowed herself to appear needy as she let Dakota take her to him. Dakota led Justice to him and gave a gentle nudge moving her closer to Joseph's side. He held out his hand and took hers. She couldn't remember him ever doing that, not even when he was wearing her she. He pulled her closer and began to describe the stillness that the snow created, even in the wind, and with snow still falling, there was a stillness. He hoped she could feel it.

Today is so cold. I can only think of how we had survived such days in the cottage. How even then without our visitors we had made it. But now it does not seem possible. I am trapped. Isn't it time I be set free? -M-

Justice tried to remember their last conversation, one that did not involve work. It had been too long. Work had become the only safe topic. Yet the kindness in his voice, the patience brought back feelings of contentment. It gave her empowerment. It warmed her from the inside out. She squeezed his hand, and at that moment, they both knew: It was time for him to tell his story.

As Justice and Dakota took him to the loom, it was more than quiet, it was still. Like the stillness, he had just described. Justice held his hand, having liked how it had felt when he took hers. She squeezed it, and he squeezed back. It felt cold, she wasn't expecting that, and shaky. Using her fingers, she began to move each one across his palm, his entire hand. It didn't feel soft but rather a bit leathery and old, Justice felt a sense of urgency as they approached the loom.

They stood still, holding hands, the loom in front of them. He had watched her hundreds of times as she would guide and encourage. He believed he knew how it worked. Even with his eyes closed, he thought he knew. But knowing just what to do, was not the same as doing. He also knew that it was her words that were needed to invite him to tell his story. Her words must guide him. It was her words alone that would let him know it was his turn. He needed to wait for her instructions.

Justice paused as she was getting ready to hand him the thread. She let go of his hand, stroking Dakota instead. He began to shake, fearful that she had changed her mind. Justice worried, unsure what his story might be and how it might change them all, she shivered a bit, too.

They had lived in the city for so long. It had been so long since they had adopted the roles they led. Justice remembered the moment she had said reassuringly that it was just the way it was meant to be. She couldn't remember either of them questioning their roles. There had been so little conversation outside of the jobs they did, the food they ate. So much had changed around them. Joseph continued to wait. Justice could feel his uneasiness; it was as if it were her own.

Whether she wanted to or not, she knew the choice was not hers to make. It was time for him to tell his story. Justice handed him the shuttle full of thread. Her hand on his she guided him through the first pass, and then she rested her head on his shoulder. She kissed his cheek feeling the dampness on her lips from the tears that fell from his closed eyes. She could taste the salt. Still, there were no words exchanged as she and Dakota left him alone to tell his story.

It was not until dawn the next morning that he called out. Exhausted but finished, he waited for Justice to come and remove it. He stood back and held out his hands. He waited for what was his. He waited for the freedom he had been longing for. He deserved it, after all, it had been such a very long time.

The story unfolded, and so, finally, did she. She pulled the hairpins from under the firm fitting mesh headpiece. Her hair falling freely onto her shoulders. She removed her shirt and unwrapped the yards of tape that, for years, had held her in place. Now exposed, she was delighted. She had set them free. She wrapped her arms around Justice so that she might feel and share the beauty she felt as she welcomed her womanhood back. And then unfamiliarly and uncharacteristically, they both sobbed.

It was so many hours I sat alone in front of the loom. Passing the shuttle of black thread back and forth. I cried letting my tears fall on the weave. There were so many years I wanted my freedom. Wanted a new story. But as I sat there I knew this was the story I was supposed to tell. This was the beginning of my freedom. -M-

Chapter 41

One step at a time, without a destination leaves room to dream

They spent weeks sitting side by side, busy sewing an entirely new wardrobe to welcome Maia back. Maia was enjoying the freedom that had for so long been hidden in the back. They sat and sewed, allowing themselves to be as creative as they wished, for this was time, this sharing was theirs alone.

There is something special about this new freedom. I have a sense of calm in what I do and choose. It is exciting to think of the possibilities. To think of all of the new adventures. -M-

At first, they worried about what story they might tell that people would believe. Who Maia was and where she had come from. How would they explain where Joseph had gone, but in the end, they said nothing. They simply sold everything they had except, of course, for the loom which they disassembled and carefully wrapped in blankets, ready to be packed up. Having decided it was time to move on. Perhaps it was time to begin again. They agreed it was time to sell their house. They waited until just the right person came along, and it was sold. After all, it was just that a house and nothing more. A building with walls and rooms, it would no longer be their home. They knew wherever they might end up would be their home. It was those that inhabited it, not the walls that housed it.

It was a bittersweet day. That is how Justice would later describe it. They had shared so many memories there, both good and bad. Memories that had been theirs alone. So many Dakotas had been born while they occupied that house. So many stories had been told and shared. But now it was time to start anew.

Chapter 42

Can any of us really go back, or must we hold fast
to who we are as we go forward

New stories waited to be told, new lives to share, new places to see, and new people to meet as they would start their journey back to Maia's home. And as the journey began, Maia told Justice, that they had a family to meet and people to reckon with.

It didn't take long for a family of means to purchase the house, giving them more than they needed with what they had saved. All that they had acquired and with the additional gifts that they had received from clients through the years.

It was enough to live, or so they believed. As they readied themselves for the move, it felt so different, it felt new. It was a choice that they had made.

There was no need to hide. They did not worry that they might appear uncivilized as they had feared in the past. They had lived in comfort among society, having left the cottage in the woods far behind. Although silently, each of them gave thanks for those times. Each silent to the other admitted to themselves, there was something they missed about it. There was something they missed about the time before. It was something that the years of simplicity had taught them.

It was the memories that clung to their souls. The hardships, although somewhat forgotten, that had made them strong. It was what had gotten them through. Then there was the care, the compassion, the generosity. Gratitude was too little of a word, too small an emotion, yet it was all they had. But this move was different; it was of their own accord. They had made the decision rather than have it made for them.

I am taking Justice back to my home. We have talked and it is time for her to meet my family. It is time for me to go back. To make amends. I can travel with pride.
I can hold my head high. When we sell our house it will be just that a house it is not our home. -M-

There would be no worries about trying to brave the elements or where their destination might be. For now, they shared a purpose and a destination. The choice was theirs alone. There were no coyotes to guide them. They didn't have to worry where they would stop or how long to stay.

We don't have to worry about the weather. About where we will go, or how we will get there. We will travel in the luxury of the railroad cars like someone important. -M-

There was no one telling them that they had to leave. Even more uniquely different was that this time as they made their way, it was not walking through the woods, along the roads, following the tracks. This time it was different. This time they would be riding the rails. Boarding a train that would take them all the way to Mississippi. They would travel in luxury—two women in cars with upholstered seats.

Sitting on the upholstered seat, Justice loved how she could feel each stitch. She moved her hands gently and slowly over the upholstery. With her fingers, she silently counted how many stitches it took. As she counted, she could not only feel the stories of each passenger that traveled before her, but it was as if she could hear their voices. Even before the travelers, she could feel the people whose hands had played such an important role in weaving and stuffing the seat itself. She loved how worn it felt, how she could feel the weight of each person as they had sat where she sat now. Dakota lay at her feet, her body swaying with the movement as the train rocked side to side, putting her to sleep.

As Justice sat happy to experience the stories, Maia told a story of her own. She watched out the window describing in explicit detail what it was she saw, her voice singing the words. Justice listened. Maia had forgotten her own voice; it had been so long. Justice, too, had forgotten its sound, but now it was Maia's voice that brought calm and peace and wrapped her in love. As they rode, Justice listened to her and wondered how she could ever thank her enough. She had sacrificed so much, she had sacrificed herself. What Justice did not know was that it was Maia who should be grateful, for even from the start, it was Justice who had truly set her free.

Justice held on to every word, savoring every detail. The green grass that smelled like the meadow where they had lived in the woods. The rushing water as they crossed a bridge made of steel, how she bet it would be cool to the touch in the shadows when there were clouds. How bright the sun was as it reflected on the glass. She asked Justice if she could feel its warmth on her skin, ignoring how it might actually cause her harm. Justice winced as she had tried to escape that warmth. The mountains—how beautiful in the distance, rising up as watchful sentinels.

"Bigger than anything you could even imagine," she had told her, "a majestic altar." And as the train sped up, "like an artist palette, all the colors vibrant and moving. A mixture so brilliant it takes my breath away." That was her song, her beautiful voice. It had been locked up for so many years, protecting the leaf that had landed at her feet the day Justice arrived. It was as if only now she too understood the magnificence of it as if she were now on a journey of her own, the journey she had started so very long ago.

I am enjoying the sights and enjoying relaying them to Justice. It is exciting and scary at the same time. Time that has passed for so long and now here I am going back. -M-

As Maia continued describing in detail what she was seeing. Each vibrant color and the endless vegetation that reached for the sun, their roots feasting on the water that flowed through the black soil, her song began to change. Justice kept listening. She got quieter, and Justice could hear her pain, she could also feel her pain. It was a pain for which she was not prepared, did not anticipate, and would never want to feel again. More than that, Justice didn't want her to suffer, to have to feel such pain, not ever again. When she completely stopped describing what she saw, the music stopped too, and instead, there was just the sound of pain. It was pain that held her prisoner in anticipation of what was yet to come.

Maia began to sob. Justice rose from the seat she had become so familiar with and moved across to the bench that Maia occupied. Justice lowered herself down so that she could sit by her side and blocked out the voices she could hear from where she now sat. She wrapped her arms around Maia. She tried to comfort her. She remembered occasions where Maia and Joseph had done that for her in years past. But there was no comforting, and all Maia could do was shake. She shook with sorrow, trembled with pain, shuddered with fear, and she shivered with loss. There was no comfort to ease all of that.

Chapter 43

When reality shows itself with little warning one can often feel lost.

The train slowed down approaching the station, Maia pressed her forehead against the window. As if she were searching for something that was not there. She thought if she got really close, maybe she would find it. Already she could see that everything had changed and as the train slowed to a halt and they prepared to get off, she was uncomfortable. She didn't recognize anything, least of all herself. Stepping off of the train was definitely not an *Aha* moment, but rather a silenced choking on her own tears.

Nothing looks familiar. Have I made a mistake again? -M-

Justice became lost in her efforts to comfort. Even Dakota was unsuccessful, nuzzling up to Maia something that had always made her smile and brought an extra rub behind the ears. Now it brought neither. They departed the train with their few bags and found a nearby taxi waiting at the curb, it seemed to be waiting for them alone. They had come so far that it seemed almost normal to take a taxicab. Maia told him a name, a hotel she remembered, the taxi driver apologized. Yes, he seemed to have remembered there being such a place, but it had closed several years ago. Perhaps they would like him to take them to another hotel in the area? Reluctantly, Maia agreed. She sat in the back, pulling at her dress, attempting to get rid of the wrinkles it had inherited from the train ride.

There is something sweet about the driver and when he smiled back at me, I felt beautiful. -M-

She could see her reflection in the rearview mirror. Sitting straight as a board, she allowed herself to flirt just for a minute, and when he smiled at her, she smiled back, thinking she still had it.

The town was newer and more prominent than Maia had remembered, and the hotel was a stand-alone building that hadn't existed when she lived there.

When the driver stopped, he got out of the car to open the door for Maia. She did not move but waited for him to reach in and give him her hand as if she needed his assistance to exit the car. Justice took Dakota and quietly got out the other side. As Maia stepped out of the car, she couldn't help but notice the group of people staring, most of them appearing quite young. She pretended to be someone famous as she made her way to the hotel entrance, forgetting that Justice and Dakota were already there waiting.

Maybe someone would play along or think she was someone special. Just a fantasy that seemed to help ease her anxiety and squelch the disappointment of what she had expected to find.

I love this feeling. This feeling of being important. I think I will make all of these people think I'm someone famous. Justice could be a fan. Dare I go in without them? -M-

When Dakota and Justice came up behind her, she attempted to brush them off with a smile as if perhaps they recognized her. Pretending she didn't know who they were. But Justice just stood there waiting, and Maia had to accept the reality. It was an obligation that she thought might go away, in her hometown. But that tiny maternal part of her could not ignore what was hers, even if only borrowed. Switching gears, Maia realized it was just as important that she had the money and wherewithal to stay in such a comfortable hotel, and for now that was enough. Maia told Justice to wait for a moment while she checked in. Again, she fought her selfishness and embarrassment as she thought twice about going to their assigned room alone. But as she walked towards the waiting Justice and Dakota, she could only extend words. Information that they would need so that they would know where they were to go.

It was at this hotel that they would stay for several days. It was difficult. Maia had too many emotions that prevented her from leaving. There was no comfort even in thought, and so they stayed right where they were in their hotel room, which was now not only a place to sleep, but they stayed and did not leave. As if frozen, not in time but lack of, it was painful just to step outside. Maia let it be known it was she who had to be ready. So silence filled the space from which there was no escape.

Helpless with space so thick and emotions so high, while Maia tossed and turned as she tried to sleep. In the blackness Justice wove the hair that Maia had saved into a beautiful wig, hoping it might make her whole. What neither of them would have expected, Maia did not accept it. She placed it back in the locked box, took Justices' hands in hers, and whispered: "Thank you, but you have already set me free."

Once again Justice has presented me with a gift.
This time a gift that I cannot accept.
I am surprised that she did not know. -M-

There could be no peace for those that occupied the area, not until Maia and only Maia felt ready. When that moment happened, it was with celebration for Dakota and Justice as they followed Maia, whose time it was to begin venturing out a bit at a time. The celebration was short-lived. Justice could tell Maia wasn't really there, not with her, not with Dakota, but someplace far away that only she could go. As they walked together but separate, Maia was preoccupied. She was always looking for something familiar, perhaps someone.

On several occasions, she reached out and held Justice's hand, squeezing at times, a bit too hard. Justice said nothing, simply tried to squeeze her back. As hard as it was for Maia, it was most difficult for Justice. With years of coexistence, Justice understood. All that was gone, all that had disappeared. All that was lost for Maia had only been out of love for her. It had been a journey that, even now, she was sure in some way, Maia would not trade. And as they continued to walk, Justice could feel how old Maia had grown, how old she had become, they had grown so old together.

Chapter 44

One must never allow fear to be their leader

I n earlier days, they would have walked. There would have been no distance that would have phased them. But Maia was tired, and the thought of walking home made her feel defeated. Fear was now her greatest emotion and her worst enemy. There was also the worry of the birds, whom Maia had come to understand, may not have ever been birds at all. Repeating to herself that final message. "Others will try to take her, we can no longer protect her," she did not feel that she could protect Justice so well either and was unsure of how well Dakota would fair.

For all these years, they had been safe, somehow avoiding them, but there was no guarantee that today would be no different. What if it was today when they had not been prepared that without warning they would come? Walking would only leave them wide open for all to see, all to take. She could not let that happen, and she was too tired to worry about it. They took a bus that would get them as close as possible. Maia watched out the window with conviction as if it were her job alone to stop time. To go back to what had been, to find something that looked familiar. She looked at Justice, who sat next to her. She could feel the warmth from her body, and it brought her some calm. She closed her eyes, wondering beyond hope that it was just a dream. But as they got closer, nothing even looked remotely recognizable.

My body is growing tired. The lack of familiarity is getting hard for my mind to grasp. I am afraid of what I will find. Or what I will not find. I am afraid for the lack of protection from what lies overhead. -M-

There were houses everywhere. Big houses, with not so big yards that seemed empty. Void of gardens and tire swings and junk that had no place to go. As the bus neared their stop, she was beginning to wonder if they should even get off. Dakota and Justice made that decision for her, more out of necessity than anything else. They just needed to breathe in the fresh air. It wasn't a long walk from where they got off the bus to where her home should have been, but just that short walk weighed her down, making it difficult for her to even move her feet forward.

Déjà vu, Maia remembered that same feeling the day after Justice had arrived, and she had run off. She had been afraid to do anything else, knowing somehow that it was this baby she must protect. Now, there was no running. She was too tired. She caught up with Justice and held onto her hand, wondering what might happen if she ever let go. Wondering who was meant to protect who.

Chapter 45

As Mary approached the Kings it was not with the baby of Joseph she held, but a child whose conception had no explanation and yet she believed

When they finally arrived, what should have been her driveway was missing. In its place, a concrete, apron, and house after house. They were so close together that Maia was sure that they could reach one another through the windows alone. They didn't even bother to go up what had once been a makeshift driveway; instead, they continued up the road. She breathed a sigh of relief. Her feet became weightless, and she felt like she was floating through the air. Justice and Dakota were left to only imagine what she saw as she walked ahead of them as quickly as she could.

I see the old cemetery down the road and it gives me a boost. I am hopeful that the church will still be familiar. -M-

The old cemetery was still there, and so was what appeared to be the original church. The steeple watching over its grass-covered parishioners needed repair. The door had an uninviting lock on it, preventing entrance. However, a new brick building was not far away. A six-foot cross was displayed on the front lawn. She cautiously approached the door. She did not say anything or stop to make the sign of the cross, she walked in. Justice and Dakota waited outside, unsure if they should follow her. It seemed wrong to enter such a building, unknowing. Justice didn't feel welcome, and Dakota seemed indifferent.

Maia was relieved to find that it was empty. She hadn't really thought about what she would have done had it been full. It was a big church, and it didn't feel warm like she had remembered her church feeling. It was silent, the music was missing, but still, she was sure she could feel something. She found her way to the front and kneeled down in one of the pews. She put her head in her hands and began to sob. The tears flowed, she felt so very lost for she had forgotten how to pray. She had forgotten how it felt to seek out Jesus through prayer. She had always been taught that he was everywhere, if she were ever lost, she would find him. But she had been gone for a long time, and even here in this holy place, she was not sure she could feel his presence.

It is more that I need to believe than thinking I can. I need to find some way to reconnect. I need answers. -M-

Justice and Dakota wandered a bit outside until they found a quiet bench protected under a shade tree. They sat and waited, while Maia was trying to make a connection so that she might once again feel the power to pray.

When a man of cloth finally made his way into the sanctuary to join her, it was not with questions. Although they would both have questions that they wished to ask one another. He was gentle, holding back his words. He cautiously put his hand on her shoulder. He wasn't sure if a gentle squeeze or a light pat would be better, so he did both. He wanted her to know that he was there. He had been waiting for her, hoping for this day.

Before he entered the sanctuary I could sense his presence. Something familiar allowed me comfort. I feel as if an older me has surfaced so that I may say my name. -M-

She held her head down, her hands still covering her eyes as she trembled. She did not look up. She could not look up. She could feel the warmth of his touch as if he held it there too long, it might burn her skin and leave a mark. He was patient, sitting there in silence, waiting for her to acknowledge him first, to say the first word necessary to communicate. Perhaps, he thought, she might make the connection.

When she began to utter the first words, he was cautious about responding. He felt it was more important for him to hear what she was saying. He listened carefully, trying to catch each word between her sobs. She began by telling him her name, a name that did not roll off her tongue effortlessly. It was a name that she had not uttered in more years than she could remember. As she said it, she felt a weight lift. She said it once more, with ease as if to make sure that it was really hers. It was a name that he already knew, but still, he remained silent, waiting for her to go on.

She, too, was quiet as she readjusted herself. She had not forgotten her manners, nor who she was and from where she had come. She stood up, extending herself fully to appear tall and then attempted to discreetly and casually smooth out her dress so that she might appear presentable.

Maia took a deep breath, being in control had been her self-preservation. Over the years, she had learned how little being emotional had helped achieve success. Emotion had never given her or gotten her anything she needed. Now she just needed to focus and stay focused. She had discovered staying focused was all she needed if there was anything for her to learn. She needed to determine what this man of cloth might know. She could not allow emotions to get in her way; she had come too far. She kept her head bowed as she began to ask questions. She asked about her family and using her fingernails dug into her thighs until it hurt. She was focused.

Like floodgates, the questions flowed a sense of relief filling their place. It was only after the last question that she became silent as she waited for answers. With a sense of empowerment, she allowed herself to look up at him for the first time. He was younger than she would have imagined, but she could see his soul was old. As she looked into his eyes, there was something very familiar. She had seen those eyes before. He did not respond, but instead, shook his head affirmatively listening as she asked about her family. Did he know them? Where did they go? What happened to the house and the belongings? The questions were endless, and yet he did not answer, he only nodded and remained silent.

I must keep in control. I must not allow my emotions to get in my way. I have so many questions that I am sure he knows the answers to. There is a sense of fear. What will I learn? What will I do with it? -M-

She was quite sure she knew him, and it appeared that he knew her. Not just the girl that went missing, but more accurately, he seemed to know her. As if he knew where she had come from and who she was now. As he listened, it was difficult for him to believe that she had made her way back.

To end up in this very church, a place where he had thought himself safe. It was what he wanted, what he had hoped for. Yet now that she was there, he could not imagine that it had even been allowed. Still, he listened, and when she seemed to have asked all of the questions she could ask when she appeared ready not just to listen, but to hear, he began to tell her what he could.

It had been such a long time ago. He closed his eyes and bowed his head, not sure where he should begin. He knew and had learned so much in doing so, he had experienced all of their pain.

"It was so hard," he told her, "that night when you didn't arrive home. When the night was already black. Black as black could be. Your mother (it was so odd to hear someone call her mama, mother) your family. Her family, even your father's family, the entire congregation, and the community as a whole, came together. They came together like never before. They came together for you." Maia listened, and with each of his words, each bit of what he said, she could feel pieces of herself begin to die.

I must be silent and listen. I think there will be too many things I will not want to hear. I hope that I will allow myself to remain in control. -M-

"There had been so many searchers. For days and weeks, they searched. Those that did not or could not search came and prayed. Your mother, she stopped eating. There were so many questions and so little to go by. You had been such a good girl."

Maia continued to hear him, and she couldn't help but wonder if there was something he knew, "You had been such a good girl," Did he mean she was no longer good?

"Even the police had no clues, there had been no sightings. It was as if you simply vanished." She was sure she saw a hint of mischief in his smile. He continued, "For years, your mother and siblings continued to search. They would not give up. Folks spoke about what a wonderful woman your mother was, such a hard worker. Your father began to drink, about that time your mother grew old very quickly. It wasn't too many years later before it was all too much for her. She died." Maia tried not to let him hear her as she held back a gasp; she was not going to let her emotions show. "They said she died of a broken heart. Shortly after her death, your siblings contracted a virus that took them, too. They all died within months of one another. Then your father drank himself to death." There were no family members left that he remembered. She looked at him, trying to hear what he was saying. She felt empty as if someone had opened her up and drained all the life out of her. With difficulty, knowing she had nothing else, she tried to hold onto her soul. There were no words to express what she was feeling, and so she remained silent. He took her hand in his and helped her up. It was difficult to make sense or justify God's hand in such a tragedy, but for now, wasn't that his job?

They cared all of them. They searched for me. Because of me they suffered. Loneliness of my unknown whereabouts, my unknown demise suffocated them. It was my choices that have left me so alone. -M-

They walked in silence as if both of them were waiting for an explanation, but it never came. Neither did the words as they continued to walk. As empty as she was, walking beside him, her hand in his, he passed her the warmth of his soul in its purest form. She accepted it, feeling the purity of his love. They walked together into the adjoining cemetery, weaving in and out of tombstones.

I am so alone as if my being did not exist.
But he is so full of love, in his presence
I am able to feel pure peace. I know him. -M-

He stopped in front of her mother's grave. She could see how surrounded she was by love as she read each tombstone. Including her father and siblings, cousins, and grandparents. Taking her breath away next to her mother was a tombstone with the inscription "My Beautiful daughter, may we walk together in the heavens." Underneath that was her name and her date of birth. They hadn't forgotten her, but instead, had made a place for her to spend eternity with them.

Weak, she let herself fall to her knees and lowered herself to the ground until she was resting her head on top of her mama's grave. It was there her moment of acceptance that she allowed herself to sincerely mourn. To let the raw emotion run out.

Justice and Dakota could hear her, the painful sobbing. With no possibility of continuing to wait and remain still. Fearful that she may be in danger of letting her soul run dry, they rose and made their way toward the sound of her heart-wrenching cries. Cries that took them into the cemetery, where like an obstacle course, they maneuvered through tombstone after tombstone. By the time they reached Maia, she had stopped crying. Her body was still somewhat contorted as she was trying to compose herself. She tried to regain control and push aside her emotions, which was what she did best. After hearing and now seeing her family lying in graves before her: the reality was that there was no one left. This knowledge brought her the closure she believed she needed. Thinking that this was the last thing she might need to truly set herself free.

I feel a crushing in my chest. The sight of my mama's grave, my siblings and father and grandparents screams with reality. The empty grave marked by my tombstone gives me an uneasy warmth. I was loved in ways I never lived. I do not know which direction I should take. Should I lay myself down? Can I allow Justice or even Dakota to be my excuse? There is so much pain. -M-

Maia was speaking to the priest, thanking him. All the while, she was trying not to stare, but she couldn't help herself. She knew she remembered those eyes. They were the eyes of a coyote. The coyote who had led them to the cottage. Who had protected them all those years and who had been lifted up and stolen away.

I know who he is. It is his eyes that I remember so well. How can it be? How can any of this be? -M-

It was Dakota who confirmed it. As Dakota came at him, he did something very unpriestly. He got down on the ground on all fours, so that he might engage fully with Dakota. They rolled a bit on the ground lovingly, playing. Maia and Dakota were both heavy-hearted as they could tell he was not the same.

There was a sense of sadness that overtook him. As if embarrassed or maybe ashamed, he quickly stood back up, just in time to see the swarm of birds begin to arrive. Hundreds of them, darkening the sky. Without a thought, without words, he grabbed Justice and ran. He ran until they were safe inside the church.

I can hear the sound as they approach, but my voice is silent and I do nothing to protect. When he sees them in an instant he grabs Justice. I watch him take her to safety.
I will follow them inside, but I will not question my actions. I have done enough. -M-

Chapter 46

When reality shows itself with little warning one can often feel lost.

It had been a very long time since there had been such a threat. The coyote who had saved Justice years earlier. Who had sacrificed himself as he had been lifted up and taken away by such a swarm. He was never seen again. He was never thought to have survived. Now it was that same coyote disguised as a Priest who stood before them. Who was once again protecting Justice.

It was as if my breath was being sucked from within. Fear consumed me like I do not ever remember. I ran as fast as I could as I attempted to catch up, grateful that Dakota ran with me. As I tried to reach Justice and her protector a part of me cried out in pain. I could not protect her. -M-

Whose eyes it was that shown through into his soul. Maia and Dakota followed them, running as fast as they could. Dakota holding back so that she didn't leave Maia alone. As they reached the church door, they hurried inside where they joined Justice and the Priest quickly pulling the door closed behind them. Justice stood there just inside, silent. All of them stood still. They were all silent. There could be no words just as there had been none previously. The Priest stood back. His hands shook as if perhaps he was unsure how to use them. He brushed the bit of dirt off of himself. Then held a finger to his lips, acknowledging the need to remain quiet. He, too, said nothing, for there were no words. He signaled Maia and Justice to join him so that he might embrace them as he held his arms open to protect them both.

I watched him. I could see how pained he was. I understood how difficult the choice was. He too had to sacrifice. He was not allowed the joy that might be his alone. I understood too well that he really had no choice. The choice had been made for him, just as it had been made for me. -M-

He turned just so hoping that he might be able to reach Dakota, wanting her. But he stopped himself. He had been taught well, there was too much need for solitude. Understanding such, he walked away. For a second, uncharacteristically, Dakota began to follow him. The pads on her paws lightly hitting the floor as if they might start to run, but she stopped. Looking after him longingly as if trying to decide. But there was no decision. She turned around and took a stand protectively at Justice's side.

It seemed like forever as the three of them waited silently for the bus to come and take them back. The sky was clear and blue.

I have decided that this shall be our new home. We will come back to where it started and find a place that will bring us peace. It will be my peace and I deserve that. -M-

Chapter 47

No matter how beautiful before may have been, there is no truth that it will be the same if we could go back

Maia's stillness had been uncomfortable as the silence continued, making the ride agonizingly long. Justice was finding it difficult to find words that might interrupt the silence. There were none. She was still trying to make sense of what had just occurred. As if she needed to understand but knew she could not ask, she was afraid of the answer. Maia's quietness meant that there were no descriptions as they rode along, making the ride even less enjoyable and longer for Justice. When they arrived back at the hotel, they went straight to their room.

Maia's only words were short and directive, as she instructed Justice "Start packing. Everything". They would need to make arrangements. It was not a conversation, but rather an order. Justice was somewhat confused. Decisions had always been discussed, figured out, and made together. That was the way it had always been, no matter what. It was one of the few times that they knew there would be communication. This new form of communication or lack thereof made Justice uncomfortable. She worried about what type of arrangements it was that Maia spoke of. Justice was not prepared for what Maia would soon enough disclose.

I must not give Justice time to think. This is the only choice she must have. I believe that going back is the only way I can keep going forward. It is my time. -M-

There was no time, not even the skipping of a beat, no asking about how she might feel or if she would be ready. There was no time to rest or weave, for they would not even stay the night. Maia could not wait, she not only insisted but pushed and hurried herself and Justice so that they would be packed up and headed back before the sunset. Justice tried to make sense of it, but her questions were met with silence, it was hard for her to understand. It wasn't until they had reboarded the bus that Maia finally spoke.

"We're going back," it was only three words. Three words that Justice would always remember. They were the words that changed everything.

Maia explained, "this time, we will be going back, not searching for my home or family. This time we will be in search of a new house that will be our home." That was what Maia had said, those were her words. But Justice heard it differently, and that is when she understood. It was for Maia that they were going back. It was to make a home for her. To make up for what she had missed all those years. To somehow make up for all that she had sacrificed of herself. Now it was her time to go back to the roots she remembered. For Justice, this had to be okay.

We found the perfect place today. It has the comfort of the cottage. The quiet of the woods. It will allow us the simplicity we both enjoy and me a place to be the woman I was born. There will be no more hiding Justice behind the layers of color. Dakota will be allowed to run. It will be our place of joy. It will be the place I will teach Justice skills she does not know. -M-

They spent days trying to find the perfect spot that they could call home. In the end, it was a quiet place that reminded Justice of their cottage in the woods. They kept it simple, the way they were both most comfortable. There was no longer anybody that they had to please, no longer anyone that they had to fool. She wore her womanhood with pride, and Justice never had to sit for what was always too long to have makeup applied that would cover up her colorlessness. Now, it was only for protection.

They no longer had to sew for clients, but sometimes they would mend a piece or two for themselves. On rare occasions, she was known to ask Justice to work with her to design a custom dress or make a gift for a parishioner the Priest had mentioned. They got chickens and goats and ate fresh eggs and drank goat's milk. They learned to make cheese.

Sometimes, she would have a male call on her. Justice always knew when this would happen because she would talk nonstop about anything as long as she was talking. She would spend a lot of time grooming herself, something neither of them did very often. But it wasn't just the grooming. It was that afterward she would wonder how she looked, worried about every detail. Justice would imagine she looked just like the school girls that Maia remembered and would sometimes talk about. There were some days when she acted like that. Justice would wish that she could tell her how beautiful she was. That she could give her the confidence, she thought Maia needed. While she hoped that someday, she too might have a caller.

It is a new feeling. Having a man interested in me. I love dressing up and going out. I love how Justice encourages me. When I leave it is by choice, it is with respect. Justice waits for me to share and together like girlfriends we laugh. -M-

Life was quite different. Not only in the place they now called home but in their relationship. They were more like girlfriends with snippets of motherhood. That was the part that Justice liked, it added something that she had been missing. But she wasn't full. She missed her outings with Dakota, the people she met, the stories they told. She missed the possibility that she might someday reconnect with the man who broke her heart.

She had never told Maia about him. It was hard for her to verbalize. There was still the pain, the lack of closure, and understanding. And there was too much that Justice felt she needed to forgive Maia for first. It was confusing, Justice wasn't entirely sure that it was forgiveness that was needed. After all, hadn't Maia allowed her to fill both roles, masculine and feminine? Hadn't Maia embraced her and cared for her? Hadn't she sacrificed all those years? But hadn't Justice sacrificed as well? Now she didn't feel capable of sharing him with Maia.

It was the fullness Justice felt when he was a part of her world that she missed the most. She knew that she could forgive him. She understood now that it was fear that had sent him away. She would often wonder what would have happened if she had known the words that would have given an explanation. If she even knew the words. If only she had known that she was so different. As Maia groomed herself, there was a bit of Justice that was sad and a bit angry that she had never been told. Maia had never explained anything to her. Maia alone could have given her the tools, the words that might have set her free, or maybe she had. Maybe by not saying anything was Maia's greatest gift, it gave acceptance to being different.

Justice thought about him, more often than she would ever like to admit. It was with the belief that an explanation would have been met with understanding rather than disgust and fear. That it might have been different. Very different, she could hope. But what else could she have expected? The memories made her sad. But the older she got, the easier it was for her to understand what he had done and why. Maia had never discussed the possibilities with her, and so she never anticipated them happening. Justice had not known to prepare. At the time, she hadn't really considered that she might be so different. Maybe that was why she had not shared. It was not something she felt that she could talk about. Often it was for these reasons that it brought her so much pain.

Chapter 48

Death holds it place, but it is not a place for those it leaves behind

Here, in this house they had picked to call home, there was nowhere to go. Apart from Maia's occasional male visitor and the Priest or an occasional parishioner, they were alone. The Priest's relationship had become quite normal, quite human. There was never talk or discussion about who he was or who he had been. Dakota was especially happy on the days the Priest visited. For Justice, this left a bit of a hole. But she wouldn't have thought of doing anything different. Maia had been her life, they had been each other's, and these new roles had a place she was sure. And so it was for the remainder of Maia's days.

With Dakota by her side, Justice readied for a day of canning. It was one of the many new skills that Maia had taught her soon after they had all appeared to feel settled into their new home. Maia thought it would be a good beginning. Now, as they were waiting the silence was especially disturbing. Dakota seemed to be out of sorts and became overly clingy even though she needed to keep moving. She paced back and forth between the kitchen and Justice's room. Justice sat quietly, waiting to hear Maia's song, some gentle words. She listened, perhaps she would hear the sound of her shoes as she skimmed them across the already worn out wooden floor. There was nothing but silence. It was quite some time before Justice allowed herself to leave the kitchen's security and comfort and look for her. In the final weeks, she had come to understand that it was best not to disturb her, but Justice felt she had waited long enough.

As Justice began to walk towards the outer hall, she could feel the air around her getting cold, a slight brush against her, left a tear on her cheek. Before she completed her walk through the house, she already knew. Dakota, who had run ahead, found Maia first. She found her cold and still, climbing up onto her bed Dakota laid her body over Maia's trying to warm her. As Justice approached, it was not Dakota she reached for, but the cold, still hand of the woman who had given so much of herself to make it possible for her to be where she was at this moment. The woman who had not only transformed but had been violated on her behalf. Justice held her hand, hoping, like Dakota, to warm her back. But the stillness did not change, even the tears as they fell on her cheek did not bring her back. Justice and Dakota sat there for days holding her. They did not want to let go. They were not ready. And they did not know-how. When the Priest arrived to pay one of his weekly visits- it was always an opportunity for him to share information about a new family who was in some type of need. But it was Justice and Dakota who were the ones he would find most needy. It was with great difficulty that the Priest had to convince Justice that it was time to let go.

Time to put her to rest, he put it: "It was time for her to go home." That was an odd thing for him to say, and Justice couldn't help but wonder who he had become. Justice was silent, trying to understand precisely what he meant. Home was wherever they were together. Maia had always made that clear. Through it all, they had each other. Justice had no way to prepare herself for what lie ahead. Most certainly, she had no way to prepare herself for saying goodbye.

Chapter 49

What is it that makes one full? Are any of us ever truly full?

When eventually Maia's story was complete, it was Justice who held onto the tapestry she had made. It was the only one that was not hers alone that she kept. She did not want Maia to have to hold onto it into eternity. The emotions were far too strong. Finding the box that held them all and using the key that she had taken from the chain which held it. The chain that had all these years hung around Maia's neck as if she were protecting a treasure. Justice unlocked it and placed Maia's tapestry among her own, before doing what she knew she had to and locked the box again.

It wasn't long after Maia's death that the sky grew dark again with the arrival of hundreds, perhaps thousands of birds. Birds who, without warning, without sound or time swooped down, covering the town in blackness. And then in a split second, they were gone, and so was the Priest. His disappearance left Justice with an unforeseen void as emptiness began to fill her. Unaware of the event that robbed her and Dakota of their friend, the Priest, Justice was reminded of what was and how quickly it could be gone. Without warning, without a chance to prepare. All she knew was that if she were to survive, it would take practice.

She felt sorrow but did not allow it to consume her. She thought about the words she had heard so many times before: "Today must also be your tomorrow. Yesterday was a gift to hold dear, a reminder of all one has and the delicious flavors that one must savor as yesterday allows us to live it over again".

Now with Maia and the Priest gone, Justice understood. It would be the gift of yesterday, living it over and over again; that would be what she would hold onto. That is what, for the moment, would keep her alive.

It took months, perhaps years before Justice and Dakota were able to be coaxed into moving on. It was not that there was nothing left, rather that there was nothing but memories to hold them. Memories that Justice held in a place that she could take with her wherever she went. The peace and quiet were comforting, a small reminder of what had been. The place she had for so long called home, the cottage, their cottage. The isolation a brand burnt into what was left of her. The isolation held her captive, preventing her from finding the people whose stories still needed to be told. Even the families and people who they had known who attended Church services had in their own rights become vacant and void. It was as if they had been dipped in vats of melted wax and left out to dry candles whose wicks would only serve to turn them into nothingness. They went through the motions, their empty prayers mimicked, played back in hauntingly lonely echoes as the belfry sounded. Echoes that moved Justice and Dakota to tears. In the end, it is what might have saved them. They packed up and moved out, moved on.

Chapter 50

When we are ready for change will we still be allowed to change our mind

It was a challenging endeavor, Justice had always been a familiar bystander. Understanding the necessary procedures it took to make moving both simple and successful. However, she had a difficult time maneuvering through the process without Maia. She knew that in previous moves, they had to sell their home and most of its contents. She had to search deep amongst her memories. Having always been an observant observer, she pulled from memories she didn't think she could get to much less make them viable. Grateful for what she often mistook as Maia's rambles, when Maia would go off on tangents. She would describe everything she did. But it was never directed at Justice nor for her. Rather Maia rambled in hopes that she could keep herself company. So much of what Justice learned was in this way. Now she was grateful for the lessons and the encouragement that Maia bestowed on her long after her death. It was in this way that Justice was encouraged to find her way to independence. And so with Dakota close by, she attempted to sell off what was left. Those things that did not hold meaning and that were not needed. In the end, all she took was the loom, and Maia's completed story still locked in the box.

It was the box she knew she had to pack. The box that had been Maia's treasure. The place that Maia had kept all of her completed stories. The box was seldom unlocked, so it was rarely opened. But it was always the first thing that Maia packed up. It always had to be protected as it was moved from place to place. Maia had always made sure of that. Justice stopped for a minute to give thanks to her again, for she knew everything that Maia did was because she believed she knew what was essential and acted on it. Justice hoped, in the end, that Maia understood that it was not so much the actions as it was the memories. After all, Justice accepted it to be the truth. The memories of a life were all that one had.

Chapter 51

Even in darkness there is light

There was quite a bit of money left. Over the years, Justice had learned to understand its meaning, its need, and its necessity, resentment, and scorn. But, it was also deserving of gratitude. As Justice remembered being forced to leave the comfort and serenity of the cottage, she learned money was what had given Maia and herself the chance to live in the manner that they did. It was money that had allowed Maia to spend her last days with Justice in a home that reminded them, each in their own right, who they were. More importantly, for Maia, it reminded her of who she had been and from where she had come. It was difficult for Justice to understand that those things alone were maybe not enough.

Keeping just a small amount of what they had, Justice and Dakota were able to get back to the city. Where it was full of the hustle and bustle with voices that screamed out. Voices needing to have their stories shared. Dakota didn't waste any time leading Justice to those whose bodies the voices belonged. Justice found pure comfort as once again one by one, she was able to set them free. At the end of the day, they both found solace in a small one-room apartment that they could own without trouble or banks or help from anyone. They had what they needed in each other. It was quieter than most places in the city, and they welcomed the stillness it often brought.

They found little need for extras, so it surprised even Justice herself with the purchase of a small electric radio. It was the kind that sat on the counter and had a dial; she could turn to change the channels. Justice never changed the channels. She would listen to the same station all the time. She was happy to hear the familiarity of the same announcers. Each morning comforted by the sound of their voices. As she sat and had her bowl of oatmeal and a cup of tea. It was always the same, and Dakota would feast on pieces of meat that somehow always made themselves available just for her. Justice always knew like Maia had learned never to question where anything came from. She understood and remembered that unwritten rule; Maia had taught her well. Justice knew that it was their assistance that added to the comfort of having Dakota. It was what made her more than just believe that she was never really alone. That there was someone always present, watching and protecting her. Making sure she was without want or need and that every effort would be made to keep her safe. There were times she may have suppressed such knowledge as if it were to give honor to Maia. Maia's ability to care and provide for her. But she always knew she could feel the hold that they had on her. Now that Maia was gone, it was indeed not her happiness that was their concern.

The days were full, and the nights quietly comforting, no longer was the isolation weighing her down. Slowly Justice was learning. There could be a new peacefulness in the space that she and Dakota had created among the chaos of the city, that they had chosen to call home. It was a place that she understood at that time was where she belonged.

As time went on, the simplicity of what was now home remained void of luxuries except for the small electric radio, which oddly seemed to bring calm to the start of each day. Perhaps she had thought, it was even simpler than the cottage had been. What she was quite sure of was that it was her spot. Her place and it was filling her with something she had been missing for quite some time. While there were often times and reminders that made her miss what had been. Times she would reach out longing for Maia, knowing she was no longer there. And she would stop herself from asking the questions she could not answer.

It was those occasions when she would hold Dakota a little tighter, rub her ears a little longer, and try not to imagine too much loss. It was on those days when she was most grateful for the voices on the radio as if perhaps they were actually having a conversation with her. Justice didn't remember how long she had listened and been comforted by them. She did not know how to prevent her heart from feeling heavy when the familiar voices she held so close began to change.

What she did remember was once again feeling deserted. Their voices no longer sang out with happiness. The conversations were at her, not with her. She could hear their undeniable distress. Day in and day out, day after day, they began to start with talk about tragedy after tragedy. Their discussions of hatred and violence were so frequent that soon it was those feelings that had made themselves commonplace. Justice was lost in the turmoil and uncertainty. The streets and sidewalks shared in those sentiments, Justice could feel it every time they went out. People were less kind, less patient. She could sense their entitlement of being me, making any talk of us or you close to extinct. Even those that were to protect her could not guide her. It had become a chore for Justice and Dakota just to go out. The emptiness was beginning to run through their bones, attempting to cool them from the inside out. They began to welcome the night time, the blackness, beyond that which was hers.

When Justice was faced with uncertainty, but fearlessness allowed her to stand extra tall, those were the times that Justice would seek them. Although she was never quite sure who they were. With all her might and all her energy, she would try to speak to them, not to question but rather to request that they listen to her. She would ask that they not only hear her words or the sounds inside, which cried out but that they take the time to really listen. She tempted them with kindness and patience, but she was tired, and after so many years, she was beginning to feel a bit used.

 In the most recent days, she had tried although with disdain to acknowledge her role, not necessarily understand it. Now it was time for truth. She was so tired, all of the loss, all of the emptiness, the lack of companionship it had been enough. Hadn't she been on this plane they called earth for far too long? Hadn't she also given up enough? Over the years, there had been so many voices that she and Dakota had succeeded in finding. All the people she had guided as she allowed each individual to create their own story as she helped to set them free. Wasn't it time? She would ask of them. To please let her go.

But her pleas were never answered, her wishes never filled. There was never anyone who responded to her cries. Instead, she would be left with her morning bowl of oatmeal and a cup of tea alongside a full teapot of hot water and extra tea bags. Justice would try to go to sleep hopeful, but in the morning, she was met with the voices on the radio. A bit more troubled then they might have seemed the day before. When the voices stopped, just for a moment when the voices stopped, Justice thought that perhaps she too might be allowed to go. She thought that maybe they had listened and might set her free. But they had not stopped talking. They had merely paused only to begin again reporting on yet another act of violence, or incident involving hate. Greed had become the daily norm as people lost their homes, beat one another, stole, making Justice feel empty and cold. Dakota would try and comfort her, but for the first time, there was no comfort. Justice could feel the life fading from Dakota as she stroked her giving her thanks. Dakota was getting old; she had never brought in her replacement. There had been no opportunities for her to go out and find a mate. It was just the two of them, and Dakota would never leave Justice alone long enough for that. There would not be another Dakota. She, too, was tired and knew she could not continue, no matter how hard she tried. They did not interfere. Alone Justice held her as she lay her head down one day and said goodbye, and they just let her go.

Chapter 52

When we open our eyes, our hearts it isn't hard to believe
the universe really does connect us all

That was the day I met Justice. I had a slow morning, and I was late when I left for work. For some reason, I chose to take a different route. I'm not sure why I was never late to anything, especially work. My routine never changed. But on that day, it was as if I had no choice. It was as if it had all been planned. As if I was drawn to her, to the spot where she walked.

As my car crawled along the city street, I saw her in a parking lot of traffic. I watched as with every ounce of strength, she moved slowly down the sidewalk, stumbling ever so slightly as she swayed from side to side. I witnessed her as she struggled with the weight of what she carried. A stream of pure light not only surrounding her but seeming to follow her. It was difficult to tell if it was coming from her or attempting to fill her. It was a light energy so beautiful it took my breath away. I watched her. Her long white hair flowing down her back. Yet it could not support her pain. I watched without choice, I was where I was meant to be, and there was nowhere else I could go. There was something so familiar about her and the energy she emitted. It was as if I had seen her before, and in that instant, I knew. She was in the story that my great grandmother had recorded on her tapestry. It was the story that she had always carried with her. She kept it close, sharing it with those she thought would listen, those she thought might understand. She carried it with her always, up, until the day she died. Now, as I watched her, I realized she was the reason that we were all here.

I pulled my car over to the side of the street, pleased that I had gotten a parking spot. I got out of the car and began to follow her. I wanted to see if I could help. While I had not noticed when I first saw her when I stopped I could see in the way she walked, in the way she held herself, she must be blind. I was especially cautious as I approached her. She was hesitant but obviously desperate. There was a sorrow that I could not comfort. I was sure no one could because it was a sorrow so deep that it could not be touched. She, too, was cautious but alone, deep in mourning. Who could she ask? That was the question she was hoping I could answer.

  She was wondering if anyone might help, she had asked me. She was trying to find a place to lay her to rest she had said, putting her head down for a minute to inhale her scent. It brought me a sense of peace when she allowed me to help even if only with the assistance of transportation. She asked me to take her to the closest woods. I was relieved that there was a reasonably accessible forest preserve not far. When we got back into my car, it was a pleasant surprise that traffic had opened up. I believe it was more than just a surprise. We drove in silence until we reached the preserve, she would not allow me to touch Dakota or put her in the backseat. Instead, she held it on her lap, stroking its still body.

When we pulled into the entrance of the preserve, she stiffened. I waited in the car and watched. With her bare hands, she dug a hole deep enough to place her in the ground only then to use her hands to replace the earth and cover her up. Her hands raw and bloody, she felt no pain only the breaking of her heart as she realized she was all alone. I was uncertain how long I sat there watching her, waiting. I saw that it was getting dark and I hoped she would hurry.

When I realized it was not the sun setting that brought the darkness but a sky full of birds flying overhead. Landing on treetops singing loudly, I panicked, I was never a fan of birds. She returned to the car slowly, but with a purpose. When she got back in, she whispered something I could not hear. I was silent as I drove her home, and so was she, so quiet that I could actually hear her heartbreaking.

She did not say goodbye. All I could do was to tell her how sorry I was as she began to get out of the car into the traffic, which had once again returned. Cars began honking at my stopped vehicle. I turned my eyes away from her for a second, and when I turned back, she was gone. I was uncertain where home was for her but felt compelled to find her and check on her. I knew that this could not be all there was. I returned to the same spot often, I drove around when I could, hoping to see her again. I continued to search for days, maybe weeks, and then just like that as if I were being directed. I would arrive in front of her building, where she stood as if waiting just for me. I knew that she could not see, but somehow she too knew I was there. I pulled over and stopped in front of her without seeming to hesitate as she got in. She placed her hands on the seat, her palms flat against the fabric. She took a deep breath and put her head back, resting it against the headrest, where she seemed to look up as if she could see through the roof of the car where she was seeking something in the sky. I watched her close her eyes and thought I could see her filling herself up with light. I watched her, grateful that there was no traffic so she could sit in silence until she was ready. She was of the simplest words and did not try to add fluff to what she would tell me. I was to learn that my new role was to drive her to any place that she would direct me.

It was always just someplace obscure. She would always instruct me to leave her there. Then with the kindest of words, she would tell me or actually ask me if maybe I could come back in an hour or so. It was as if she knew I would do it as if it was expected, but she wasn't comfortable with that. I could tell that, like me, she was doing what she had to. She was a giver, not a taker. It was usually a quiet ride, but there were some days she would just want to talk, and some days she would want someone to talk to her. Those were the days when I tried to make conversation without asking too many questions.

She was a brilliant woman, gifted, I'm sure, full of compassion, equality, and forgiveness. In her world, there was no room for discrimination on any level. Often she would laugh awkwardly and ask me if I thought that perhaps folks just didn't understand? That question would always accompany a tear running down her cheek. She would always follow with the same statement, "that everyone had the same bodily functions, and no matter what, they all bled the same color." Over the years, she grew sadder. There were fewer days when she would ask me to take her somewhere. Instead, she would ask me up for tea. I enjoyed those days the most, although it pained me to see her like that.

Her apartment was sparse, with a single table and chair in a kitchen area-a radio, a small stove, and a refrigerator, with cupboards just full enough for her daily needs. A small cushioned chair, a bed, covered with a beautiful coverlet that she proudly shared might be over 100 years old. It was Maia's she told me. There was an amazing artisan loom that surely had been handmade that she would rarely talk about. A box with a lock on it that she never opened that had been with her for as long as she existed. She was a private person and humble. Her colorless hands had surely seen their days of work but still were soft to the touch. I knew this because she would often reach out and take my hand as if to gift me a bit of all she had, herself. Sometimes when she asked me in, she would ask me if I knew why they would not let her go. I didn't understand who she was talking about and thought it best not to pry. Or maybe I was actually afraid to know. I only visited on the days I was summoned or directed. It was more often on some days than I was prepared. I was not allowed to choose my time.

She crumbled after hearing the announcer on 9/11. I am quite sure that day alone pushed her even further. She would ask daily for them just to let her be free. But I suppose more stories needed to be told, and only Justice had the gift to unlock what they needed so that they might be set free. And so she had to stay.

When the radio announcer talked about the gay killings in Orlando, she sobbed. With the massacre in Nice, she felt numb, the murder of innocent black children, and the marching full of hatred in Charlottesville, she could take no more. Each morning the announcer shared more stories equally as disturbing. Soon I could hear her from outside as she begged in pain for them to please just let her go.

When the day finally came, it was not my turn to go and visit. I was not summoned or directed, I was not allowed. She died alone, I hope that it was them, whoever they were, that finally gave her the peace she begged for, I hope it finally set her free.

I didn't arrive until they were bringing her body out. I have yet to know who notified the authorities. She was covered up, and they would not allow me to see her body, although I longed to hold her hand. I didn't go up, right away, there was nothing I could do. I just stood on the sidewalk for a bit, quite numb, wishing that I had told her how loved she was, although I think she knew. As I stood there, someone, or maybe it was something, came running out the door holding the box, her box.

They stopped only long enough to put it in my hands as they whispered to me, "You must be the keeper of the box." It was with great difficulty that I held it, it was much heavier than I expected. And then there was the question of what to do with it. I had no idea what treasure it held, and yet somehow, I felt solely responsible for its contents. There was not much time to ponder it. I could sense that something magnificent had already begun, and it would now be my job-keeper of the box- to be ready. I waited because I didn't know what else to do. I waited until I was directed or guided to do something. I really am not sure how long I remained there on that spot as if it held some extraordinary power.

Eventually, I did go back inside. I collected the pieces of papers, and journals, the history that she had said was all Maia had documented, she hadn't yet shared it with me only told me about it. But I am sure she would have wanted me to protect it.

I remember going home, my hands stiff from holding the box so tightly. I didn't let it out of my sight, and although it was quite challenging to get comfortable, I even slept with it. I would be lying if I said that while waiting to be given direction, I did not attempt to open the box. But no matter what, that was not going to happen. It wasn't going to budge, and there was no way I could break the lock. For days I kept it with me taking it wherever I went. I could not work. I was consumed with its safety. It was on the seventh day that the blinds flew open, letting the sun in as it rose, pulling me out of sleep. I didn't waste any time getting dressed. Then as if without choice, without consciousness as if being moved like a chess piece ready to call *checkmate*, taking the box, I drove to the park that took up residence in the center of town. It was there that I parked in a parking spot that I am quite sure had been reserved for only me. I got out of my car, the box securely in hand.

Still being directed, I followed a line of people, not sure where it would lead me. I did not get in line but rather was instructed to walk parallel to those who were waiting. It was a line so long that it wrapped its way for city blocks. Passing person after person, I made my way slowly to the front, the box seeming to grow heavier with each step I took, with each person I passed. It was as if each person I walked passed was filling up the box. When I finally reached the front of the line and made my way inside, it was then that I realized that all of the people standing in line were actually celebrators. Each one held a story of their own waiting their turn for one final goodbye, one last time to give her thanks. A chance to celebrate her and all she had done.

I made my way to the front where on a low wooden bench of sorts was the plain wooden box in which she lay. I stood there proudly as if I had been assigned the grandest job of all, the sentinel of her departure. She was beautiful lying there in the simplest of wood boxes! There had been no alterations to her being in the preparation of laying her to rest. I was grateful for that. I had witnessed so many others so many times before. Plastic replicas of who might have been.

Her skin was even more colorless than I remembered. Was that even possible? As she lay there resting, I could see the slightest smile. A smile that she was to wear forever. I found peace in this gesture as I knew that she must have been thrilled when they had let her go quietly and without a fight. Peaceful and free.

PART II

The Celebrators

Faith

The screams had been so loud and so shrill that even a deaf Dakota was aroused. Justice listened painfully, each scream sending a shiver through her being. Like Dakota, each second that passed without silence, caused her to wait on edge. She hoped that the screams might stop. Joseph wasn't home, it had been an unspoken rule of which there weren't many, and she wasn't sure if they should leave.

It had been sort of an agreement early in the move, and although Justice really had no fear, she knew how worried he would be if he were to come home and find that she and Dakota had ventured off alone. She knew that it would most likely cause distress should they leave without telling him where they were going. Justice found it difficult not to abide. But as the screams continued, Dakota began to howl. It was too painful to wait. Justice listened, trying to hear through the screams. Such a desperate call. When she realized that it was her that the screams were summoning, she could no longer wait. There was no way she could keep her word. Gathering herself, she let Dakota know that they were going to find the source. Together they followed the screams and the penetrating vibrations.

Despite that the sun was trying to rest for the day, there was still just enough light to be pulled in close, causing the reflections to bounce from store window to store window. Then landing just right light shone into the alleyway. The alleyway that Dakota and Justice had been led to. Laying on the ground curled up in the fetal position was a small body just barely moving. A pair of dirty little hands covering what appeared to be its head. A dirty blue blanket was lying just out of reach. It seemed oddly misplaced as if ripped off and tossed away from what was undoubtedly a very needy child. A small, frail woman stood over it, looking too vicious for her size. She held her arm raised with what looked like a club of sorts, held firmly in her fisted hand (later it was discovered it had been a rolling pin). She was just about to deliver another blow upon the child, when Dakota, who had arrived first, jumped in between the two and angrily bared her teeth. Justice without Dakota by her side followed the sound which had gone from screams to a muffled whimper. The woman her arm still raised, turned her attention on Dakota. Dakota let out a low deep growl. Frightened, the woman dropped the club. But before running off, she was able to kick the child with such force that it rolled over. Dakota turned her attention to the child while waiting for Justice to find her way. As she waited, Dakota positioned herself so that she stood protectively hunched over the child, her breath hot. She lowered her head and gently nudged with soothing compassion, but the child who was now on his back face up drew his arms and hands up to cover his face. He peeked out ever so slightly only to see the dark eyes and white fangs of Dakota within inches. Petrified, he might be eaten, he quickly rolled back onto his stomach and resumed the fetal position. Trying to make himself as small as possible, he tried not to cry out and not to scream. He squeezed his eyes closed tight, dirt filling his tear ducts as he waited for certain death. Justice arrived seconds later, making her way to Dakota. She stood beside her, a hand patting her head. Dakota pulled back so that she might make way for Justice, who, with pure love, approached the boy. As she lowered her body, she kneeled down so that she might comfort the child.

With great caution, he allowed himself to open his eyes. Slightly, peeking through the small opening where his head,was resting on his arms. Trying not to cry out as the now dry dirt scrapped both his eyeball and his eyelid. He could not believe what he was seeing. Kneeling over him, beside him, was the most beautiful sight. Just like the ones he had seen at church, was an angel!

Justice sat back on her feet and motioned for Dakota to join her. To lay down beside her. Justice knew all too well how frightening Dakota might be to a young child, especially one who did not know her. Dakota responded lovingly. Moving closer, she lay down and rested at Justice's side. Justice repositioned herself so that she was sitting cross-legged on the ground, making herself a buffer between Dakota and the child. Gently reaching out, she lifted the child into her lap. Pulling him close until his head was resting against her chest. She wrapped her arms lovingly and protectively around him. She stayed that way for several minutes before she began to rock him back and forth while she sang just loud enough for him to hear. As if time did not exist, she waited in that spot doing nothing else but being protective and loving. She wiped his face with a corner of her blouse, she wiped his tears, his nose. She held his hands in hers, and together they let Dakota lick them clean. He giggled a small yet contagious giggle.

Dakota left to retrieve the blue blanket and brought it to him. Dropping it over his shoulders as he held onto Justice. She pulled the blanket around him, hoping that it might keep him warm or bring him comfort. Helping him stand up on the ground next to her, she took his hand in hers and began to walk back home, Dakota protectively walked alongside them.

As they walked, he just kept looking up at her. He remembered thinking he was holding the hand of an angel. And this angel was taking him home. There was never a question that she would invite him into their house, and as she made him some hot chocolate and gave him a biscuit, Joseph arrived home. Certainly, the child heard the conversation, the questions. For a second, the raised voice which made him wince, and a wet spot grew in his pants. Joseph looked at her, he was tired but knew all too well that this was what Justice was to be doing. He stopped himself from being upset and kneeling down to the boy, asked if he might like a fresh pair of pants. Justice smiled, knowing what it was she needed to do.

Joseph took the boys hand and assisted him in changing his pants. He made him a warm meal and sat down as if he had something to say, but they sat in silence as the child filled himself. Justice sitting at the table with them saddened that there was so much silence. She remembered their own lack of communication and wished that perhaps there might be a book he would think to read the child, but he did not. After the child was clean, his stomach full, Justice with Dakota close by, took the small boy's hand and walked him over to the loom. Justice carefully removed her own unfinished tapestry tying off the ends before she re-warped the loom, preparing it for a new story. She pulled the child lovingly onto her lap and whispered in his ear. This would be his story. He could make anything he wished, make his story anything he wanted. He giggled not so much at the idea of making something, anything he wanted, but because he could feel the words of an angel in his ear.

Justice put the shuttle of black thread in his hand and guided him for the first few passes. She felt him look up at her and knew that it was his turn, it was time to leave him alone. She moved him lovingly from her lap to the chair and left him there so that he might tell his story.

The child folded his knees under himself as he created. His small hands trembled not so much because it was difficult for him to work the loom but because he wasn't comfortable. Even as he worked he wasn't sure what his story should be. No one had ever told him he could do whatever he wanted. But the angel had told him. She had said to make anything he wished as long as it was his story. He was afraid that his mama wouldn't like his story, afraid what she might do to him. He was afraid of the pain that she might inflict or the punishments she would give. But in the end he decided to make his story. His wish, a strong and happy boy who would grow strong in spirit and size, who would no longer have to live in fear, who would instead be surrounded with love.

As he finished, he reached down to stroke Dakota who had been laying at his feet and allowed her to lead him to Justice. She was waiting. A peaceful smile filling her and lighting the way in what had become a darkening room. The child cautiously reached out and took her hand, together they returned to the loom where his story waited. Joseph came too, following them. Not invited and not requesting permission but because he felt it somehow his right. As Justice removed the child's finished tapestry from the loom, carefully and with grace finishing off the edges, she handed it to him. His story came to life. The most beautiful colors had shown themselves where the black threads of his storytelling had laid. He was in awe as she placed it in his hands, and as this child held it close, a tear ran down his cheek. His hand touched hers, and he could feel something he never had before experienced, he felt whole. He looked at Justice and knew he had been correct all along, she was an angel, and she had been sent to save him.

The child held onto it. He knew he did not need to ask if he could keep it, he understood that it was his. He held it close, worrying if he was going to have to return home would she take it from him. Would she beat him until it was hers? But Justice knew it was the child's. It was his story, and it would protect him if that was the story he told. Without many words, she reassured him that it was indeed his, and no one could ever deny him that right.

Joseph watched once again, witnessing something he did not understand. Something he knew he must not question. He stood there, witness, to this child whom Justice had saved and watched the tapestry come to life as if he knew. It was as if that was why he was, and for this, he had to be honored.

Now at the age of 92, this child stood in line, the tapestry, his story held close to his chest. It was worn from so much use, just as the hands that held onto it. Over the years, it had helped him out of some tight spots. It had given him faith. He had been strong, he had been blessed. He had an angel that had watched over him. Now, as he stood in line, he thought about how much he would miss. He wondered how he would get by without the phone calls. Calls that came every year on the anniversary of his story's creation and the day he had been set free. No matter where he was, Justice had always known how to find him. He had changed on that day, he was no longer afraid. He knew his mom could no longer hurt him. Over the years, they had even grown to understand each other. He had learned to forgive, and on the day his mother had died, there was an extra phone call from Justice as if somehow she had known.

Now here he was an old man standing in a long line. As he stood there, he didn't feel so strong. His knees felt as if they might give out, yet he forced himself to stand. After all, it was his story, and he had to say goodbye.

Gold

There were more than a dozen people, family members. No two shared exactly the same skin color or the same age. There were men and women, girls and boys standing together, not sure if they should allow themselves to express the excitement they were feeling. Or if they should stand quietly, giving respect to the woman who for years they had all heard so much about.

In the end, what they all agreed upon was how honored they felt standing there in line. All waiting not only to say goodbye but each one of them waiting so that they could give thanks in their own way.

For this family, it was a story that they had all heard. It was repeated over and over again. A story that had been passed on from generation to generation.

Before Rosa Parks, it had been their very own relative, Bertha. Bertha was tired of being told where her place was as a negro, and she had had enough. So she decided it was time to stand up (or in her case sit down) in protest against the segregation of blacks and whites on city buses. It was a young Bertha who had refused to give up her seat to a white woman. Ironically it was a white woman who had sat beside her. It was this white woman who they all now stood in line waiting to give thanks. Waiting to say goodbye.

In doing so, they celebrated that they might let the world know and understand what she had done.

They stood hands joined in camaraderie as if each of them had been there listening to Bertha tell her story. As if they could hear her words, and perhaps they could. The story was always told passed on by whoever was telling it as if it were Bertha herself speaking. And so in a robust slow voice, she told Bertha's story.

"You know me. Myself, well, I wasn't overly afraid. You all know, don't you, there had been others who stood up before me. Others stood tall to protect their rights, others who lived to tell. But my oh my on that day, it was all against me. You know there were more white people on that bus than blacks. (everyone liked that she had called them blacks). All those black folk they had taken their seats in the back of the bus, just like they were supposed to. But they didn't want no trouble, and instead of standing beside me, they all remained seated, not a one of them did nothing.

No siree, they chose not to interfere; instead, they just sat back and watched. The next thing I know, some young very white woman, she must have been blind I figured as she had one of those seeing-eye dogs I think, anyways she came and sat down next to me. Now I was thinking but didn't want to say nothing, I was thinking, mam you best not be sitting there, I'm a negro, yep that's what I told her. I believed she could not see and might get herself in trouble, being blind and all. So I said it out loud, but in a whisper, ya know so that no one else would hear. She smiled and didn't say anything. But then the driver asked me, well he didn't really ask, he ordered me to move to the back, just as another white woman boarded.

Well can you just believe it, this crazy white girl reached over and just took my hand in hers and held it. She done held it like she wasn't ever gonna let me go. When the driver repeated himself, he was real stern now, no care that this white woman was holding onto me. Next thing this crazy blind white girl she done rose up out of her seat, still holding my hand, and she done told him to stop the bus.

Just like that, she stood up my hand done stuck with hers and told him in a voice that meant business to stop the bus! She startled that bus driver so bad that he stopped the bus so fast that we both almost fell over. She held my hand sorta tight, and her and her dog led me off the bus. Now there I was thinking about how was I gonna get home when the next thing I knew, she was still holding my hand and walking with me down the sidewalk.

I wasn't sure what was going on, and I had no idea where she was done taking me. And then just like that before I even know what hit me, I'm in her house, sitting at her table having a cup of tea with her. We done talked for hours and then she takes me into a room, she said it had a loom in it, and she wanted me to see it. It sure 'nough, there it was, she wasn't kidding, the biggest loom I ever seen, almost took up the whole room. (laughing) but that there room was a bitty thing. She put her arms around me, handed me some thread on a stick of sorts, and told me to tell my story. She helped me with the first few passes and then just went and left me alone to do my thing, tell my story. I dun stood there for quite sometime. I wasn't sure what my story should be. I stood my hands trembling something awful. For sure I didn't want my story to show my anger, I didn't want my story to have any hate. I let myself think of that girl in the other room, that white girl. I let myself sit on the bus as I told my story. And the funniest thing; Can you just imagine using only black thread? This was the story I told. Can you just imagine, don't even know what gave it so much life. Funniest thing is that white girl once she said goodbye and helped me home. I thought I was finished with her, but she done found me every year. She'd write a letter or call me on the phone and always want to know how I was doing. Blind and all and she done cared about how I was doing."

"When Bertha died, so did the calls and the letters ceased coming as if she knew."

Whoever it was that told Bertha's story showed the tapestry to all.

That was why the family now stood in line, holding Bertha's story among themselves, protecting it as if it were gold. They were waiting to give their thanks to this woman who, until she died, was the unknown hero in Bertha's story.

Confidence

She was the woman whom he had come to love. As she pushed him in his wheelchair, he was sure she loved him too. They were together, and for the moment, that was all that mattered. She pushed him forward a little at a time to conform with the slow-moving line.

When they stopped again to wait, she let go of his wheelchair and placed her hand on his shoulder, giving it a loving squeeze. He tilted his head as far as he could and looked up at her. He remembered how lucky he was. He remembered her kindness and what it had taken to get to this point. She loved him for who he was. It didn't matter that he weighed 500 lbs and needed her assistance to do everything, including to push his chair. She baked the best butter-crusted, cream-filled pies on the planet and never once considered telling him that maybe he shouldn't have one. In fact, often, she'd bake them just for him. He had been on a roll in the weight loss department when they met and had just celebrated his 275 lb loss. He was so proud of himself. It had been quite an accomplishment. She was a big woman, and she understood the trauma involved with name-calling and bullying when it came to being so overweight. She understood the extra skin that seemed to have nowhere to go each time the fat disappeared. Still waiting for the line to move, she reached inside her purse for a Milky Way bar and offered him a bite, he shook his head. A tear rolled down his robust cheek as he reminded himself that it was here and now that he would have to say goodbye to her. For it was not her love for him that he must embrace, but his love for himself. Somewhere along the way, he had forgotten that. It was here in this line with hundreds of others that he waited, for like himself, he was sure that they had each been given a gift. It was a gift that they held dear, a gift that gave them the ability to see, change, and accept. Each of them must have lived it well. Each of them must have had a story that they had been allowed to tell. For so long, he had let himself forget. But now, as he waited in line to say his own goodbyes, it was time to remember. He looked back at her and asked her for his story. His story that she had insisted she hold onto. Hesitantly, she reached in her bag. Less cautiously than he would have liked, she pulled it out and put (sort of threw it) on his lap. With more difficulty than he would admit, he moved his hand until it rested on it. Protecting it the best he could. He closed his eyes and letting his fingers read it; he allowed himself to remember.

He had been walking. He remembered that it was more likely waddling down the sidewalk. At that point, he was using a cane to help him balance his 500 lb. plus body. The city sidewalks were busy, and more people were walking than he had anticipated. It was a slow waddle as he attempted to stay as far as possible to one side of the sidewalk so that others might pass. But he was too wide. As he tried to maneuver his way to cross over to the other side so that he might get to the bus stop, a businessman came hurrying by. There was definitely no room on the sidewalk for them both. They bumped into one another. That was all it took. That slight bump knocked him off balance, and he found himself crashing anything but gracefully to the ground. The businessman hesitated for a split second before moving on. There wasn't even a word, just a look of disgust. He remembered how little room there was for humility as he attempted to get up. He could hear the gasps of passers-by, their comments, the intentional or unintentional feet that stepped on him, instead of over him. He remembered having difficulty breathing. Holding back tears, trying with desperation to get up. So many people, so little compassion. And then in the blink of an eye, he was standing. She stood behind him, steadying him as if he were a piece in a giant Jenga puzzle that you didn't want to fall. When he felt he was finally steady enough to stand alone, she let go. He turned around to see who it was. Who had saved him? She was a tiny thing with a smile as big as himself. She had reached out and handed him his cane, taking a few too many minutes, she didn't seem like she was going to leave. There was an awkward silence before he allowed himself to look at her. Really look at her and muster up the courage to say, "thank you." What happened next would be the moment that had forever changed him. It was the moment that he had allowed himself to forget for too long. It was the moment that he had allowed himself to be distracted from, so he might be allowed to forget. It was in that moment that someone had not only looked at him but had actually seen him as the person he was, despite the grotesque, obese body he filled.

As he sat there in line, remembering he could almost hear her laughter. It was not really a laugh but a polite and inviting giggle that was hers alone. A giggle that said, "join me, life is full of joy."

Now all he could do was remember as if it were yesterday. Or maybe now at the moment, perhaps she was there just as she had been the first time they met.

She had waited for him to steady himself through the awkwardness of words and then asked him to join her for tea, a question that he might be allowed to consider and to decline if he so chose. He had tried to remember when the last time a person had invited him anywhere, let alone to an establishment that had offered food. Not even his own mother had done that in as long as he could recall. With more than a little trepidation, he had accepted. He remembered thinking that his acceptance had actually made her happy. That was the first of many tea dates. He wondered how, through all the stares, all the whispers, she never really seemed to notice his obesity. She would spend hours walking with him, encouraging him to move. There was an ease with which he was able to talk to her. She was so easy to talk to that he was quite sure that after some time, she could possibly know more about him than he knew about himself.

 It was those talks that he would remember now as he sat in line, waiting. He now understood it was those talks; she had used to guide him. Talks that encouraged him to be not only healthy but happy. That was what she had always told him, at the end of each tea, "The most important thing in life is to know that it isn't what others think about you, but rather what you think about yourself. What you do with your own life, that is what will make you happy and proud of who you are." She would pause each time after she said it, she would pause as if deep in thought and then complete our time for the day with "To love one's self, now that is pure gold."

 It was over the next several days, weeks, months that each time they were able whether a planned or accidental meeting, he would begin to learn to do just that. It was during one of those get-togethers, he laughed out loud, remembering that he had thought perhaps she had wanted more of a relationship when she had invited him to come home with her. He couldn't have been more wrong. It was there that she invited him to tell his story. She had so kindly and so patiently guided his hands until he was comfortable, and then she had left him alone and allowed him the freedom to speak. His hands were overly plump and although he had thought he was comfortable, he was everything but. His behind barely fit on the delicate wooden chair which held him, causing him constant worry that his weight might break it. He tried to plant his feet onto the floor but even that didn't help him to balance. The fullness of his fingers made it difficult for him to make the passes. It was hard to include the intricate designs that seemed to weigh him down even more than the weight of his own body. What he really wanted was to please her. But he could hear the echo of her words, not only remembering them but knowing that they were true. For the first time it was who he was and what pleased him that mattered. And so like him, his weaving went quickly, each pass helping the one before it. Nimble he would wrap his arms around the woman who gave him birth, break bread with those less fortunate, compliment those that bullied, heal the victims. He would run to the aid of a crying child, pained human or a wounded animal. He could be whoever he wanted and love freely. For it need not be simply a strong body but a strong mind, heart and soul. It would be with these strengths that he might support and heal himself and others.

Now he could feel her in the stitches of his story that lay under his fat fingers the story which he held on his lap. It was a story that had more than once allowed him to stand tall and walk alone. It was his story, and it gave him not only the incentive but the strength to do just that, to stand tall and walk alone. He had lost more than 300 lbs.. He loved the way he looked and the way others looked at him. Most importantly, he loved the way he felt. He looked forward to the day that he could share with her, who he had become. But it had become only an occasional phone call and a yearly letter that kept them connected. During those calls, she would try to keep him encouraged and remind him how much value he had. But something happened, and once again, food became more of a love than he did. And then, of course, he met her, and she filled him with desserts. She flirted with him, she thought him sexy. That was all that mattered as she encouraged him, and he began to gain pound after pound. And with every pound he gained, she seemed to love him more and more. Still, every once in awhile, she would call, ashamed he wanted to tell her. He tried to seek out her help, but he couldn't. It was this woman who pushed him in a wheelchair that made him feel whole. Who would never leave him alone long enough to speak to her so that he might ask for what he needed most. The encouragement to love himself again. Eventually, he could not even take the calls, embarrassment, and shame prevented it. Now he could hear her voice, her giggle, he could feel her hands picking him up, holding him until he was ready to stand on his own. He knew that the woman he thought he loved was more of an enabler than a helper. That staying with her would never allow him the freedom he needed to stand alone and love himself. It would be a painful goodbye. She had been there for so long. But it was time and so too was it time to focus his attention on her, to give thanks to the woman that everyone was waiting to see.

As he waited in line to say his goodbyes, he realized he had never bothered to ask her about herself. He never really knew who she was, this woman who had cared enough to literally pick him up and change his life.

$\mathscr{P}$eace

There were so many people, he wasn't sure how that felt. He stood in line, the corner of his story crumpled tightly in his fist. He wasn't sure who he was angriest at. He toyed with the thought that perhaps he really wasn't that special after all as he let himself remember how they had met. He allowed a tinge of guilt to surface. Instinctively he pulled the collar up on his overcoat. Pulling it together, sorry it did not have a button or snap.

He thought about it, knowing it would have been such a simple task for her to have added either. He looked around, trying to keep his head down a bit, hoping no one knew him. He knew when he allowed himself his own honesty and let his emotions loose that he might feel or acknowledge that he was most uncomfortable with the path he had chosen.

So many people coming to him, asking forgiveness. When it was he who had so much he needed to be forgiven for.

He replayed the first time he had seen her. She had been quite a distance from where he sat. He remembered how as far as he could tell, she appeared to be an angel. He could see the halo of light that surrounded her, thinking only an angel was worthy of such a light. Even then, as he looked, he was sure it wasn't just surrounding her, he was quite sure that it was she alone that glowed. He stared at her for some time, thinking about how utterly beautiful she was. How perfect she was. He was afraid to even move, scared he would lose sight of her, the thought of trying to walk over to her temporarily paralyzed him. He had just sat down and was drinking a cup of coffee and trying to pretend to read a book. All he wanted to do was watch her, breathe in the moment and let her beauty etch itself into his soul. When she got up and started to walk away, he knew he had to do something. In an instant, he found the courage he needed to actually start running just so he might catch up with her. He found himself running so fast that he feared how to stop. He didn't think it was even worth trying to slow down. The next thing he knew was that he had accidentally run into her. Literally ran into her, knocking her down and then catching her before she hit the ground as if he were the hero, not the perpetrator. He was confused and unsure how to respond when instead of anger or fear, she giggled, non-judgmental, and pure. When she regained her footing and started to stand up, he offered an apology, and a helping hand, she giggled more. She didn't laugh, but giggled, that delightful sound a child makes when they've tasted ice cream for the first time. When they watch the puffy white on a dandelion scatter after it's been blown on. She reached out, he was hopeful that it was so she could use his waiting hand to help her up. He allowed her to put her hand in his, and he gently folded his fingers over hers as he pulled. Her hand was so soft and warm. He could actually feel the blood running through himself as their hands touched.

He remembered how, unintentionally, as she began to let go, he held onto her a bit tighter. He never wanted to let her go. At that very moment, he was quite confident that his fate had been decided for him. As he continued to hold her hand, his entire body was in ecstasy. He felt things in places he didn't even know he had.

She was so simple yet sophisticated. He was delighted when she agreed to go for a cup of coffee, although she had asked if it would be all right if she had tea.

As if it would make a difference, he tried to pull his collar closer around his neck, remembering as if it were yesterday.

They had sat for hours. She was an excellent listener, he wondered if he had listened as well. He wondered if even now he listened that well.

For weeks they spent almost every day together. Usually, drinking coffee and tea and discussing world events, personal likes, and dislikes. He couldn't actually remember anything she did not like. They talked about dreams, and they held hands. He loved how touching her made him feel. She was electric and warm. She was soft and so full of everything good. She seemed to always watch him as he spoke. Not just looked but really saw. He was flattered as he could tell she was genuinely interested in what he had to say. They talked in-depth about his schooling, about why he had chosen the path he had. He explained to her how he had always believed that God was calling him, and he had no choice but to obey. On the other hand, she wasn't so sure she asked lots of questions. She didn't even hesitate when she asked him, "who was God?" As he fingered the Bible he carried with him, it was the first time that he could remember that he ever questioned his calling. He was physically uncomfortable and could feel beads of sweat on his brow, still, or perhaps because of it, he couldn't help but love her. There was a uniqueness about her that held him, intrigued him, kept every time that they were together new. They would take long walks together, sometimes she would bring Dakota, a dog that seemed to talk to her, and she back to it. They understood each other, and sometimes it made him jealous, that was how much he loved her. He wanted to be that person that made her life as complete as he felt she was making his.

He took her home to meet his family. She could not have been any more charming even with the onslaught of questions and apparent dislike. She was kind and warm, full of compassion. They had made it difficult, there was no doubt. She was more cautious and wanted to wait before taking him home to meet Maia. He thought it odd and found it a bit uncomfortable that she never spoke of a mother or father, and she made it clear that hers was not a family of size, just the two of them she had explained. Still, he was anxious to meet her for his decision had been made, and he was ready to ask for her hand.

Months passed, and they grew closer, she let him kiss her, and she seemed to like it. He told her that he had decided to change his vocation, that priesthood would never work, not now when he was so in love when it was she whom he wanted to spend his life with. She had been so quiet, he wondered why he hadn't really noticed, and maybe there was a sense of sadness that he didn't want to see.

So life went on as it had for so many days, so many months. It was New Year's Eve he remembered. An uncontrolled shutter made him visibly shaken, and it felt wrong, especially now, especially here as he waited. Neither of them had ever drunk before. But now that they were together celebrating the beginning of the New Year and what he was sure would be a new life together, a new beginning. They allowed themselves to get pulled into the festivities, which included the drinking of champagne. So they drank, the champagne's bubbles made it an enjoyable beverage they both agreed. It was fun to make a toast and have a drink, soon they found themselves toasting to everything and anything they could think of. She giggled. They had rented a room for the night certain it would be safer than traveling anywhere, even on foot.

They were both more than a bit giddy. Although she was extremely shy, they had decided to spend the night together, neither of them actually intending to sleep. They were both too proper in their own rights.

But they had both had too much champagne, and both felt the effects of the alcohol found it difficult to control any desires that they might have had. She was so beautiful he could no longer refrain from the feelings that he had or the needs he felt, he wrapped his arms around her and kissed her, when she kissed him back he knew he had made the right decision. As they got more comfortable with one another, she allowed him to unbutton her blouse, revealing perfect breasts, ones that he had only dreamed of and never seen, let alone touch. They were soft and full, and when she allowed him to feel them, they filled more than just the palm of his hand. He was lost with emotion. He kissed her neck and let his tongue slip out, tasting the salt of her as he followed it down to her breast, where it was met by her perfect hard, pink nipple as if waiting for him, inviting him. He began to suck. She, too, was lost in emotion and awkward with what she should do with her hands. Carefully, she unbuttoned his shirt and putting her hands inside, she wrapped her arms around him. She kissed his ear, and as she caressed him, he remembered thinking he felt a tear. But he didn't stop, he couldn't stop, he put his hand up her skirt, moving it to her underpants where he reached in to do what he had always wanted to do. He reached in to explore. She was wet, and that delighted him, he inched his finger closer, trying to insert it into her vagina when he felt it. Resting against his investigating fingers was what he was sure was a penis as hard as his. He pulled his hand back, and did the unthinkable, he pulled her underwear down. No, he ripped it off of her. He didn't wait for words or ask questions, he didn't bother to comfort her as she cried, sobbed. He simply pulled himself together and left. He left her there, alone and without explanation. He left her to cry herself to sleep. It was just weeks later that he took his vows and joined the priesthood, confident that she had been the devil in disguise, and it was a test which he feared he had failed miserably.

He looked around at all the people who were waiting to say goodbye to her. A tear ran down his cheek. He never called her after that night, he could not allow the devil to entice him again. Years later, she came to him. She had found him at his church. She just walked in and waited for him after the service had ended. She was full of forgiveness and more beautiful than he even remembered. She asked if he would join her for tea. He told her he'd join her for coffee, and she giggled. The sound of that giggle brought joy to his heart, but so did it bring such painful memories. He tried not to remember. She must have decided not to forget. She didn't ask him any questions about that night, she only wanted to make sure that he was happy and that he was at peace. At that moment, and for that moment, they rekindled their friendship. He could not imagine how much he had missed her. She invited him home with her, sad that he would never meet Maia, she so wanted her to know. But now it was his turn. She took him to the loom and helped him with the first passes. And then explaining that he could tell his story, she left him alone to work. She left him alone so that his tears might flow freely. His entire body shook with emotion. It was difficult for him to see through the tears that uncontrollably poured from his eyes. He snorted trying to stop the snot from running into his mouth. There was no control, years of guilt, lost love. Avoiding contact that meant one must feel. He could not allow himself that. His was a story of redemption, of the power to imagine, to regress. It was the ability to let forgiveness be his leader not his enemy. His story could be nothing more for the reality was he had lost. She left him alone until he was finished, and then she removed his work, and as she handed it to him, it came to life. So much pain, so many lonely days and nights. So much love. It was his story, and even after what he had done, it was a gift so great that he could not even begin to thank her.

That was the last time he saw her. It wasn't that he didn't try it was that he didn't know how to find her ever again. As if she vanished, leaving a hole in his heart that grew with each day of his life. And now here he was waiting like so many others to say goodbye. But for him, it was more than goodbye for him; he needed to find peace. He knew that he had to find some way so that he might be allowed to grant himself forgiveness.

Acceptance

It was a sea of different size crotches and waists, even a few knees, some more colorful than others, but a sea in which she could not swim. For the first time in as long as she could remember, she felt small. Even standing on her tippy toes, there was little she could do. It was a feeling that she hated to remember, but also a feeling that reminded her of why she was there.

She pulled her story closer, afraid that if the line moved and she lost her footing or wasn't paying attention, she might be trampled. She thought even worse, and probably more than likely, she would lose her story in the commotion that would inevitably ensue. She fidgeted a bit more than usual and considered the very real possibility that it could happen. She decided to be smart and began jumping up and down. She hoped that perhaps someone would notice and be kind enough to protect her. She was getting quite anxious afraid that if she didn't do something, she would be damned. She tucked her story into the front of her pants, tightening her belt to make sure it was secure. Protectively she tucked her shirt in over the top of it and began jumping up and down. She jumped with vigor waving her arms every which way. Almost ready to give up. It was so exhausting when the woman behind her noticed and looked down at her. Certainly, her first reaction was not to laugh, but ignoring her wasn't an option, not here, not now. The woman knelt down respectfully, asking if she could help. As she picked her up, she pulled out her own story, and together they waited.

Pride

D akota had been gone for days, Justice kept insisting that maybe she was hiding. It was inconceivable to her that she could be gone. Justice didn't just miss Dakota, but she, herself, was lost. It was not only the loneliness that Justice felt, but with Dakota gone, she was truly lost.

They had been together for as long as Justice chose to remember. They had served each other's needs, Dakota serving as Justice's eyes and Justice as Dakota's ears. With Dakota gone, she could not see. They had been together, inseparable from the beginning leaving one another only on rare occasions when they would decide to play hide and seek. But now Joseph knew Dakota wasn't playing, she was missing. The house was unusually quiet. He had never seen Justice so empty, so lost. He couldn't remember feeling so entirely useless. Then as if it were just another day as quickly as Dakota had disappeared, she returned. She came running in carrying something in her mouth, a dirty blue piece of cloth and a shoe. Upon closer observation, Joseph identified it as a child's dress and with it a scuffed up white dress shoe. He could do nothing, he knew that. It was not his place, and the uselessness morphed into helplessness.

250 I AUDREY N LEWIS

Whimpering, Dakota placed the items on Justice's lap. Justice elated by Dakota's return was not concerned with what she had brought home with her. She was too busy indulging herself with joy to listen to Joseph's description and urgency. Dakota, however, would have nothing to do with such self-indulgence and continued to whimper nudging the items Dakota had placed in Justice's lap. A low growl forced Justice to stop and listen, she understood. Justice moved her hands to focus on the items she held. Then without warning or words, without even time for another sigh of relief, she stood up and followed an anxious Dakota out the door. A difficult task to be sure as Dakota chose to waste no time as she ran to locate the person that the items belonged to, and Justice did her best to keep up.

As they had started out the door, Joseph had thought about following them, it was his amazing self-control that allowed him to stop himself. While he was not sure what it was that he actually knew, he had come to understand that it was best just to let them be and wait only then might there be an opportunity to help, or to be offered to tell his story. So without knowing why, he did know it was best for everyone if he did not follow.

It was several blocks before Dakota stopped, Justice had been sprinting behind somehow able to keep up. It was Dakota placing herself in front of Justice that alerted her to stop as well. Stopped, Justice could hear the breathing of a young girl whom they had found sitting visibly uncomfortable on the step of an old tenement house. She sat shivering a bit, wearing what appeared to be an old dirty slip and one scuffed up white shoe. Her dirty face streaked with tears, snot dripping from her nose, she tried to stifle her cries.

Her curly red hair half fallen from the clips that had been holding it in place, and they now hung, on her shoulders and around her neck: a knotted mess. Dakota slowly moved closer until just at the girls' feet she laid down. Justice was holding onto the dress, and shoe Dakota had brought home. The girl reached down without fear and began stroking Dakota, her sniffles stopping with each stroke. Justice standing right next to Dakota, lowered herself down so that she was sitting on the ground next to Dakota. She listened as Dakota happily welcomed the young girl's attention. Justice held out her hand and waited for the girl to take it.

Now she too stood in line, waiting to say goodbye to the Princess she remembered. It had been her dress that Dakota held. Her mama had ordered her to stay clean and proper when she sent her to the store for Sarsaparilla. She had felt so grown up being asked to pick up something so special and allowed to wear her brand new church dress. She had only just tried it on for the first time. It had just arrived, and she loved that her mama had surprised her with a blue dress, her favorite color. She loved the softness of the material and the pleats on the front that made it look extraordinary. She didn't like to dress up, but this was the perfect dress for her if she had to. She remembered that she had tried really hard to stay clean, really she had. But as she headed to the store to pick up the Sarsaparilla, there had been a group of boys playing kick the can. She loved that game, and she was good. She knew she was better than any of those boys would ever be. She had stopped to watch, trying to stay still and clean. Trying to just watch. But when the can landed at her feet, she couldn't resist. She took off running, volleying the can between her brand new white shoes maneuvering her way down the street. And just as she was about to kick it into the goal, she felt someone pull her back. She heard a rip, and turning around too quickly had caused the dress to rip right off, her shoes scraping the ground as she fell. The boys didn't waste any time in taunting her, and she wasn't going to let them see her cry. She stood up her slip dirty and wrinkled, her knee scraped and bleeding. She reached forward to grab her dress, but they wouldn't have it. They weren't going to make it easy and began playing keep away.

All she had to use to fight back was her shoes, so she took one off to throw it but that backfired, and now they had two things to taunt her with. She had tried to stand tall, forgetting for a minute that her mama had warned her. She was really going to be in trouble, she had to get her dress back. And just as they threw it again trying to keep it just out of her reach, Dakota came running out of nowhere. She lowered her head and bared her teeth at the boys, who scattered in all directions, taking the dress and shoe with them. She ran too, in the other direction, not sure what she would say. What she would do. She certainly couldn't go home without her dress and only one shoe. Her mama was sure to beat her. So she ran and ran until she had come to a stop at the tenement house where Dakota and the Princess had found her.

As she stood in line with hundreds of others, the very same blue dress tucked safely away next to her story in her purse which hung by a strap on her shoulder, her hand securely holding onto it, she remembered.

Dakota had been so gentle, but not as gentle as the Princess was delicate. She remembered her so well. She had hair that glistened with gold and elbow-length white gloves. Her voice sang out harmoniously, a comforting song, more than just spoken words. Her eyes were like rubies under the most beautiful golden lashes. She wore a flowing dress but was happy to reveal to her that underneath she wore pants. It had made her giggle, and the Princess had loved her smile. When the Princess had offered her hand it was genuine she could feel the love and joy, and it made her heart skip a beat as she walked with them, forgetting that they might be strangers and she should stay clear, she was more than happy to go wherever they might take her. The house they took her to looked like a castle and they had been met at the door by a handsome knight. She wondered if they were in love, the knight, and the Princess, like in the fairy tales her mother had read her. The fairy tales that always ended with her mother reminding her that those types of things would never happen to her. But they did happen.

She was a guest in a real castle with a real Princess, where she was not only offered but served delicious food. As dirty as she was it was the Princess herself who helped her to a glorious bath with real bubbles. But the very best part came just before she was to go back home. The Princess sat her down in front of a table that held a beautiful loom. She gave her a spool of black thread and guided her hand through the first few passes. She told her that it was time for her to tell her story. She could tell any story she chose, and then the Princess left her alone where she worked for what she was sure was hours creating her story. She was giddy from the experience of the day's activities and more than excited at what the possibilities of her story could be. Somewhat cautious she did a quick scan of her surroundings before spitting into her hands and rubbing them together. It wasn't because she felt the need to spit as much as because she could. She was replicating what she had witnessed so many athletes do. With more confidence than thought she worked the shuttle back and forth. The speed with which she worked was a great match for the story she told. There was no perfect little girl but a strong and powerful woman. A person not afraid to win, to excel to show both her masculine and feminine. Someone that others could look up to as she lived with pride. When she was finished the Princess returned, Dakota never leaving her side. The Princess carefully removed the finished tapestry from the loom, and then carefully and with grace, she finished off the edges, and as she handed it to her, her story came to life. The most beautiful colors had shown themselves where the black threads of her storytelling had laid. The Princess stepped back admiringly, and she held it to her heart, feeling it beating with life. As if that wasn't enough the gifts continued as Dakota, and the Princess got ready to take her home, the Knight presented her with her blue dress, good as new, clean and mended and the pleats perfectly pressed. The Princess helped her on with her dress and with gloved hands smoothed out the slightest wrinkles. The Knight helped her on with her shoes, just like in Cinderella, which had both been polished and shined like new. The last touch was an addition, a blue ribbon to tie in her freshly washed and brushed hair. Holding onto her story, they took her home. When the Princess said goodbye she touched her ever so slightly on the forehead ever so lovingly, and she knew whatever happened it would always be all right.

As she continued to stand in line, she stood strong, she had let go of the need to be the perfect little girl her mother had always wanted. She celebrated the fact that it was more than okay for her to not only excel in sports but to win even if her opponent was a boy. She knew that it was okay for her to wear pants and yell and have fun, after all, she had received the approval of a Princess, royalty. She would miss the phone calls, the ones that came every year on the date that they had met, no matter where she was, the Princess always knew how to find her. She had changed that day. Now she held onto the memories, her story and that mended blue dress, she let a tear fall down her cheek as she waited in line to say goodbye.

Equality

The street was busy, and a crowd had begun to gather. Everyone just stood around watching as if what they saw was entertainment. Two young men lay on the pavement barely able to move as a small group of insecure males, arms raised, fists ready, garbage pouring out of their mouths, stood over them. There was no letup as they were undoubtedly enjoying themselves as the hitting and kicking continued.

Neither of the young men lying there ever saw it coming. Neither of them had a chance to protect themselves. Now they lay there struggling, their eyes were swollen, their faces bloody, moving the only thing they could, their fingers. Despite the pain of what was surely broken bones, they inched their fingers towards one another. Reaching out with all their might until their fingertips were touching. The only thing each of them wanted was for the other to know they were still right there. That love was stronger than anything and that no matter what, each of them refused to die alone.

Yet it was the act of holding hands that was the reason they were laying there, to begin with. The reason these cowardly males with underdeveloped brains and uneducated words were beating them. Just as their fingers found one another, one of the men lifted his boot-covered foot, ready to bring it down hard, prepared to break not only their fingers but also their souls. Just as he was about to crush them, Dakota came running out of nowhere, leaving Justice behind to have to catch up. Dakota could not wait. Without warning, she lunged at the male knocking him onto the pavement falling directly next to the man he was beating. She turned and bared her teeth a paw heavily placed on the male's chest as she waited for Justice to arrive. Just as the men began to turn on Dakota, Justice arrived a light following her into the circle. With total calm, she knelt down a hand lovingly stroking Dakota before leaning over the two injured men. They could barely see, but Justice's presence, her touch as she wiped away some of the blood from their faces renewed them and filled them with all they needed to roll over and slowly and painfully lift themselves up. The crowd was silent, the males dumbfounded. Justice helped the two men up as Dakota still baring her teeth to let everyone know she meant business continued to growl. The men hugging one another, tears released in a combination of pain, relief, and love. Justice put her arms around them, shielding them as she and Dakota leading the way led them away from the crowd. As if the parting of the Red Sea, the crowd moved out of their way one by one. More in amazement than by choice.

With conviction, they forced themselves to stand tall, never letting go of each other's hand, they stumbled. They remembered it was a painstakingly long walk before they arrived at the entrance of a building. Neither of them recognized but gladly accepted Justice's invitation to go in. They were a mess, bruised and bloody, but grateful that they were alive. Inside, Justice showed them to the bathroom, supplying them with fresh towels and fresh clothes. She turned on the water in the bear claw tub, making sure it was not too cold and not too hot. She left them to soak for as long as they wanted or needed telling them she wouldn't be far if they needed anything. She was not concerned with how long they might take and prepared a fresh pot of water for tea. The refrigerator had a fresh plate of fruit and cheese waiting. On the counter was a plate full of fresh cookies. Today especially, Justice appreciated the kindness. It had been a while since she had invited anyone to tell their story. Now, as she waited, she thought how long it had been since there had been two at once. She was getting tired, and yet these two young men deserved so much more. She wondered if allowing them to tell their story would be enough to set them free.

As they stood in line holding hands, they couldn't have been prouder or felt freer. They held onto each other, not a reminder as much as a show of strength. It was with broken hearts that they stood in line, holding onto their story. Together waiting to say goodbye.

Lifeline

It had been a busy day, not too much different than all of the previous days. He had gotten up extra early, excited to go to school. The project he had been working on for weeks for the science fair was complete, and he was sure his hard work would pay off. He had given his mom and dad separate invitations in case they decided not to share. He had told them the project was a secret, but he was pretty confident he would win or at least place. He was pretty stoked.

The morning of the fair, he was secretly hoping to be met with a special breakfast, a few words, "see you later," "good luck," but instead, like usual, the house was empty. He poured himself a bowl of cereal and ate it dry, an empty milk carton sat on the counter. He retrieved his project from his closet and carefully carried it out the door, hoping he wouldn't have to run too fast to catch the bus. In the back of his mind, he kept hoping that they would surprise him and were waiting in the car for him to come out, in his heart, he feared the truth.

Catching the bus was hard enough. He stumbled, barely catching himself and saving his project from meeting an early demise by hitting the concrete a bit prematurely. Even from the street, he could hear them laughing at his clumsiness, and once he climbed the stairs to enter the bus, they were louder and more aggressive, pointing and shouting. He did his best to block them out as he found himself focusing on how to maneuver over and past the army of legs and feet that suddenly took up the aisle. He just had to protect his project; that was all he cared about. He didn't dare attempt to catch the driver's attention for fear of taking his focus away from the situation even for a second. Yet, he imagined it would help, knowing all too well, he didn't care. In fact, there had been several occasions when he had seen the driver himself laugh at the other kids taunting him.

He was relieved when he found the first empty seat was not too far in the back. Protecting his project, he sat down, holding onto what was his, for now letting nothing else take that away from him. He focused his energy and thoughts on the science fair and his presentation. He tried not to let anything else distract him, although the boy in the seat behind him continuously hitting him on the back of the head did not help.

He didn't remember how he had gotten out off of the bus and into the school building, he was that determined. He did remember standing in front of his project, presenting it, and trying to stay focused. He scanned the room, which was already full of proud parents and family members. He searched, but he didn't see his mom or dad anywhere. Their absence made it a bit more difficult than he imagined, and he was finding it hard to stay fully focused. Even though he began to stutter as he presented his data, everyone was quite interested and impressed. He demonstrated how the filthy water moved through a vacuum filter. The toxins removed, and it came out not only as clear as possible but also tasting incredible. The teachers and administrators asked him challenging questions. He knew all the answers but was finding it difficult to recall them. He appreciated their patience. Each of them asked to see its operation again so that they might actually taste the water. They were more than satisfied with the result.

When he was presented first place, he wasn't sure if he could muster a real smile when all he felt was abandoned and unloved. He felt more like crying than smiling when alone he accepted the award. Making things worse, out of the corner of his eye, he could see the boys from his bus that morning. Watching him through the glass wall, offensively motioning to him, which caused him to reject any bit of pride he may have had.

After the ceremony and everyone had left, he hung out for a while in the room, wandering around from exhibit to exhibit. As if he were interested when all he wanted to do was pass the time so he wouldn't have to ride home on the same bus with them.

He waited so long he almost missed the second bus, the last available bus whose route would still take him home. When he finally made his way out to catch the bus, he scoured the driveway and parking lot. Hoping perhaps one of his parents might be waiting or would pull up in their car apologetically with a valid excuse. But that did not happen, and as he boarded the bus home, he allowed himself to be grateful that it was less crowded than the bus in the morning. He found comfort knowing that there was no one on board tormenting him, ultimately this allowed him to relax. It allowed him to dream, to watch out the window, and to be lost in his own thoughts. He was looking, but he did not see, and somehow he missed his stop. Anxious, he began to not only look but watched as he noticed buildings he did not recognize and landmarks he had only read about. He wondered if he had boarded the wrong bus altogether. Indeed, this was a route he did not recognize.

The bus stopped, the driver announced that it was the last stop. He did not move. He could not move. In a rather authoritative voice the driver informed him, it was the last stop and he'd have to get off the bus. He had always been taught never to speak back to authority and was now afraid to ask for help. There was no one else on board, and hesitantly, he got off the bus. Before his feet were even firmly on the ground, the bus sped off. He had no idea where he was but found relief that his project was now on display at school, that he no longer needed to be concerned about its safety. He had always been so worried as he had to transport it back and forth while working on it. Now his hands were instead full of books, he was lost. He hadn't noticed how long he had been on the bus, it was getting dark, and with more than a little uncertainty, he walked south, thinking that was the way home. He had never been more wrong. He ended up in a neighborhood that he did not know. Where people were speaking loudly in a language, he was unfamiliar with or didn't understand. Worse yet, no matter where he stepped, he seemed to be in someone's way as they pushed past him on the sidewalk.

Frightened, he began to walk faster. The faster he walked, the less attention he paid to where he laid his foot, and the next thing he knew, he had tripped on a large crack, which had made the sidewalk uneven. He fell hard, his knee hitting the concrete, ripping his pants, and breaking the skin. His hands scraped up as well when dropping the books he had been carrying. His arms were wrapped tightly around them as if somehow they might protect him, and he might protect them. He had put his hands out as he tried to catch himself. The books flew several feet away. He could hear his glasses crack under the feet of a passerby, one oblivious to their actions or merciless to his predicament.

It was difficult to control the tears which had begun to overflow from his eyes and run down his cheeks, he held his breath so as not to let the sounds out. He attempted to grab what might be left of his glasses and tried to pick himself up. Intellectually, he knew the only choice he had was to remain in control. However, he found that quite difficult, he stood still trying to console himself as he took a breath and gathered his thoughts. He put his head down, defeated for just a minute, and when he looked up there, he was, standing directly in front of him, a big dog by his side. He had gathered up the books that had scattered and was holding onto them. A smile on his face, eyes sparkling.

Standing in line now, he couldn't help but chuckle as he remembered.

He had held out his hand, not letting go of any of the books, and then he began making funny faces. It had made it hard not to laugh. He had helped him up, and they had walked together. He insisted on carrying the books for at least a while. The gentleness of his voice was such a comfort, it made it easy to talk to him. And as they walked, it was as if the floodgates of emotion opened. Without thought, he began to tell him about what had led to him winding up here, wherever here was.

As he told him about his parents' lack of concern or attention, weights began to fall from his shoulders, his heart became lighter. It was as if for the first time that he could remember the words and emotions were able to flow freer, than they had ever flowed, and it felt good. He listened, he knew he wasn't judging, but his interest was genuine, he could feel it. They must have been about the same age he imagined. However, he was a bit thinner and slightly taller and most obvious, much wiser than anyone he knew. He walked him to the bus stop and waited with him for the correct bus to arrive and then he surprised him by getting on the bus with him, still carrying his books. Together they watched and listened for the right stop. Together they got off, and he walked him home as if he knew exactly where he lived.

But what was truly amazing was what happened in the days and weeks that followed. Every morning after he had breakfast and walked out of the house to go to get the bus, he was there his dog by his side waiting. He was waiting at the sidewalk for him to come out of the house so that they could walk together so he wouldn't have to be worried anymore about the bullies on the bus. He'd wait there with him until he got on the bus and then he'd be there waiting in the afternoon when he got off. He never did say where he went to school, or he didn't remember if he did. Thinking about it, he wasn't sure if he ever asked.

They spent many hours together, mostly laughing. He could tell him anything, but he remembered that he didn't say much of anything back. He recalled being selfishly grateful that the tormenting had moved from himself to his new friend, although he wasn't sure why. The tormenting grew louder every day, both going and coming. He would look out the window and see the hurt in his friend's eyes, but he did nothing, and on one occasion, he even participated. He wondered why they did it, why anyone would want to be so cruel, it didn't feel good. There was that one occasion that he saw a tear run down his friend's face, and he was sure that would be the end of their friendship, certain that he would not be waiting when he arrived home. He was wrong; he was still there waiting for him that afternoon, and the next day after that. Not too long after that incident where he had found himself participating, he could not forget, not explain, and had a hard time forgiving himself. His friend invited him to walk with him to his house.

He gladly accepted, and when he got there and went inside, his friend took him in a room that housed a big wooden contraption. It was here that he sat him down and handed him something with black thread wrapped around it and told him it was time for him to tell his story. He took his hand and helped him with the first few passes, but then left him on his own. He wasn't quite sure what he was supposed to do. What he meant by "time to tell his story." At first he didn't feel worthy of the privilege that was being given him. But he knew he could not leave until the task was finished, so he continued with the passes, using the pedal to raise and lower the threads. Faster and faster he worked hoping that the momentum would trigger what he wanted his story to be. It was difficult because he had a hard time getting through the anger he felt at himself. Angry for allowing himself to follow the crowd, to experience bullying from the bully side. To have caused hurt. Yet here he was being presented with the greatest gift from the one he bullied. When finally he let the anger turn to sorrow the tears flowed freely his story began to unfold. He worked until he felt his story was to his satisfaction. A story where he was allowed to invent anything he chose and where his parents would embrace him and encourage him. A place where his experiences allowed him to mentor. Where there were no bullies or victims, but humans. Then he waited anxiously for him to return. He came back, his dog close by his side, and he looked at him and at his story, and he cried. He removed it from the loom in silence; he finished the edges and handed it back to him, and as he did so, brought it to life. He walked him home in silence. He never showed up again. But every year, he would call him, once sometimes twice just to check up on him. Those calls were like a lifeline always there when he needed them, somehow he would know, and now they would stop. He wondered what he would do. And as he stood in line, his hands gripping his story, held close to his chest, he wondered how he would summon the strength to say goodbye.

Grounded

She was nervous, and she found that she was having a difficult time just staying in line. She continually dropped things from her pockets and purse just so she could bend over to pick them up. Her eyes darted from person to person, she didn't just wonder who they were, but it was as if she had to know. So many people. Could she be in the wrong place?

She looked at the hundreds if not thousands of people and worried, they all seemed to be holding a story of their own. Both anxious and restless, she fidgeted. Perhaps she was not so special after all, just that thought felt like it would kill her. She began to pick at a piece of skin on her fingernail, pulling at it ever so slightly but with enough force to draw blood. Moving along to the next nail enabled her to restrain herself from pulling on the threads from her story, she knew she best not allow herself to go there, after all, it was all she had to give.

As the line began to move ever so slowly, she grew more anxious. She could feel the eyes of people in front and behind her as they watched her but were trying not to stare. She was becoming agitated. It was apparent that it was a behavior she could not control, and it was noticeable that she was not comfortable with it.

She had felt this way when he had walked up and stood by her. Unable to keep her hands to herself, they crossed the line going into another student's space. They had no patience or acceptance of that behavior or the person demonstrating it. In this case, that would be her. She was unkempt and unclean, her body odor overwhelming. It was difficult enough to eat in the same room, let alone sit at the same table. But there were only so many seats, and that meant that anyone arriving just a wee bit late would be stuck.

She couldn't understand why they talked so loudly over her, never to her. She was confused that the conversations passed her by. She didn't understand how each day she wound up at the very end of the table, it never seemed to matter how many times she started in the center. In the warmer weather, everyone moved to tables in the courtyard. Still, she was the one that no one chose to have to sit with, and would, in fact, do what they could to stay away.

Day after day, Dakota would walk with Justice and stay as close to the school fence as she could, and then she'd stop. She would sit and watch, her head bowed down, her tail between her legs, she would sit, Justice's hand on her head understanding but unsure what to do. But on that day the gate lay open the students pouring out as the bells sounded all too early, she sat alone, not following them out onto the sidewalk. No one noticing, no one seeming to care. She sat alone, her tray in front of her. Dakota taking Justice's hand in her mouth, moved her past the crowd and into the courtyard. She was stuffing her mouth with not only the food on her tray but also what was left on the others when Justice sat down. Dakota put her head in her lap and gave a nudge, she was about to scream when Justice laid a hand on hers. That was when she looked up and saw him. The most handsome man she had ever seen, and it was her hand he was holding. For an instant, she thought perhaps she was dreaming, and she lay her head down, oblivious to the food that was in its path. Dakota couldn't help but catch the crumbs and morsels as they fell. Justice could hear her devouring each drop and smiled. She couldn't hold back, allowing herself a slight giggle. When she lifted her head up from the table, he gently wiped the food off of her face. He didn't seem disgusted like the others but genuinely seemed to care. She just stared at him until another bell rang, and she knew it was time to go. He followed her out of the courtyard and back onto the sidewalk, holding her hand gently, his dog was close by.

As they walked past several students who still lingered, she held her head high and squeezed his hand, making sure it was real. Justice squeezed back. They walked for several blocks before she stopped. She was quite happy but confused, more so when Justice let go of her hand. She remembers looking at him, looking into those beautiful eyes when he told her he would be back tomorrow. She didn't remember going home that day, she thinks she may have just gone back to school and waited. She was starving and tired when he arrived, bringing sandwiches and juice in a beautiful picnic basket. She made room for him at the table, making sure that no one would push them out. For several days he joined her, and she became less anxious as she waited for him to arrive.

Becoming more anxious, she tried her best to maintain some type of control. Remembering she thought about the day that he didn't show up, she had pulled several clumps of hair from her head and had more than just a little trouble finding her way home. As she turned the corner onto her street, she could see him and his dog standing there waiting for her. When they went into the house together, she could tell that he had already met her mom. She worried that maybe she had told him something terrible. But it was more likely not as they both seemed quite happy to see her and they seemed to like each other.

It was the first time she actually remembered wanting to take a shower when pressed by her mother. She was also eager to put on the clean clothes her mother had laid out on her bed. Just as she did every day, always hoping something would make a difference; perhaps there might be a miracle. He was waiting downstairs with her mother when she came down showered and dressed. It felt good to have him notice her clean hair and new clothes.

He stayed and had dinner with them. She watched his every move attempting to follow his lead. Each mouthful was taken with a fork or spoon, and she was careful to keep to her own plate, asking for more when she was finished. He continued to visit them for weeks, and then one day, she was invited to visit his home. He had been so kind to her, to her mother. His house was inviting and smelled like fresh bread. His mother had laid out a dinner fit for a queen, and together they made her feel like one. It was in his house that night that she learned a valuable lesson, to believe in herself. That whatever she did or whoever she was, it was okay.

He sat down with her and talked about the art of weaving, she knew he wanted her to understand on a level she might accept before showing her how to use the threaded shuttle. It was a real concept she understood, an art form she might enjoy. His hand on hers, he showed her how to use the threaded shuttle to pass thru the strings on the loom. After several passes, he had told her it was her time. She alone must tell her story, any story of her choosing. As he left her there alone, he told her that she was to call him when she was finished, he would be waiting. It was hard for her when he left her there alone. She had loved his hands on hers as he taught her the correct process. But alone she found it difficult to focus and it took a great deal of energy for her to proceed. She was nervous, afraid that she would make a mistake, that she might disappoint him. Afraid that she didn't know what her story should be. But as she worked to make it clear she was grateful that the story told itself. Learning to enjoy the experience of self care and concentration, opened doors to places she had never been. To have friends who shared in her many accomplishments. Her story allowed her to be a member of those who had previously shunned her and taught them that they too should be grateful for accepting who she was with only gratitude. Her story allowed others to walk beside her accepting and with love in their hearts.

When he returned, he removed it from the loom, she remembers the pride as it came to life. It was hers, he told her, hers alone.

Through the years, it was what kept her grounded and allowed her to go on with her daily life. Reminding her that she could do anything.

She proudly took it home and everywhere she went, always keeping it folded so she alone could see it. Now standing in line, there was so much to remember. She had showered and was wearing clean clothes. She smelled her armpits making certain she smelled good, and she wondered and worried about what she would do. He had called her often, in the beginning, a pleasant reminder of how important she was, later it was once or twice a year mostly as needed. But he never forgot her, never forgot her birthday that was always a day she could count on him remembering her, always. She tried not to fidget remembering those calls, his words, but it was useless, she didn't know what to do with the anxiousness. There were too many people, she understood that they too each had a story. Like her, they stood in line, and she guessed that they also must have come to say goodbye.

Gratitude

They all wore black and stood together so closely that it was difficult to tell how many of them there were. Their clothing weighing them down but not as much as their sorrow. It was difficult not to be affected by the sound which they produced in deep wailing cries. A sound that was so shrill and penetrated so deeply that you could feel it as it touched your soul, paralyzing your very essence.

As if that wasn't enough, add the noise from the crowd, which had begun to fill into and around their space. You could actually feel yourself caught in a cyclone of emotions, unsure what or who to hold onto without being carried away. Each person stood there, not just observing but rather actively trying to get close enough to make out what it was that they were saying, what it was behind the wailing. Each word spoken as if in song more intense than the one spoken before and still behind the words, the constant wailing. And in each of their hands, you could see that they too held onto their stories as they stood huddled together in mourning to say goodbye.

For them, it had been in the midst of a vicious attack. The men had pulled their car over along the side of the road and gotten out. Each of them laid down their individual prayer rugs to face east and then lowered themselves down and began to pray. It wasn't long before a group of young boys had seen them praying and pulled their car over parking it behind theirs. They grabbed baseball bats from within their car. Each held one in their fisted hand as they too got out of their vehicle. They walked along the shoulder of the road until they had surrounded the praying men.

There were no words, only the anger, and hate with which they began not just swinging but using their bats to beat them. With steel-toed boots using all of their might, they kicked them. The praying men did not fight back, they could not, all they could do was continue their prayers. Another boot made contact with one of the men's ribs when from nowhere, Dakota arrived teeth bared emitting a low deep growl. She stood on her haunches, a distraction as Justice quietly without sound made her way behind the young boys who had chosen to be these attackers. She approached them, fearless, larger than life. The attackers were taken off guard by her presence, but once they saw her, they returned to continue their attack. They weren't concerned after seeing her slight stature and short height. Never expecting what happened next. One of the boys turned away from her. He raised his bat again, ready to take another blow to the men whose bloodied hands now covered their heads. Justice stepped forward without hesitation, she reached up and placed her hand on the boys 'wrists just as he brought the bat back, ready to swing.

Startled, he spun around. Justice was swift, catching him off guard. She lowered her shoulder and using her entire body gently pushed him back. Dakota, who was now positioned against his calves, held her ground, Justice pushed one more time. As the attacker losing his balance began to fall backward, he began to fall onto Dakota. Dakota quickly moved out of the way. It was too late for the attacker to catch himself. Dakota backed away and watched as he hit his head on the solid ground. By this time, the other boys hearing the commotion had turned around fast enough to watch him fall, but not fast enough to help. They watched as blood began to seep into the ground.

Dakota stood again between them, and the boy, baring her teeth, she emitted a low deep growl. They remained frozen, fear holding them hostage just long enough for Justice to move towards them. Justice waited until she heard their stillness before attempting to go help the men who had been praying. The men were more than surprised. They were a bit confused, even hesitant as she reached for their hands. It was difficult for them to accept that it had been a woman who had come to their rescue, who had stood up for them, who had set them free—a woman who now wanted them to touch her as she reached for their hands.

It was equally painful for them to accept her invitation when she invited them for tea. Still, they had no choice, for gratitude was beyond their religious preconceptions that they had studied. Together, they walked with her, shared in her hospitality, and gratefully took thread in hand and told their stories. Stories that opened their hearts with acceptance. Stories they now held to their hearts as they wailed waiting in line with so many others to say goodbye.

Beauty

Perhaps it is not just the act of bravery that defines a hero, but the heartfelt compassion that often may lead up to the act.

For the woman who stood alone, her face fully exposed so all could see, she did not falter. She held her story against her chest, and let her face show so that all could see her most peaceful and loving smile. She stood tall and proud, there was no embarrassment or shame. There was only peace and joy. She loved the way the sunlight felt against her face, and how it shined against her skin, she thought it was beautiful how it made her scars glisten. For there was no shame, she did no wrong.

She did not remember how it happened or why. She did not remember who the perpetrator was or how many of them participated.

She had been in the United States for several years, having been the recipient of many anonymous and generous donors. Not to mention a team of doctors who had spent hours, weeks, months actually years in an attempt to make her whole again.

But it was the kindness of a stranger that she remembered.

Standing in line, remembering that day brought tears to her eyes, and she glanced around curious what gifts the others had been blessed with.

It had been an unusually hot and humid day. Her clothes were sticking to every possible contact that they made with her skin making it painful to stay covered. She had been waiting for the bus for several minutes and found it hard to keep herself concealed. As the bus pulled up, she waited for the others to board first, contemplating if she would be able to tolerate the bodies of the already overcrowded bus, let alone the heat; still, she boarded. There were almost as many people standing as sitting when she found a small spot in the front of the bus.

She remembered the small boy sitting on his mother's lap. The dog snuggled up under the seats as far out of harm's way as possible, and the woman whose head was bowed she assumed in prayer or sleep. With each bump or turn, it became more difficult for her to hold her covered body in place. The little boy, too, was having a difficult time staying on his mommy's lap. When the bus turned a bit too sharp, the little boy reached out and accidentally grabbed a corner of her scarf, pulling it from her hidden face and dropping it on the floor. Everyone around her gasped. Not only could she hear the comments, but like icicles being shot at her, she could feel the coldness of their stares. It was without control that tears tried to run from what remained of her eyes. She tried to shield herself as she attempted to bend down to find her scarf, she struggled, her hands whose fingers were fused from the burns were met by the purest, softest white hands she had ever seen. Hands that had already found the scarf and were carefully picking it up off the dirty bus floor, she gently moved the standing feet out of the way. She was afraid to grab it, and she didn't want to make a scene, so she just stood up her head lowered, trying to reach her pockets so that she could at least hide her hands.

The woman with the white hands stood up from her seat, her dog raised its head as if to acknowledge. Carefully so that she would not frighten her, she reached into her pocket for an instant so that she might hold her hand as she whispered to her that it was okay. She had offered her her seat and even assisted her in sitting, making sure she was comfortable. Once she was seated, she gave her back the scarf, gently placing it over her lap, smoothing it out she leaned over. She whispered to her, "you are the most beautiful woman on this bus, there is no reason to hide your beauty." She squeezed her hands, unbothered by the disfigured digits.

For the duration of the ride, she stood as if guarding over her, smiling. Her dog lay at her feet all the while its ears raised, listening. It rested its head on its front paws, but showed readiness should there be the slightest indication of confrontation. They rode this way for several blocks, and when the bus stopped for her to get off, she and her dog got off too. They walked together silent at first, her scarf once again covering her head and face. But when she finally spoke aloud, not whispering, the power of her words stopped her as if she must listen and hear all that she was being told. She held out her hand, waiting for her to take it, and together, they walked hand in hand until they had arrived at her house.

She was invited in for tea, it was so lovely a home, bright with a slight breeze that took away the heat. She was served tea in the most perfect teacup, one that she did not have to fight with to take a sip, nor one that was too small for her disfigured hands. It was as if it were meant for her alone.

They spent hours together, sipping tea and laughing. They shared secrets, and she was comfortable beyond words. She felt no need for her scarf and loved to expose her arms and roll her shirtsleeves up. She felt so free. It was in that moment of freedom when for just a second, she had forgotten the attack, the pain of the acid as it burned through her skin, her bone. It was in that second that she was given the threads and invited to tell her story whatever it was she wanted her story to be.

It was in that second that she created her story. There was not a moment's hesitation as she created. There was no pausing for breath. Hers was a story full of light and warmth. Wings of birds on which she could take flight, soaring. The brightest of day, and the brightest of night. It was her story and it was in that moment that she felt truly free. When she had completed it, tears of joy ran down her face, and she could taste the salty tears. As she removed the story from its frame and handed it to her, she bore witness to its beauty, to her beauty. She held the story to her chest, leaving her scarf behind. Several times she had tried to go back to find the house and the woman, this stranger who had so generously and with such compassion and wisdom given her renewed freedom. But it seemed impossible to find.

When the phone calls and cards began arriving with words of wisdom and encouragement, she would ask if she could visit. But it was always at the end of the conversation when she had already said goodbye. Those words on the other side of the phone had been a lifeline, a reminder. Those cards a treasure, filled with praise, verse, and encouragement. "There is no other whose beauty shines brighter than what she holds within." "May each breath be a reminder of not only your strength but your beauty." "Share every day a bit of yourself, for you are a gift to the world".

She shook her head, letting her human hair wig bob just right, and she smiled. She smiled for all to see. She would miss her special friend but would remember to always stand proud and tall in her honor. She held her story close to her chest for one last time, knowing it would have a special place when she reached the front and was able to say goodbye.

Freedom

D akota had found the young woman and led Justice to her, stopping Justice just short, not allowing her to take another step. The young woman lay in the alley on a pile of bloody gravel.

In recent months the alley was being used as a parking lot of sorts hidden back away from the street. Justice squatted down and touched the young woman's hand, she could feel the coolness, life escaping. Using her other hand, Justice reached down to steady herself, her hand getting wet from the blood that had not yet seeped into the ground. The blood flowed all too freely from between the young woman's legs.

Dakota attempted to lick it off of Justice's fingers and gently and lovingly as her own mother had to bring compassion to the woman by cleaning her. Justice sat still for a moment when she heard muffled angry voices coming from somewhere behind where the young woman lay. She was trying to listen, hoping she might learn something when she heard the young woman moan. Justice with only compassion cautiously lifted her head onto her lap and trying to hear what she might have said she leaned in close. She felt her breath on her cheek, in and out, lightly.

Justice began to breathe with her and waited until their breaths were one. She continued to breathe with her, trying to calm her, touching her forehead gently. But as the voices seemed to grow closer, Justice felt desperate to get out of their way knowing she'd have to take the young woman with her. Justice helped the young woman to her feet, gently and yet with urgency. The young woman was not capable of standing, let alone moving. Justice somehow picked her up and carrying her as best she could hurried so that they might get away. Dakota stayed behind and stood her ground, standing over the pool of blood, she waited, ready to bare her teeth.

Standing in line, she shuttered remembering. Her granddaughter pulled at her wanting to be picked up.

It had been hard times, she had so much she needed and wanted to do with her life. She was nowhere and in no way ready to be a mother, let alone a mom. They had been in love but were not prepared for the responsibilities that came with parenthood. Both of them had plans for a prosperous future.

She remembered how she had thought that she had no option. How when she learned that she wouldn't have to travel too far, she had been so grateful. She had almost been elated when she learned she didn't even need to leave the city. After having made up her mind, they talked. He was undecided, he wasn't so sure he felt the same way. She had decided to go alone.

It had been a seedy-looking building, and she had hesitated before entering. It was a bit of a relief when the room she walked into, perhaps it was the reception area actually looked clean. It wasn't quite so bad; in fact, she thought she might even believe it welcoming. Someone had actually taken the time to hang pictures on the walls and put plastic flowers in vases scattered around on unmatched tables. The chairs covered in bright plastic colors appeared clean, despite the visible cracks, evident from way too much wear.

The woman who had greeted her had had a beautiful smile. It had been the same woman who had reached out and told her about the man who would soon perform the procedure. She was the one who had stayed by her side, she had held her hand. There had been some comfort in having her there, a motherly substitute. But as she watched the man wiping off a plastic knitting needle, one like her grandmother used, she couldn't help but think, her mother wouldn't allow it. She remembered trying to pull her hand away, trying to get up. The man screamed profanities at her demanding she lay still. He yelled in some foreign language at the woman who was holding her hand. She was squeezing it even harder. Soon two additional men entered the room. They had been summoned to hold her down.

She remembered trying to fight any way she could, she knew this wasn't going to be good, she had heard of these back-alley procedures but had been assured this guy was on the up and up. She tried with all her strength, with all her energy to squeeze her legs closed. She tried with all she had to fight it. But they were way too strong, and there were two of them and the woman. She could feel their firm hands on her ankles and thighs, their fingers holding her legs while pulling them apart. She could feel their fingers digging into her skin. It was over before she could fight anymore. She remembered lying in the alley, too weak to move. She thought she was dead. A beautiful young girl cradled her and told her it would be okay. The girl had been so small that she thought for a second that perhaps she had died, and this was an angel. (She wondered if she had made it into Heaven despite it all.) While she wasn't sure and couldn't explain it, she remembered that this beautiful small girl had carried her blocks to the hospital. Could it be anything but an angel that was able to perform such a feat? Who stayed with her for hours, hours which turned into days. In fact, she thought she didn't remember if she had ever left her side, not even once. Each time she awoke, there she was, a hand ready to hold. A peaceful and loving smile gave the assurance that, indeed, everything would be all right. She could almost remember how it felt, the warmth of her hand in hers. The nurses and doctors said she saved her life, had she not gotten there when she did, she wouldn't have made it.

As she looked at her granddaughter, standing there with her, she was reminded that she did more than just save her life.

She was there with her by her side, even when they released her from the hospital. Her sweet Dakota waiting for them both by the front door. Justice escorted her home, making sure that she was settled in. She thought now how selfish she had been. Never even realizing that perhaps she might have needed help herself. She didn't see her again for years. And always wondered where this savior of sorts might have come from? Where she might have gone, even who she was? Then just like that, Justice showed up on the day of her college graduation, Dakota, at her side.

As valedictorian of her graduating class, standing there looking out at the audience, it was Justice who she saw. Suddenly she found herself changing her entire speech.

After everyone had left the stage, she waited and watched Justice, who was sitting so tall, so quiet. It filled her heart, seeing her there for her, she could see how filled with joy she was. Justice continued to sit quietly as she made her way to her. It was there at her graduation that she learned the most authentic and purest of humanity. Justice's head was bowed, her hands folded comfortably in her lap. As she approached, Justice was humbled and proud as the young girl whose hand had ultimately breathed life into her stood before her. Having accomplished so much, having made it so far.

The two of them spent hours talking and walking around the city, and then Justice invited her home. It was more than just an invitation, it was also an introduction. She had wanted them to meet. There was something that seemed so special about her, and Justice had hoped perhaps they would connect, and maybe his stories too might finally be put to rest. It did not go as Justice had hoped. Joseph didn't want Justice to bring another person into the circle. He didn't want to talk about it with anyone else. He was not ready to share.

 She tried to reach out, be understanding and calm, but there was so much noise and commotion. Justice knew only that it was time and led her to the loom where in hopes of healing at least one of them, she sat her down and offered her to tell her story, whatever story it was she chose to tell. An emptiness that had long filled her. A void that could not be filled. Without knowing, with her heart broken and heavy she wondered if it would truly ever heal. In her soul, she feared would she ever stop hating. As she told her story all of it. There was anger that morphed into peace, darkness that became light, ugliness that rose to beauty and as she came to finish she felt almost weightless and for the first time she understood forgiveness. She stayed there at that loom for hours, asking for additional thread. She worked through tears and, ultimately, laughter as Justice joined her and carefully removed her efforts. As she was handed the finished story, she did not know how to respond as she watched it come to life. Justice walked with her for a bit before saying goodbye.

She held her story up to her chest, tears falling, her granddaughter tugging on her coat. She wondered now, realizing she never knew how every year she would get a phone call, or a letter, sometimes both. When times were tough, or she was unsure of herself, or just remembering and being sorrowful, she'd hear from her. There would be words of encouragement and pride. She never saw her after that day, the day she told her her story, but the contact never stopped. She looked around. Unable to see how many stood before her—each seeming to be holding a story of their own. The same was true of those behind her, where the line was so long she could not see where it ended.

There were so many people, so many stories, so many waiting like she was to say goodbye.

For a second, she remembered and thought about him, the man Justice had wanted her to meet, to share with, and she hoped perhaps he too had found freedom and was somewhere in line with his story. She imagined it would be just as hard for him as it would be for her to say goodbye.

Protection

He had been running for his life. Several men were chasing him, including the police. He could hear them screaming at him as he was almost out of sight. He was little and fast. He had stopped for an instant to catch his breath and see how far back they were, calculating how much time he had to refuel his body. He could see them in the distance. It had been only an instant, just long enough to have turned around to look. But it was when he turned back to start to run again, that is when he had stepped out in front of him, stopping him in his tracks. There was nowhere to go.

He remembered thinking he was a giant, after all, he barely reached the top of his thighs. His hands weren't only big but strong. They were heavy as he rested them on his shoulders, squeezing gently. He wasn't sure what to do, afraid to try and get away, yet fearful of the circumstances should he stay. When he looked up, he saw big red eyes looking down at him. It was the devil himself, of this, he was sure. In that instant, he could hear the men running, getting closer. He cried those men were going to hurt him. And just as they were getting close, he remembered being swept up into those massive arms. He had never felt so protected. He lay in his arms as if he had suddenly turned into a rag doll, never had he been so relaxed. He felt so good, so secure. As the men approached, he could feel him rocking his body back and forth. They looked at him. He could feel their eyes on him, they were so close he could feel their breath as they asked if anyone had seen him. They must have pointed at him lying in his arms, he held him tighter, and he could feel him shaking his head. And when they passed, he put him down, they looked at one another face to face, eye to eye.

It was then that he saw the gentleness, too gentle and kind to be the devil. He walked with him for a bit in silence as if there was no need for words, and then he invited him to go home with him. It seemed like that was what he needed to do, almost like he was supposed to, and he went without hesitation. It was then that before they entered the house, he dropped the watch from his pocket, the one he had taken, and the men had tried to get him for stealing. Now, as if it never happened, it lay on the sidewalk outside his house. He took him into a small room with a big loom and sat him on his lap. He remembered sitting there a bit uncomfortable for some time. Each time he squirmed just a bit to get away, he put his hands around him and held him tighter. Eventually, he remembered they just sat there in silence, and it was peaceful. He whispered to him that it was time for him to tell his story. He was quite young and did not understand the magnitude of the task he had at hand. It was difficult to allow himself the honesty which he was asked to tell. Everything good and valuable could never be his not unless he tried to take it for his own, yet here it could not be taken. Here taking would not and could not be allowed. In the moment as he told the story that was his, speaking out there became there was no more taking only the ability to freely give. It would be a story that only he could tell, and with that said, he handed him the spool of black thread and helped him with the first few passes. He stayed for a bit to make sure he was confident with the process and then did not return until he was done. The results were his story, full of life for only him to see, to keep to remember.

He would always remember that day and that gentle giant. He would remember all of the phone calls reminding him that he mattered, that kindness was good, and that the devil did not exist. He pulled the worn story from his pocket, his story the one he needed so badly to tell, his hands wringing its very fibers. He took a deep breath, swallowing hard. He continued to wait in line, knowing that soon it would be his turn to say goodbye.

Friendship

They held hands, the two of them. In fact, when asked, neither could remember ever being together and not holding hands. Each of them had reached out to the other as they lay on the roadside broken. Witness to the accident that spared them but took their parents.

They had been so young and yet so full of wisdom. They held hands and prayed, for prayer was all that they had been taught. And as night grew and cold air formed the steam that came from their mouths as they breathed, they could do nothing more but wait and pray. As the sun slowly rose, they could see their parents 'stiff bodies. They scanned the road and watched as a slow-moving shadow walked toward them, a large dog by its side. It was some time before it was close enough for them to make out that he was just a small boy, perhaps older, but certainly not much bigger than they were.

The dog seemed to sprint forward approaching first. They remembered that it was such a gentle dog. It was the dog that first touched what was left of their parents, it was as if she were there to give permission, but it was him that found something to cover them, respectfully and with care. It was he who spoke softly. Words that they could not hear. They did not understand. But words they understood gave permission to their parents to move on. As they were quite sure they could see their souls rising out of their bodies, hesitate and then float away. It was he who knelt down, opened his arms, and held them. He didn't hesitate to pick them up one in the front and one on his back as he carried them away from what would be their very last memory of those that they loved most. They didn't remember, neither of them. At what point, he blessed them with the time and material, even the place in which they each made their stories. But certainly, they had.

It had been the stories that consoled when they were not able to be together. It had been the stories that brought back all that had been lost. It had been the stories that truly set them free. For years he would call, first one and then the other just a reminder that they were so loved, that yes it was indeed their parents that they could feel watching over them. It had been more than comfort those calls, those words. For each of them, it had been a lifeline. And now, as they stood in line holding hands, each of them holding their own story, they wondered what they would do without him. They wondered how they could possibly let go again to say goodbye.

Humbled

H e stood in line wearing a worn letter jacket, purple with a yellow V, it was the same one he had earned in high school several years back. He fingered the zipper, thinking about how hard it might be to zip it up now that he was so much heavier should he actually need it.

Today, though was a day he hadn't hesitated to wear it, he thought it seemed only appropriate to have it on. The woman behind him sneezed, he was sure he could feel her snot on the back of his neck. He wanted to turn around, he could feel himself getting hot, his face getting red. He automatically clenched his fists. It had been so many years, he tried to remember each detail. He took a deep breath as if just remembering would take him back and calm him down.

His dad had promised to be there and true to his word, he could see him standing in the stands tall and proud. His mom wouldn't show up. She never did, she hated football, she hated that he played. She said that she was always afraid that if she ever watched him play, it would be that game in which he'd be injured, and she would be there to witness it. She would shutter, she couldn't even handle the thought. On that day, there were rumors that there were college scouts in the house, and some said it was him that they would be watching. He had been focusing on warm-ups throwing the pigskin to his best friend and receiver. He tried not to notice the cheerleaders as they were apparently trying to get the receiver's attention, not his. He could feel himself begin to lose his temper, he knew how important this game was, and his performance would be critical. But as he prepared to throw one more practice shot, it happened.

It happened so fast he wasn't exactly sure how. He had already pulled his hand back when the receiver turned away to hear what the cheerleaders were saying. He couldn't stop. The ball had already left his hands. His anger propelling it a bit harder than usual, and then like a bullet, he could hear it hit. It was a freak accident hitting him at the base of his helmet, his head propelled forward and back, and his body followed, he was down. He stood there watching as chaos took over, the sidelines filling up quickly with coaches, parents, and players. It wasn't until he heard the sirens that he actually made an attempt to go to his friends 'side. His dad rushed down to the field to be with him, he could feel his dad's disappointment hiding under his concern.

The game was postponed as they took him off the field, his body not moving secured to the gurney, his head strapped down. The field was silent, he was sure he could feel the blaming eyes on him. In the locker room, the coach was sympathetic and supportive, encouraging him and the team to go out and win, "win it for Josh, you owe him that" he was sure that those words were meant for him alone. He owed him that. But the game didn't go well, he couldn't focus, and each time the ball left his hands, it barely carried. He was sacked time and time again, with each sack wishing it would be the last, his last. He let the cold get to him. He tried not to look into the stands. Tried not to see his dad's face.

At halftime, his coach benched him. It was the last time he started and one of the last times he played at all. After the game he and his dad went together to the hospital, the waiting room was full. He joined the crowd of concerned family, friends, and fellow students. He was sure that all of them were looking at him and wondering how he could even show up. His dad put his arm around his shoulders, but the weight was too much, and he collapsed. It was impossible to understand what happened next. It was a severely burned young person who was there when he came to, a glass of water held in hands with fused fingers, an offering. Through the layers of scar tissue and what was left of a nose were those eyes, the kindest and most gentle, compassionate, and forgiving. He didn't hesitate to reach out and allow the glass to be put in his hand. Or for the assistance to put the glass to his lips so that he might have a sip.

He remembered times when he had bullied someone so grotesque that their physical being disturbed him and made him fearful of their presence. Someone so monstrous was certainly not someone he would expect to reach out to him or someone he would allow to reach out. But there in that moment, in the stillness and sterility, he was vulnerable, making the frailty a contrast to his athleticism an ideal opportunity. He allowed this young person to help him up, his dad stepping back, watching. Watching the son who hated to be helped, who hated his space to be invaded by strangers, and yet there he was, he was allowing this young person to take his hand. He watched as his son allowed himself to be guided to an empty couch where they sat down next to one another. Eyes began to divert, leaving them alone in a room so full.

He tried to remember that moment the conversation, but all he remembered was the feeling of peace and forgiving himself.

It was weeks later when this person showed up at a football game and tried to get his attention as he sat on the bench. They nodded at one another as the coach put him in. They won that game, he threw the winning touchdown. When he went back to the bench, he was gone. Years later, after he had graduated, decided that football was no longer a career option that they once again met, no longer so young, this person covered with scars invited him over for dessert, for a chance to reminisce. It was there in the humblest of homes that they ate the most decadent of desserts. It was there that their conversation led him to make the decision to volunteer at the hospital that took such good care of his friend, the receiver. They helped him through a long and painful recovery. It was there, in that humble house, that he was taught to weave and invited the opportunity to tell his story. Sitting there ready to weave what would be his alone, he thought sure he felt ready. But it was harder than he would probably ever admit. His fingers were not so nimble and he felt that if he did not seek acceptance he would fail. It had been a difficult journey in so short a time. He was not clear on how he would accept his own failure or how it would be to forgive himself. How it would feel to accept that the course of events had played out not because of who he was but because of what he had done and the reactions he demonstrated. He sat at the loom as if frozen the emotion too hard for him to let go of. The guilt too hard to allow forgiveness. He sat there waiting to breathe, having found himself holding his breath. And as slowly as his body returned to what he knew to be normal he began his story, realizing it would be accepting his new found sensitivity that would surely guide him.

The story he now held, not sure how it would feel to let it go.

He never saw that person again, but throughout the years, no matter where he was, he would get a phone call or a letter, a note, a reminder that he mattered and that life counted.

The woman sneezed again, and once again, he could feel her snot on his neck, but this time he turned around and reached out, offering her his handkerchief. He stuck his hand in his pocket and fingered his story, knowing how hard it would really be to say goodbye.

Innocence

It had been several weeks since Justice, and Dakota had been out. The weather hadn't been cooperating, and the humidity had been affecting both their joints, perhaps an indication of age. Maybe it was fatigue or lack of enthusiasm that had kept them in. Now that they were out, they found themselves enjoying a quiet spot in the park.

They were happy to be able to choose a park bench in the shade. Dakota lay down, surely the sun had not found that spot for some time, and the concrete sidewalk had benefited remaining dry and cool. Equally refreshing was the park bench.

Justice loved how it felt against her legs when she pulled up her pants just a little, cooling all of her being. It was unusually quiet, and Justice appreciated the time to breathe in the freshness, sitting there alone with Dakota's company. She was getting tired, she could feel the years taking a toll on her. Dakota could feel it too. So many Dakotas had come and gone, she leaned over and rubbed behind Dakotas ears, a favorite spot. As she stroked, she couldn't help thinking that she didn't want to have to say goodbye to another. Each of them had been such wonderful friends. Now sitting in the park, she wondered if she had given enough back. She didn't realize that tears had begun to run down her cheeks, when without warning, not even Dakota had time to react, out of the quietness, a child came running right at them.

Not hesitating for even a second to perhaps stop, she jumped right smack onto Justice's lap, and that is where she parked herself. She wrapped her arms tightly around Justice's neck. And she planted a kiss on Justice's cheek, her tongue protruding a bit added a bit of saliva to the kiss, leaving Justice's cheek a bit wet. Startled Justice smiled, she put her arms around the child and breathed in her small stature. She sighed a slight sense of relief, thinking had this child been any bigger with how much excitement she carried in her when she jumped up, it may have just been a little more than her aging body could handle.

It wasn't often that someone would reach out to Justice first, yet this little girl was full of love. Even from a distance, she had seen Justice's tears and just wanted to give her a hug. Justice could hear someone running and assumed it was a parent, most likely a woman from the lightness of the step.

Apologies were profuse, but Justice didn't mind at all, even the drool that dripped onto her hand as she held her was not disturbing. Justice felt the child's face. She was a bit confused as her features did not seem to match the face she might expect. Her eyes seemed to slant a bit, she wasn't an overly muscular child, and Justice liked that just fine, it was so much easier for her to hold her on her lap.

Her speech was not articulate, and she was a bit slow in getting out the words, but Justice was the perfect listener. The mom joined them on the park bench, Dakota moving a bit to make room. She was out of breath and welcomed the seat. The four of them sat there for the good part of the day. As Justice listened to the mom, she thought of Maia, something she hadn't done for quite a while. Memories came reminding her of how Maia must have felt. All that she had given up, perhaps not so much a sacrifice as a duty. She listened to the mom and realized how much love she had for her daughter, and she could only hope that Maia had truly loved her if only a little in that way. As the sun began to set, Justice and the mom realized how late it had gotten, both of them enjoying the time together, but knew it was time to say goodbye.

Justice thought about Maia. As she listened to the love and beauty this mom held for her daughter, she couldn't miss an opportunity to have her tell their story. Especially when it was a story that needed to be told, and so she invited them over before calling it a day/night. Oddly there was no hesitation, and the little girl insisted on holding Justice's hand the entire way. She walked with a sense of purpose and pride. Justice offered them tea and was sorry that she didn't have something more suitable for a child. But the little girl was thrilled with a teacup of her own, and the mother assured Justice that it was the perfect beverage.

Dakota snuggled up to the little girl as she laid on the floor with her, and they cuddled. Justice took the mother to the loom. She gave her the spool of black thread and showed her the proper way to start. She told her it was her time to tell her story. She could take all the time she wanted, she was happy to play with the little girl. When the mother was finished, Justice removed the story, and together they all watched it come to life. The little girl was ecstatic as it changed, jumping up and down, squealing for a turn of her own. Justice took the little girl's hand, but the mother was apprehensive.

She held her story in her hands and feared what her daughter's story might be, would she even have a story? Justice still holding the little girl's hand put her other hand on the mother's shoulder. She looked up at Justice, a sense of peace overcoming her. She saw the big smile on her daughter's face. The slanted eyes and full cheeks, her tongue sticking out of her mouth ever so slightly. A drop of drool falling down her chin, her simple expression, and she thought how beautiful simple could be. But it was not so simple a story she told when Justice removed hers from the loom. And her mother's reaction not only brought tears to her eyes but brought her to her knees.

The little girl ran to her, knocking her over so she could give her a hug. Justice always remembered to stay in touch with each of them. A simple note that said "hi" a phone call that asked mom for updates. A gesture that made them normal beyond the regular "feeling sorry" words that always seemed to accompany such kindness.

The little girl was grown now. Her tongue still hung a bit from her mouth, and drool ran down her chin. Her stubby fingers held her elderly mother's hand as she watched everyone around her, her mom held her hand a bit more tightly, with so many tears she wasn't quite sure what she might do. The mom held her story to her chest, and the little girl held hers to her chest in mimicking fashion. The mother knew that they had come to say goodbye, but she wasn't ready, and as she looked at her daughter, whose smile was so big and heart so full, she realized perhaps there was no such thing as goodbye.

Rebirth

She was confused as she observed those in front of her and those behind her. For it was the baby lying at her doorstep that she was there to say goodbye to. She brought no gifts, she had no story to hold onto. It was the simple act of faith that had made her open her door, and now she felt perhaps in some way she had borne witness.

It had been months that she sat alone in her house, blinded, not by the loss of sight, or the darkness of day but by the inability to either give or receive love. There had been too many failures, too many losses. There had been joyous anticipation, followed by days of grave despair. There was no one left, and soon there would be nothing, just the quietness of space. She had convinced herself that the quietness would be her salvation. She had spent days, weeks, months, and she thought perhaps all her years practicing for that moment. The moment when beyond blackness, beyond the stillness, it would be the unimaginable quiet that would be the last thing she would hear. And it was at that moment, just as she was becoming lost in the blackness, becoming one with the still.

It was just as she was ready to give in to the quiet, it was only then that she heard it. Like an echoing whisper as if it were coming from every corner of the house, yet so far away, perhaps an echo of her own heart beating. For a few seconds, she could not move, the blackness had already begun to consume her, and the stillness seemed to hold her captive. Yet it was a sound that she could not ignore. Through the quiet it grew, its intensity increased; with great effort, she freed herself. It was a laborious task, just putting one foot in front of the other. Over and over again, she moved, making her way by holding onto the furniture for support.

She could hear it on the other side, it was not in the house, not within her walls. She faltered, unsure of what to do. The sound, although still muffled, continued, louder and louder. Painful. Lonely. As she reached the front door, she felt the blackness in its fullest form come up behind her, reaching its fullness around her, attempting to once again consume. And then there was the stillness that held a place just for her. For just a split second, she forgot what she had heard and almost allowed the quiet back in. Almost allowed it to absorb her entirely. With difficulty, she forced her hand to make contact with the doorknob. It seemed to call to her as if the door itself were calling to her, seeking her aid. As if waiting for the knob to turn faster wasn't fast enough. Yet the simple act of touching it was undoubtedly not enough. Not sure if she was more fearful of the noise or of what the sound belonged to.

To be sure, fear held her tight, squeezing her hand as she attempted to turn the knob and open the door. To open it into the unknown, a sea of fear, an ocean of wonder, an entire world waiting to attack, yet struggling, she turned the knob and pulled. There on the other side of the world, just within her reach, lay a basket. Its flat bottom laying on the cracked and deteriorating concrete, a stark contrast to the neatly folded rainbow-colored blanket that lay over it.

Still, fear held onto her making her afraid to lift the blanket off. She stood in the stillness for what seemed like hours. Just the thickness of silence stood between her and the basket. The sun was just beginning to set, the dark of night creeping in. At some point, she allowed herself to sink down, her back leaning against the house's exterior wall. Her legs so weak, like rubber, fell beneath her, the weight of her thin body resting on them. She stayed there wondering how she would ever get up. Yet, she couldn't take her eyes off of the blanket, apprehensive of what it might be hiding. The basket was big enough, and then there was the noise.

The undeniable sound was what had first caught her attention. A howling cry, yet the basket and blanket that covered it were still, still and silent. She continued to stay stuck where she was, against the wall as if all that was important was to sit there in that particular spot.

In the quiet, the noise began again, a stiller, quieter howl, really a whimper. Hiding behind the basket creeping slowly toward her was a forlorn-looking coyote, behind her was the pack. The coyote was Dakota, who inched her way forward as the pack retreated. The coyote appeared hungry, she wasn't sure if she should try to move, what if she would need to run? Where would she go?

She was without energy or desire to do any more than lean against the wall. She wasn't quite afraid but could not put an emotion on what she was feeling. There was something about this coyote, something that said she was sadder than hungry, and then with her head lowered. Her tail trying to wag, she inched her way forward until it was possible for her to lay her head into her lap, which is what she did.

Fear was nonexistent, and she could do nothing short of love her as she positioned her head under her resting hand. For quite some time, they sat together, feeding off one another, speaking without sounds. They sat until their hearts began to beat as one, and then together, they pulled the blanket off of the basket. It wasn't clear whose silent scream came first. There lay a beautiful baby, quiet and still. She picked her up and held her, while Dakota licked at her bluish skin, trying to lick life back into her, but there was no life left. In the quiet stillness, they held her. Together they cried, together they wept.

And now they were together, waiting in line, sorrow filling their very souls as they waited for her to be put to rest.

Keeper

I stood there and watched as each individual, each family, came forward. Some seemed confused, while others seemed not to notice, yet no one said a word. For the person that they had come to say goodbye to was not necessarily the person that lay before them. Yet, without hesitation, each story was placed around her, a final word, a finality as they each let go.

I continued to hold the box because that was what I was meant to do. It became heavier and lighter with each guest saying their goodbyes. It would move as if coming to life with some and made funny, loud noises with others. And the more stories that were left, the more colorful the room became. It was as if she, herself, was changing. For a moment, I thought perhaps she was getting color in her cheeks. But it was the stories coming to life in colorful bursts, a thousand tapestries. A thousand stories left to be laid out and sewn together, to tell the most significant story ever.

As the last person reached the front, they were without a story, but instead, she stood there with her dog. I was sure I recognized the dog, for it was actually a coyote. I looked as closely as I could without notice. I was quite sure that it was hers. It looked just like the one I witnessed Justice bury on the day I met her. There had been something unique about its eyes that I would never forget, almost human and each a different color.

This coyote had the same eyes. I wanted to call it by name and see if I was right but thought it best to let it go. As they approached her laying there in her glory, something happened. Everything began to stir as if a massive wind had allowed itself in and was taking control. The tapestries blew with purpose like kites flying every which way, and the coyote began to howl. Somehow in the chaos, someone or something ripped the box out of my hands. Together, they disappeared.

Now, I spend my time piecing together the stories and waiting for the box to be returned. So that someday I might find the actual keeper of the box.

Acknowledgements

There are so many people who have supported me and to whom I give thanks. Susan Burghes for encouraging me to finish and believing in "The Tapestry" so strongly from the start.

To Shelley Share for always finding time to be my sounding board and staying with me from the first draft to the last. Always encouraging and complimenting and holding true to her word, being honest. To Annie at WordWolves for understanding my voice and working tirelessly through the editing process. To Hrvoje Butkovic author of A Wizard's Dream, for your kindness and amazing direction.

To my son, Garett and my daughter, Casey for always putting up with me and supporting me no matter what.

About Author

Audrey Lewis is an award-winning author, proud mother, and passionate adventurer who loves to push boundaries, take risks, and inspire others. Whether she's climbing mountains or camping out on billboards in Times Square, she's a dreamer and a giver who has proven time and time again that she's not afraid to break the rules. As the author of the critically acclaimed short story collection "Everybody has a story... These are ours", Audrey's work has been featured in hit magazines including Short Story Town, Weird Mask Magazine, Spillwords, Active Muse, Evolving, Dissident Voice and Cephalopress.

Armed with her natural-born creativity and a deep passion for her craft, she enjoys nothing more than sharing stories and providing readers with thought-provoking new perspectives. She's also the founder of the non-profit Cure SMA, where she served as the executive director for 23 years. Audrey currently resides in Illinois, where she enjoys spending her free time growing vegetables, beekeeping, designing dream catchers, finding vintage treasures, or enjoying a good game of scrabble. For more information about Audrey and her work, visit her website at audreynlewis.com.

CPSIA information can be obtained
at www.ICGtesting.com
Printed in the USA
BVHW032054121222
654086BV00004B/25